WHO WAS NIGHTSHADE?

I0547157

Eamonn Vincent

ARBUTHNOT BOOKS

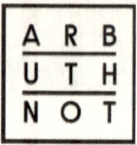

This edition published by Arbuthnot Books

https://www.arbuthnot-books.com

ISBN: 978-1-9164813-5-0

Cover illustration: Eamonn Vincent

For Anna and James.

CONTENTS

FORDHAM MARKET

TONY SMALLWOOD, CODENAMED HEMLOCK, sat nervously on a bench in St James's Park and watched the ducks on the lake. He was not looking forward to the rap over the knuckles he was certain to receive for his failure to locate the Mother Goose dossier.

A smartly dressed older man, Michael Rafferty, codenamed Larkspur, approached the bench and sat at the other end. Without acknowledging Smallwood, he said, 'Moscow is not happy. They are adamant that Nightshade's true identity should not become known. Sadly, they seem less worried about our own situation.'

Smallwood nodded glumly, but said nothing. It sometimes seemed to him that Nightshade was a mythological character. He certainly had no idea himself of Nightshade's true identity, which was probably for the best. Rafferty, on the other hand, rather prided himself on knowing Nightshade personally. Smallwood was not convinced, although he accepted that there was no simple way of testing the truth of Rafferty's claim.

'What's the problem, Smallwood?'

'Mother Goose's papers are guarded by a family retainer who lives on the premises.'

'Surely, you are trained to deal with these eventualities?'

'Yes, and he has now been evicted, but it has not been easy. This is a remote corner of rural Hertfordshire which is struggling to free itself from feudal power relations.'

'Smallwood, spare me the sociological analysis and reassure me that the next time we meet I will be able to tell Moscow that the Mother Goose dossier has been located.'

'Yes, Rafferty. You can rely on me.'

'The only thing that makes me half believe you is that your own name is very likely in that dossier. If it were to fall into the wrong hands, that would be the end of your brilliant career in British Intelligence, which, when you come to think of it, is a bit of an oxymoron.'

Smallwood tittered uncomfortably. 'I am about to spend a couple of days in Fordham Market with unfettered access to Wyvern Hall. If there is a dossier there, I will find it.'

Rafferty stood up. Before walking away, he said, 'Remote corner of Hertfordshire indeed! If you are ever unfortunate enough to get to know Siberia, you will understand what a remote corner really is.'

Tony Smallwood munched thoughtfully on his sandwich. Not the first time he was starting to regret having taken the Soviet shilling.

THE LITTLE VILLAGE OF Fordham Market lay snoozing in the late July sunshine. Fordham had been mentioned in the Domesday Book, and some said that the Warren family had been lords of the manor since that time. Now, in 1963, there remained but one scion of that noble pedigree, Richard Warren, who at the age of thirty-five had so far shown little enthusiasm for continuing the line. But worrying about who would inherit the estate on his own demise was the last thing on Richard's mind on that particular sunny afternoon, as he sat in his Lagonda in the car park at Puttenham Junction, smoking furiously while he waited for the three-thirty train from London to get in, bearing his old Cambridge friend, Tony Smallwood.

Stubbing out his cigarette in the car's ashtray, he folded the letter he had just been reading and stuffed it pensively into his inside breast pocket. It was from Agatha Ponsonby. They had been close during the war years. Her parents were old friends of his mother's and Agatha had been evacuated to The Priory at the start of the war. She had been two or three years older than Richard and although things had not started well, she soon became the big sister that he had never had. Richard's parents had been only too pleased to have acquired a combination of playmate and governess for their unruly offspring. But if they thought that the scrapes that Richard was always getting himself into might be reduced by the supervision of this older and supposedly more sensible teenage girl, they were sadly disappointed. Where, before Agatha's arrival, Richard's difficulties had been as a consequence of his tendency to daydream, thereafter it was because of the devil-may-care attitude that Agatha now introduced into their adventures in and around Fordham Market. But somehow it was always Richard who was caught red-handed.

As they moved into adulthood and each went off to university and then, in Richard's case, did military service, they continued to stay in touch. Neither was particularly surprised by the direction their respective sexualities took. It had become fairly obvious when they were teenagers that though close, indeed surprisingly intimate, there had been no spark of sexual attraction between them. In more recent years as Richard's career as a country solicitor foundered, they had lost touch with each other. So, it was a surprise to get a letter from Agatha announcing that she had decided to pay him a visit and would be arriving in a fortnight's time. She apparently had a matter of importance to discuss with him, a matter that had the potential to change their lives profoundly. Richard was genuinely pleased at the prospect of seeing Agatha again, but was slightly irritated by her enigmatic tone and the timing of her visit.

Because Richard had more than enough on his mind at this juncture. The previous year, his parents, with whom he had had an uneasy relationship, had died in a car crash, leaving him The Priory, by some margin the biggest house in the village. The problem was that The Priory and its estate were severely encumbered with debt. His father had been an enthusiastic but incompetent speculator and had squandered the considerable fortune that he had inherited on the death of his own father. Richard might live in a grand house, but he was strapped for cash.

It didn't help that he had also lost his position with the firm of solicitors by whom he had been employed as an assistant solicitor over the matter of inconsistencies in the client funds account. The matter had been hushed up, and the partners had made up the deficit but had forced Richard to resign. It was put about that he had some obscure illness, but locals didn't buy into that explanation. He was much too frequent a figure at Newmarket, local point-to-points, and at the so-called turf accountants that had sprung up with the relaxation of the gaming laws a few years earlier.

More recently, to add to the bereavements in the Warren family, Cuthbert, Richard's uncle and also a resident of Fordham, had died of a heart attack. Cuthbert was the owner of Wyvern Hall, the next biggest house in the village, and Richard was his sole heir. In the normal run of things, the property would have passed directly to him, the sale of which might have been expected to generate sufficient funds not only to fix the hole in his finances, but also to enable him to do up The Priory.

Unfortunately, Cuthbert had added a codicil to his will, witnessed by Richard's parents shortly before their deaths, allowing Cuthbert's loyal servant and general factotum, Neville Smith, known to all and sundry as Nippy, to enjoy a life interest in the property. That meant that Richard would be unable to dispose of Wyvern Hall until Nippy died. Nippy himself was not young, but these country folk had a nasty way of lingering. It would be fair to say that Richard Warren's thoughts towards Nippy were far from charitable. His first impulse on reading the will was to destroy it, but he assumed there must be a copy at Wyvern Hall, his uncle's residence and also with Loveday and Stoker, the firm of solicitors in Standon that had acted for the Warren family over many years. Fortunately, he was the executor of the will and so there was scope for him to drag his heels before he began probate.

And then a few weeks earlier, out of the blue, he had had a letter of condolence from Tony Smallwood, who had seen Cuthbert's obituary in The Times. The letter was followed a day or two later by a long chatty phone call. Before he knew what he was doing,

Richard had found himself inviting Smallwood to come and stay for a few days. He was a little perplexed by the rekindling of this relationship. It was true that they had been friends at Cambridge, but they hadn't seen much of each other in the intervening 15 years. The most recent occasion before the visit following Cuthbert's death had been seven or eight years previously at a college reunion. Still, one never really stopped being friends with the chaps one met at varsity. Furthermore, while Richard didn't know exactly what Smallwood's job entailed, he knew that it was quite an important post in Whitehall.

But the fact was that this second visit of Smallwood's was dashed untimely. Richard had more than enough on his mind with what to do about the inconvenience of Nippy's life interest. In addition to which, his creditors were pressing and it was getting increasingly difficult to deter them from extreme action. He kept on telling them that it was just a matter of cashflow, but they were adamant in their refusal to extend the mortgage on the estate and were now threatening foreclosure. It would be ironic if, just as he had become a property owner of consequence, he was forced to sell that same property.

It was true that their reunion a month earlier had been surprisingly successful. And Smallwood had come up with a good solution to the problem of Nippy. Smallwood had suggested that Richard simply act as if there was no amended will and instruct his solicitor to give Nippy notice to vacate Wyvern Hall, offering him instead accommodation in an estate cottage. Nippy had been outraged, it would seem, but wiser heads in the village had pointed out the benefits of the move. Nippy remained obdurate. It appeared that it was not the loss of his apartment in Wyvern Hall that he minded so much as loss of access to his perpetual motion machine in the barn to the rear of the Hall. Following approaches from a number of village worthies in this connection, Richard had grudgingly allowed Nippy access to the barn. Nippy had finally moved his things to the cottage the previous week.

Richard recognised that the solution had been Smallwood's, but now that he had adopted it there was really no need for Smallwood to be further involved. In fact, he was feeling irritated with himself for having confided in Smallwood. He realised that he had given

Smallwood a certain amount of power over him, not that he imagined Smallwood would attempt to blackmail him. He seemed much too upstanding for that. On the other hand, Richard had been a little surprised that Smallwood had not shown the smallest scruple in conniving in the suppression of an entirely valid will. It did suggest that his ethics were somewhat flexible. Richard had expressed his thanks and tried to make it clear that no further support was needed, but Smallwood had insisted and Richard had eventually given in.

They would have to take their meals at The Fox, of course, but that was not such a penance either. Indeed it was a long time since there'd been a cook at The Priory. Richard no longer even had a cleaner. Shortly after his parents died, he had dispensed with the services of Doreen Hammond, the wife of Fred, the local butcher. The house might now be covered in a film of dust, but it meant that he no longer had to find the pittance he paid her nor put up with Terri, Mrs Hammond's brat of a daughter, who seemed to think that she had the run of the place. That had been his father's fault. He had doted on the girl, especially when she was younger. Well, Richard was immune to her charms, whatever those were. It was true that she had recently turned into a young woman in that alarming way young females did. But that was not the kind of thing that Richard was interested in. His only reason for even giving her the time of day had been so that he could feast his eyes on Mike Smith, her brawny swain. Sadly she had transferred her affections to Flo Hodges' great-nephew, the previous summer, and while her new young man was not without his charms, he lacked the guardsman's physique that Richard found so compelling in Mike.

Sitting in his magnificent but rusting car, Richard brooded on how drab life was with insufficient funds. At that moment, he noticed Flo Hodges' light blue Morris Traveller putter into the car park. Flo, who lived at The Croft which abutted the Wyvern Hall estate, was another of Fordham's cast of eccentrics. It was rumoured that she and Cuthbert had been sweethearts during the war. It seemed unlikely to Richard, but they had certainly remained good friends until the day of his uncle's death. The worst thing about her was that with her brisk manner and her no-nonsense approach she had the ability to make Richard feel like a grubby schoolboy.

He dropped down in his seat and stubbed his cigarette out in the hope that she might not notice him, but it was pointless, really. His car was far too distinctive. The dotty old dear must be meeting someone off the train too. He checked his watch to see how much longer it was before the train arrived. Three minutes. That was a relief. He had no relish for pointless chitchat. With luck, because of her gammy leg, she would decide against passing the time of day. But Flo was not so easily deterred. She was already hobbling towards the Lagonda.

Oh, well. Best make an effort. Richard wound down the window. 'Flo. How lovely! Meeting someone off the train?'

'Yes. My great-nephew. You may remember him. He spent last summer with me and did rather well in the annual cricket match against Standon. Quite turned the heads of some of the village maidens, including the fiery Terri Hammond.'

'That can't have gone down well with Mike Smith.'

'Probably not, but I think Mike is not short of admirers.'

Richard wondered what exactly Flo was hinting at. It seemed she was not just referring to the village youth. 'Well, it's very brave of you. But by the end of the summer, you'll be quite fed up with the dreadful music these teenagers listen to now.'

'Oh, I'm quite looking forward to being introduced to this pop music.'

'Well, I wish you well.'

Flo thanked him. 'And you're meeting someone too?'

No, you silly old bat, I came here for a quiet smoke!

'Yes, an old college friend. He fancied a weekend in our glorious countryside. He's an amateur architectural historian and wants to know all about The Priory and the Hall.'

'Well, you've plenty to show him.'

Just then, the big green diesel locomotive with its bright yellow snout hove into view. Flo bade Richard farewell and slowly made her way to the platform, while he continued to slump in the driving seat of the Lagonda, drumming his fingernails on the steering wheel. By the time Flo got to the platform, the train had creaked to a halt and three or four doors had swung open. Flo was standing near the first-class carriage from which a brilliantined young man emerged. He raised his trilby to Flo and glanced across to the car park. A jaunty toot from the Lagonda brought forth a languid wave from him. Flo frowned. There was something familiar about the newcomer, although she couldn't quite place him. But at that moment, she caught sight of a tall, loose-limbed teenager with a rucksack on his back and a guitar case in one hand emerging from a carriage further down the platform. She waved at him and a few moments later Peter, her great-nephew, was giving her a big hug.

'My goodness me, Peter, how you've grown. You're probably fed up hearing such things from us oldies, but you really must have grown several inches in the last year.'

Peter laughed. 'Yes, Mum is starting to get worried. She says she won't be able to afford to clothe me soon.'

Flo laughed too. 'It must be the Hodges genes.'

And indeed Flo was herself an imposing figure, tall and still good looking. Peter's mother had said that Flo had been in the Wrens during the war and was a little eccentric, putting a curious kind of stress on the word *eccentric.*

They walked towards the Morris. Flo noticed that Richard had emerged from stowing his guest's luggage in the Lagonda's boot and was drawing his attention to Flo and her own guest with a nod of the head and smirk. Flo instantly understood that it was not she who was the object of their attention, a perception that was confirmed by the unpleasant chuckle this elicited from the trilbied one and the way he dug Richard in the ribs. Fortunately, Peter seemed oblivious to the reaction his arrival had provoked and put his rucksack and guitar in the back of the Morris.

Until the previous summer, Flo had not really known Peter all that well. She had seen him a few times, mostly when he was still only a tot. But she was fond of Doris, her niece, and keen to help a relation who was also a single parent. Peter's father had been killed in the Korean War. Doris had not remarried and had brought Peter up on her own. This had certainly made life harder for her and in the early years had limited her to part-time jobs. But when Peter started secondary school she had been able to take on a full-time position and was now doing well in her career. The previous year Doris had been promoted to a position that required some overseas travel. She had been keen to accept the promotion but was reluctant to leave Peter in the flat on his own for a large part of the summer holidays and so, much to Peter's chagrin, it was agreed that he should spend the summer with his great-aunt.

Peter had resisted the arrangement, mainly because he would miss his friends over the summer, but in the event he and Flo had got on famously. He had even won over the local youth with his heroics in the annual cricket match against Standon. Somehow, although Flo had never understood the mechanics of this particular occurrence, he had also smitten the self-proclaimed princess of Fordham, Terri Hammond, who had forsaken her former boyfriend, Mike Smith. Flo supposed that London boys had a certain cachet for country girls. It had certainly involved an overall improvement in Terri's manners and appearance, even though she still displayed a tomboyish tendency.

Flo was already in the driver's seat. Peter climbed in on the passenger side, and they set off. Flo was a careful driver, keeping close to the verges, which at this point in the year were foaming with midsummer cow parsley and nettles, the unfamiliar aniseed and citric scents of which filled the car. It was all quite different from the dusty London streets and choking diesel fumes that Peter was more used to. They hadn't gone very far when Peter became aware that another car was tooting at them from behind.

As a long sleek car overtook them, Flo tut-tutted. 'Oh, that's Richard Warren. Always driving much too fast. One of these days he'll end up in a ditch. Or worse. I saw him at the station. He was also meeting someone off the London train. One of his fancy friends.'

Having passed Flo on the outskirts of the village, Richard roared up the high street, turned left at The Fox public house, then right at the ancient parish church of St Mary's, skirted the cricket ground, and eventually turned in through the impressive gates that led to The Priory. He swept down the drive and pulled up under the *porte-cochère*. A short while later, having deposited Smallwood's bag in the lobby of the house, the two men proceeded to take a quick turn around the grounds, delightful even in their current unkempt condition. Back at the house, Richard showed Smallwood to his room, apologising for the lack of staff, which Smallwood dismissed with an airy wave of the hand.

'Much better not to have one's habits too closely monitored.'

Richard agreed. 'Please make yourself at home. I'm going to have a nap. We can rendezvous on the terrace at six o'clock for an *apéritif*, then take a stroll around the Wyvern meadows to work up an appetite for supper in The Fox. I've booked a table for seven-thirty.'

Smallwood smiled. 'My dear chap, you are the perfect host. And if I recall, the food at The Fox is excellent.'

'It is,' said Richard, exuding an unwarranted pride, as if personally responsible for the bill of fare. 'The produce is locally sourced and the meat is from Hammond's, the butcher's in the high street. Fred really does know one end of a hog from the other.'

A little while later Smallwood was lying on the bed in one of the guest rooms of The Priory, reflecting on the situation. There was no doubt that Richard Warren, his old college chum, was a fathead, but Smallwood rather envied him. Even if the Warren family had contrived to squander their inheritance, Richard Warren still had a magnificent house in which to live and the informal status of lord of the manor, which brought him no special privileges other than the right to open the annual garden fête, but gave him a standing in the local community that his own qualities could not have earned. Now, with the demise of Cuthbert Warren, he had the means to restore those empty coffers by selling his uncle's estate, and in a curious turn of events, it was Smallwood's task to help him achieve that as a way of fulfilling the wishes of his Soviet paymasters. Of course he could not divulge to Richard the real reason for this apparent altruism. It would seem to Richard that they had the same goal, whereas in fact it was the locating of two completely different documents that they were intent upon; Smallwood to locate the Mother Goose dossier, Richard to locate his uncle's amended will. And if the net effect of preventing Mother Goose's ancient retainer from enjoying a life interest in Wyvern Hall were to turn Richard Warren into a wealthy man, Smallwood could hope to be recompensed in some appropriate way.

MEANWHILE FLO AND PETER were turning into the drive of a thatched cottage set in its own garden and surrounded by lawns and flower beds.

Flo switched off the engine and said, 'Welcome to The Croft again, Peter.'

'It's great to be back, Flo. The cottage looks even more lovely than I remember it,' Peter said, with evident sincerity.

The house had at some point been a lodge for Wyvern Hall, perhaps accommodation for the estate manager and his family, but this must have been in the days when the Wyvern Hall estate was a going concern. A separate freehold had been created earlier in the century for a previous owner and Flo had bought it when she had retired from the civil service a few years previously.

It was by no means spacious, but was more than adequate for a small family or a single person who had the occasional guest. To the left of the hall that led from the front door was a kitchen where Flo took most of her meals. At the rear of the kitchen was a small utility room, which contained the boiler and a washing machine. There were hooks for coats and a rack for boots, a clothes horse, a small sink unit and a broom cupboard. To the right of the front door were a further two rooms, a formal dining room overlooking the front garden and to the rear a cosy sitting room with inglenook fireplace and French windows onto the back garden.

Upstairs were three bedrooms. The small bathroom boasted the usual facilities but also a walk-in shower cubicle, decidedly exotic from Peter's point of view, but essential for Flo because her gammy leg made it difficult for her to get into and out of a bathtub. The bedroom that Peter had occupied the previous year was at the back of the house with views of a row of mighty trees at the bottom of the garden and glimpses of a large meadow between the trees. Peter dropped his rucksack and guitar in this room and went back downstairs to join Flo.

The big kitchen table was spread with a selection of sandwiches, a handsome-looking pork pie and a large chocolate cake. Flo invited Peter to sit down, poured two strong cups of tea and then took a seat herself, passing Peter a large plate of sandwiches.

After a moment or two, she said, 'Well, as you know, there have been a number of changes since you were last here.'

Peter regretted that he had not conveyed his condolences sooner. He knew how fond of Cuthbert Flo had been.

'I was so sorry to hear of Cuthbert's death.'

Flo's earlier cheerfulness evaporated. 'It's still so recent that I haven't really come to terms with the fact yet. He'd always been so fit and well. He just didn't seem to be the kind of person who would have a heart attack. It wasn't as if he'd been having chest pains or difficulty in breathing. And, of course, Nippy is very distraught, not only because he feels that he ought to have kept a closer eye on Cuthbert, but also because he's now had to move out of the Hall.'

Peter was shocked. 'Where has he gone to?'

'Oh, he's still on the estate, but Richard Warren asked him to move to one of the estate cottages. Actually, in many ways it's a better place for him to be and I hope that Richard is not being disingenuous when he says that Nippy can stay there for the rest of his life. There was some talk of Cuthbert making specific provision in his will that Nippy would have what is called a life interest in the estate, but no such will has come to light. The only will that the local solicitors have leaves everything to Richard.'

'So does that mean that we can't go to the Hall again?'

'I'm afraid that's exactly what it means. Richard is about to start sorting out Cuthbert's affairs and I don't think he will be as tolerant of the youth of Fordham using the estate as an adventure play-ground as Cuthbert was. What worries me, though, is what his longer term plans for Wyvern Hall might be. He can't live in two large houses in one village. And in any case, I fear that his financial situation is not particularly robust, which might prompt him to dispose of the estate. That might be for the best if a sensitive buyer could be found, especially one with enough money to restore the buildings. But we will have to wait and see.'

'But what about Nippy's machine?'

'Well, apparently he has made some kind of breakthrough recently. Don't ask me what is involved. Not having access to the barn upset him more than having to move out of the Hall. But Richard relented when he saw how upset Nippy was and said that he could continue to have access to the barn. How long that arrangement might last is not clear at the moment. But at least it means that Nippy has calmed down a bit, even though he continues to say that the Master put something in his will that gave him the right to stay forever. So go easy with Nippy when you see him.'

'I'm hoping to see him as soon as possible.'

'Even before Miss Hammond?'

Peter blushed. 'Well, maybe not.'

Flo laughed. 'I'm surprised that she hasn't come around already. Fred says that she hasn't talked about anything other than your visit for several days.'

'Would you mind if I went over to the Hammonds' after tea?'

'Of course not, dear. I think you will find that she has changed quite a lot. Not quite the tearaway tomboy she was last summer. But then you have changed a lot too. A year is a long time at your stage in life.'

Peter wasn't quite sure what Flo meant and was a little worried. Was Terri now wearing glasses or had braces on her teeth? Flo could see the signs of consternation passing over Peter's face. 'Oh, I'm sorry, Peter. I didn't mean to worry you. I think you'll approve.'

Peter helped Flo with the washing up and then said, 'Is it okay if I go and see Terri now?'

'Of course, dear. Supper will be at eight. You're welcome to bring Terri.'

RICHARD WARREN AND TONY Smallwood were sitting at a small table on the terrace of The Priory. They were enjoying the first drink of the evening, large whiskies on the rocks for both of them.

Smallwood sat back in his chair and said with quiet satisfaction, 'Well, now that we have Mr Nippy out of Wyvern Hall, we can make a thorough search for Cuthbert's amended will, if such should exist.'

'Thank you, Smallwood, but I'm perfectly capable of doing that myself.'

'I think you'll find that in such cases two pairs of eyes are better than one. Anyway, I have been doing some research and it would appear that the Warren finances are in a sorry state.'

Richard was irritated. 'Smallwood, I hardly need you to tell me that.'

Smallwood smiled patronisingly. 'From what I saw of it, as we drove by, Wyvern Hall is indeed a charming house and small estate, ideal as a stud farm or sporting estate. And I look forward to seeing it in greater detail tomorrow. And even if it needs some work doing on it, it should enable you to extricate yourself from your current financial predicament.'

Richard sniffed. 'Considering we haven't seen much of each other in recent years, you seem to be rather well informed about my affairs, Smallwood.'

'Well, as I say, I do have access to sources of information not available to everyone.'

Richard was uncomfortable that such information was available, even to a Foreign Office mandarin. 'But probate has not yet been granted and I remain nervous that a copy of the revised will might still surface.'

'Which is exactly why we have to assure ourselves that there is no copy in Wyvern Hall.'

'There might be other people who have a copy of it.'

'Who? You seem to be Cuthbert's only family and Nippy his only servant.'

'The old dear we saw at the railway station. She was his neighbour and they saw a lot of each other. Some say she was his former sweetheart.'

'But if she had a copy, wouldn't she have come forward with it? Especially since you are the executor.'

'That's true, but perhaps Nippy's assertions will jog someone else's memory.'

'But does Nippy's word carry weight in the locality? I mean, a man who is building a perpetual motion machine is hardly a reliable source of information.'

'Well, it is true that he is seen as an eccentric and a loner, but there is a degree of affection for him too.'

'Which you have recognised in housing him in a delightful estate cottage. To an impartial observer you cannot be faulted, my dear chap.'

'No, I suppose not,' said Richard, not entirely convinced.

'Look at it this way. When Cuthbert made his will, he hardly supposed that both witnesses to the codicil would predecease him. No doubt in due course he might have made a new will, but the Grim Reaper caught up with him too. So at the time he amended the will, a copy at The Priory and one at Wyvern Hall would have seemed a reliable enough means of transmitting his pentimento in relation to a life interest for Mr Nippy. If he didn't bother to send one to the family solicitor, it is unlikely he gave a copy to his neighbour, even if she was an old flame. Fortunately for you, once we have found the Wyvern copy, we will be in a position to modify his wishes to reflect what would have been his attitude once he'd been aware of the threat to you and to The Priory.'

'Do you think so?'

'Yes. I am pretty sure that were you to go to law over the matter, the court would accept the argument that Cuthbert had not intended Nippy to enjoy sole occupancy of the entire estate and find in your favour. But why line the lawyers' pockets? And, after all, you have made over to Nippy accommodation that is much more suitable to his needs. If you also grant him a life interest in the Wyvern cottage, you will have honoured ninety-nine percent of Cuthbert's wishes.'

Richard realised that Smallwood was trying to make him feel better about the suppression of the amended will, but he was unable to dismiss a certain apprehensiveness. He looked at his watch and said, 'If we're going to get our walk in before supper, we'd better get a move on. I'll give you a quick *tour d'horizon* of the Wyvern estate before we broach Cuthbert's papers tomorrow.'

Smallwood leapt to his feet. 'Raring to go, old boy.'

WYVERN HALL

I⊤ WAS A FEW minutes past six o'clock by the time Peter got to the back lane that gave access to the Hammonds' flat over Fred's butcher's shop. He rang the doorbell and even before the echoes of the bell had died away, the door had opened and Terri Hammond was standing there, beaming at him. For a moment he was tongue-tied.

'Well, don't just stand there, come in and say hello to Mum and Dad.'

She grabbed his hand and pulled him into the entrance hall of the Hammonds' living quarters. Before turning to lead him into the living room she turned and gave him a little kiss on the cheek. A few moments later he was being given a hug by Doreen, Terri's mother, who kept saying how much he'd grown. The door to the shop opened and Fred came in. 'Well, well, well, look what the cat brought in, Fordham Market Cricket Club's secret weapon.' He shook Peter warmly by the hand. 'What have they been feeding you at that school of yours in London? I rather think that you're taller than Mike now. You might well find yourself playing for the first team, if your cricket has improved in proportion to how much you've grown.'

Peter had been dreading this moment. 'I'm afraid I'm not play-ing cricket for the school any more. I'm in the athletics squad. I'm a miler.'

18

Fred's face fell. 'That Peter Snell has a lot to answer for,' he harrumphed.

Peter tried to soften the blow. 'I'm not saying that I won't play, if you're short of players again, but I haven't been doing any cricket practice this year.'

Fred regained his composure. 'Peter, you can do whatever sport you want. Middle distance running seems like hard work to me, but if that's what you like doing, that's fine. Just don't think you can come around here and take my daughter out, having given up cricket.'

It was Peter's face that fell now. He wasn't sure how to take this last statement until Fred burst out laughing. 'As if I'd have any say in the matter.'

Terri punched her father's arm. 'Dad, don't be such a tease. Pete's only just got here.'

'No, I'm delighted. No reason for you to mope around here so much now.'

Fred went back into the shop and Doreen patted Peter on the arm. 'Don't take any notice of Fred. You know what he's like when it comes to cricket.'

But Terri was tugging Peter's arm, saying, 'C'mon Pete, let's go for a walk.'

As they went outside Doreen called after them. 'Terri, will you be back for supper? We're eating at eight.'

'Don't know, Mum. If I'm not back by eight, eat without me.'

Once outside they stopped and looked at each other properly for the first time. Peter noticed that although Terri was wearing jeans, zipper jacket and plimsolls as she had the previous year, she now looked more grown up and less tomboyish. And not just because her hair was longer. The fact was she could no longer disguise the fact that she was a young woman. Her own assessment of Peter was that he was not only taller, but also more muscular. They smiled awkwardly at each other. Terri was the first to break the silence. 'Where shall we go?'

'I understand that Wyvern Hall is off limits now.'

'Yes, I'll tell you what I know later. But the railway cutting den isn't, even if it is on the edge of Wyvern property. We can get there by the footpath from the rec.'

Terri and Peter made their way through the village, but instead of turning towards The Croft, picked up a footpath that ran along the edge of some allotments that abutted the railway line. At the far end of the allotments they ducked through a wire fence and continued in single file along the flat verge at the top of the railway cutting. Strictly speaking they were trespassing on railway property, but there was no one to see them and they were sensible enough not to try and cross the tracks, even though the branch line service was now very infrequent. They soon reached the thick hedge that marked the corner of the Wyvern meadow. Here the ground started to rise more steeply but at the same time the verge became wider enabling them to walk side by side and resume their conversation.

Terri said, 'I've been getting the den ready. I've restocked the supplies chest, got a new groundsheet, and, most importantly, some beers, crisps and bars of chocolate.'

Peter was impressed, especially by the mention of beer. 'Wow! That's brilliant.'

Terri shook her head ruefully. 'I wanted it to be just like last year but with beer, and one other feature.'

'What's the other feature?'

'You'll have to wait and see.'

Peter was intrigued. 'So, we can't swim in the lake?'

'No. And the pity is that Cuthbert had it dredged in the autumn, so that it'd be safer to swim in. If it was just a matter of making sure Richard wasn't around, we could take our chances, but he's also informed my dad and Flo that swimming in the lake is now banned. My dad would be furious if he thought I'd been in the lake. He takes a very deferential approach to the Warren family.'

'Surely it'll take Richard a while to find a buyer and for everything to be sorted out. You would have thought he might have allowed people access to the fields and lake until the property was actually sold. What's the hurry?'

'I think things might be moving quite fast. He's had some kind of poncy advisor from London staying with him.'

'Presumably Nippy still has access, if he's living in one of the estate cottages.'

'Only the barn and the path that leads there from his cottage.'

'Not the house?'

'No, Richard has had the locks changed.'

'That's a bit heavy-handed.'

'Yeah.'

At that moment they reached a point where the ground levelled out and was covered in short grass rather than the long rye grass they had been walking through on the way up. Here the hedge, a thick tangle of hawthorn, dog rose, bird cherry and blackthorn, was set far enough back that not only was the track no longer visible, but anyone sitting or even standing in front of the hedge could not be seen from the trains that trundled through the deep cutting. In fact the location was so secluded that the only point from which it was visible was a section of the grain field on the other side of the cutting, which other than at harvest time or when the farmer was out shooting rabbits was seldom visited.

It was for this reason that Terri had made it the base of her operations when she was younger. The hedge at that point had formed a kind of cave which over the years Terri and her gang had enlarged by the judicious use of a pair of secateurs. She had also made a kind of tunnel so that you could get into the neighbouring field, where a bench was situated at the highest point of the Wyvern estate with a fine view across the lake to the house and the barn, without walking all the way to the next break in the hedge. When she and Mike had been going out she had persuaded him to drag a large wooden box with a hinged lid and a padlock all the way there in which they had stored refreshments and a variety of useful bits and pieces. The box had been more a way of keeping rodents from attacking their supplies of biscuits and crisps than keeping things dry, because the roof of the hedge was thick enough to keep off all but the heaviest rain. In fact there had been occasions that Mike, when he had been having problems with his parents, had slept out there. He had tried to persuade Terri to join him, but she, suspicious of his motives, and not wishing to get into hot water with her own parents, had wisely rejected his suggestion. Even so she had envied him.

Warm from the climb up to the den, Terri took off her zipper jacket and said, 'Welcome back to Fordham and to the den. No one will bother us up here and we can have a proper talk.'

Peter, rather obviously delighted by the tight tee shirt Terri was wearing, said, 'Doesn't Mike come up here any more?'

'No, he spends most of his time in Standon. He and Jacqui are going out. His dad got him an old banger when he passed his test. But Mike and Jacqui spend more time snogging in it, than actually going anywhere. Anyway there's no way that he'd get Jacqui to come up here. She'd be too worried about her clothes and hairdo.'

Peter took off his own jean jacket and laughed. He had got to know Mike and Jacqui well enough the previous year to realise that what Terri was saying was probably entirely accurate.

Terri threw her jacket on the ground. 'So, do you fancy a beer, then? I've got some bottles of Pelham Pale Ale in the box.'

'Terri, you're amazing. The next best thing to BBA.'

'Well, I thought we ought to celebrate the start of our summer together, even if it's not going to be quite as brilliant as it would have been if Cuthbert were still alive and Nippy still living in the Hall. It looks like we'll have to find another way to make it memorable.'

She disappeared into the opening in the hedge and returned a few moments later with a groundsheet and a couple of beach towels. 'Here spread these out and I'll get the beer.'

Peter unrolled the groundsheet and the towels and threw himself down on one of the towels. Terri reappeared with the bottles of beer. She pulled a pocket knife out of the front pocket of her jeans and flipped off the caps with the bottle opener tool. She then handed one of the bottles to Peter and stretched out beside him on the towels, propped on one elbow. They clinked the bottles together and took a couple of swigs of beer. After a moment savouring the bright-tasting beer, she said, 'You didn't tell me in your letters that you'd grown so tall.'

Peter took another swig of beer and said, 'I didn't think that it was worth mentioning. Anyway you didn't tell me that you'd grown too.'

'I don't think I'm much taller than I was last year.'

Emboldened by the beer, Peter said, 'In other respects.'

Gratified at the effect that removing her jacket had had on Peter, Terri said, 'I'm sure I don't know what you're talking about. And when did you stop being the shy boy I got to know last year? Does this mean that you've been out with girls in London and not told me about it?'

Peter was indignant. 'Some of the people I hang around with are girls, but I haven't been out with a girl in the way you're implying.'

'So you haven't been out with a girl, just the two of you.'

'No.' Peter felt he should fight back. 'What about you? For all I know you might have tried to get back with Mike.'

'What? And have that big lunk trying to get his hand under my shirt all the time.'

Peter felt he could hardly blame Mike, because he had aspirations of that kind himself, although he had no idea how one actually got to that point.

Terri mistook the quizzical look on Peter's face and said, 'What's the problem? Don't you believe me?'

'Of course I do.'

'Then what?'

Peter hadn't anticipated that it might take them a while to re-establish the rapport that they had had the previous year. The relationship during the intervening year had been conducted mainly in writing and the occasional telephone call, so it was quite possible that things weren't going to work out unless they could adapt to the fact that they had both changed, perhaps in incompatible directions. And with the unexpected changes at Wyvern Hall, the possibility of a disappointing holiday loomed on the horizon. Peter wasn't quite sure how to negotiate this new terrain. Maybe they should talk about something else. He decided to find out more about what had happened to Cuthbert.

'Did you go to the funeral?'

'No, it wasn't held at St Mary's. It was at a crematorium. Very few people went. Just Flo and Nippy of the Fordham people. Oh, and Richard Warren, of course.'

'How sad.'

'And then a few weeks later Richard Warren gave Nippy notice to leave the Hall.'

'Flo said the cottage he's been given was rather nice and might actually suit him better.'

'Yes, it's true. It might have been quite spooky being in the Hall on his own. But Nippy was furious and kept saying that Richard was up to no good. I helped him move his stuff. I'll take you around there tomorrow.'

They fell silent. They were both conscious of the awkwardness that had arisen between them, but neither knew how to discharge the tension. Peter wondered whether another beer might help and was just about to suggest it, when the sound of two male voices just the other side of the hedge stopped any further thoughts in that direction. Terri put her finger to her lips. 'It's Richard Warren and his smarmy friend,' she whispered.

Peter said under his breath, 'What shall we do?'

'Just stay still and keep quiet. We don't want to draw attention to ourselves. They have no idea we're here. It sounds like they're sitting on the bench.'

Richard's friend was speaking. 'Cigarette?'

'No thanks, Smallwood. I must say, those are very odd cigarettes that you smoke. They smell like old socks.'

'Balkan Sobranie, dear boy. Finest cigarettes in the world.'

'Well, I think I'll stick to my Rothmans, if you don't mind.'

There was silence for a while as the two men smoked their cigarettes and contemplated the view. Peter noticed that the smoke that was drifting through the hedge was unusually aromatic. He presumed that was what Richard meant by the phrase *smelling like old socks*.

Richard and Smallwood resumed their conversation.

'Warren, what a delightful place this is. Thank you for the quick look around the estate. It is quite clear to me that someone will be prepared to pay top dollar for the estate. It has bags of potential.'

Richard was not so certain. No doubt the property would fetch a pretty penny, but he felt far from comfortable about parting irretrievably with an important part of his birthright. 'Wyvern Hall has been in the family for generations. It won't feel right not to have a member of the family living here.'

'But, if I am not mistaken, you are the last surviving member of the family and something tells me that you are unlikely to have issue.'

'You never know, Smallwood, I might do it for Queen and country, as it were. Some of these county girls just see the coupling business as a disagreeable chore to be got over and done with in the interests of continuing the line. We probably wouldn't have to do it very often, just enough to produce a brat or two and then we could call a truce and suspend conjugal relations *sine die*. The little lady could get back to the horses and I could find occasional respite with a bit of rough down in the Smoke.'

'Fine words, Warren, but another matter entirely when you are required to screw your courage to the sticking place, as it were.'

'Oh come on, Smallwood, how hard can it be?'

'Perhaps not hard enough to do the business when faced with the cuckoo's nest in question, if you see what I mean.'

'Smallwood, I find your remarks unseemly and insulting.'

Smallwood realised that with the passage of time his old comrade, who in the past could be relied on to enjoy a bit of smut and innuendo, had become decidedly strait-laced.

'I'm sorry, Warren, my comments were in poor taste. And we are getting away from the main point. Let's do our best to find this darned will. Or at least assure ourselves that there isn't a copy in Wyvern Hall. We wouldn't want a copy of the will coming to light which would support Nippy's contention.'

'You can say that again, but I don't think you realise the extent of Cuthbert's papers. It might take us a while to go through everything.'

'So be it. I have some leave owing to me. I can stay a day or two longer if necessary.'

Richard wasn't delighted by the prospect of Smallwood staying at The Priory for longer than absolutely necessary. But there was no point fretting about that right now. Smallwood stubbed his cigarette out and flicked the butt into the bushes that shielded Terri and Peter. 'Shall we make a start before we go to The Fox?'

'I suppose we might as well.'

The two men rose to their feet and made their way back down the hill to Wyvern Hall. Terri moved to a point of the hedge where she could see through it. When she had assured herself that Richard and Smallwood were out of earshot, she returned to Peter and said, 'What a pair of twisters!'

Peter was sure she was right, but he wasn't quite clear why. 'Yes, it would be terrible if they sold the estate, although it sounded as if Richard wasn't so sure about it.'

'It sounds like they're worried about a copy of Cuthbert's will saying exactly what Nippy has been saying all along, which is that he has the right to stay at Wyvern Hall as long as he lives. So that would mean that Richard wouldn't be able to sell the estate.'

'But it sounded like they didn't know whether there was one or not.'

'I've got a feeling that if they find a copy of Cuthbert's will in the Hall, it won't survive very long.'

'You mean you think they'll destroy it?'

'That's exactly what I think.'

'But what can we do?'

'We could try and find it before they do.'

'And how are we going to do that?'

'We'll get into the Hall.'

'But they're starting their search now.'

'They won't get much done in the next hour or so. We can wait until they've gone and then get into the Hall and search for it ourselves.'

'But I thought you said that all the locks have been changed.'

'I know a secret way in. Let's clear all this stuff away and then we can be ready to go when we see the car driving off.'

'The trouble is Flo is expecting me, and you, as a matter of fact, for supper at eight o'clock. I can't let her down on my first day back.'

Terri was only briefly nonplussed. 'Alright, we'll do it after supper. My parents are often fast asleep by the time I get in and I bet Flo goes to bed even earlier. You could say you're walking me back home and we could nip over to the Hall then.'

Peter wasn't enthusiastic about the plan, but agreed to it in principle. He knew from the previous year how difficult it was to deflect Terri from a course of action once she had set her mind on it.

RICHARD WAS POINTING OUT some of the finer features of Wyvern Hall to Smallwood. 'It used to be a lovely old house, but Cuthbert let it go, especially in recent years. Seemed to spend most of his time hand-cutting jigsaw puzzles.'

Smallwood was perplexed. 'Sorry, old boy, did you say he made jigsaw puzzles?'

'Yes, he seemed to have one of those minds, intricate. Or devious as my old Pa used to say.'

Smallwood nodded. 'Yes, I can imagine that, somehow.'

They went up to Cuthbert's rooms on the first floor. There were three interconnecting rooms at the front of the house. The most imposing room was Cuthbert's study. A large desk dominated the room with a view of the lawns in front of the house. The walls of the room were book-lined, with a number of old prints and several modern paintings filling the sections of wall not given over to bookshelves. To the right of the desk were three large filing cabinets and to the left a battered leather armchair. The door to the right of the desk led to a small sitting room and the one to the left to a bedroom.

Richard waved a hand around. 'He spent most of his time in these three rooms. Nippy, his manservant, had rooms up in the attic. There is a kitchen and utility room on the ground floor at the back, but most of the other rooms are empty. If he had his own copy of the will, it would most likely be here.'

Smallwood was full of enthusiasm. 'Well, let's make a start. You take the filing cabinet furthest from the desk and I'll take the one closest. Let's do it systematically, so we don't have to go back over what we've already checked. We'll have made a good start if we can do the top two drawers each. We will work up a good appetite for supper.'

They set to. The conversation became desultory. When Smallwood had finished the first drawer, he said, 'Do you mind if I have a cigarette? You're very welcome to have one yourself.'

'No, I'll have one of my own later.'

'As you wish.'

Smallwood took a small silver lighter out of his pocket and lit his cigarette. He drew on it heavily and then, exhaling a stream of fragrant smoke, sat down in the leather armchair and surveyed the room. 'The room is clearly that of a gentleman and a scholar,' he mused, 'but the paintings strike a jarring note, somewhat naïf. Did he collect a particular artist?'

'The paintings are his own handiwork. They were the images he used for his jigsaw puzzles.'

'Ah, that would explain it, tending to craft rather than a fine art aesthetic.'

Richard was defensive. 'They're highly sought after around here.'

Smallwood said, 'I can imagine.' It sounded more equivocal than he had intended.

He finished his cigarette and started work on the second drawer.

Richard had already finished his top drawer and now had the second drawer open. He pulled the first two folders out, and saw that one of them was labelled 'BILLS'. It seemed unlikely that Cuthbert had misread 'BILLS' for 'WILL', but it was true that latterly he had been getting a bit doddery and maybe his eyesight had been starting to fail. Probably best to check he hadn't misfiled the amended will in the 'BILLS' folder. He opened the folder and leafed through the assorted rates demands, water rates demands and electricity bills. No sign of a will. But just then he caught sight of the electricity charge for the most recent quarter. It was enormous, several times that of The Priory. That must surely be wrong. He found the three or four previous bills and they were all equally high. It was only when he got back to the first bill for 1962 that it dropped to about half of what The Priory was regularly charged.

He waved the sheaf of papers in Smallwood's direction. 'Here's a strange thing, Smallwood. Uncle Cuthbert's electricity bills are incredibly high.'

'I thought you were looking for his will, dear boy, not analysing his energy usage. He probably had electric fires on in every room during the Big Freeze. It must be difficult keeping these old houses warm.'

'Well, that's true. And it's also true that the bill for the first quarter of this year is higher than any of the other bills, but the odd thing is that for the last eighteen months the electricity bills for

Wyvern Hall are three or four times as much as those for The Priory, which is a much bigger house. And I should know, because I was shocked by the first electricity bill I had to deal with after my parents died.'

'I'm sorry to hear that, Warren, but we are hoping to put all such tedious matters behind us, once Wyvern Hall is up for sale.'

But Richard wasn't really listening. 'My grasp of physics is a little hazy, but I presume that you can't have an electricity leak like you might have a water leak.'

'I don't think so, old boy. Heaters, big electrical machinery, they're the sort of thing that use a lot of electricity.'

'Well, we've both been over the whole house. One didn't get the sense that there was a part of the house in which an electric heater had been left on.'

'Perhaps there is some kind of agricultural machinery that is powered by electricity in one of the outhouses. I don't know, a thresher or incubator of some sort that Mr Nippy attends to.'

'The only machine that Nippy attends to is his infernal perpetual motion machine and that is supposed to use little or no power.'

'There you are. Nippy's machine is a hoax and he's powering it with Cuthbert's or, rather, with *your* electricity.'

'Do you know, Smallwood, I think you might be on to something here.'

'Perhaps when we have dealt with the matter of finding the will, we should have a little talk with Nippy.'

'Yes, indeed.'

Smallwood returned to the close inspection of the contents of his own filing cabinet. Within a few minutes, he said, 'By George, I think I've got it.'

He pulled out a folder with the word WILL handwritten on the outside and waved it in Richard's direction. He opened the folder and, removing the top document, proclaimed, 'Last will and testament …'

He handed the document to Richard to check that it was indeed what they were looking for. As Richard cast his eye over the will, Smallwood glanced at the other documents in the folder before closing the folder and throwing it on the desk.

'Looks like we've struck gold even before we sat down to our supper.'

Richard could hardly believe it had been so easy. 'Thank you, Smallwood. Supper's on me tonight.'

Smallwood was magnanimous. 'Well, if you insist. Tuck that document safely in your inside pocket and let us repair to The Fox.'

As they drove back to The Priory, Smallwood was thinking about the folder he had left on the desk in Cuthbert's study. He was pretty certain it was the Mother Goose dossier, or at least a part of it. It was strange that it was in a folder marked WILL, but maybe Cuthbert saw it as part of his legacy. Smallwood had been reluctant to draw attention to it, lest Warren ask to see the contents, but he needed to secure the document and get it into Rafferty's hands as soon as possible. There was only one thing for it; he would have to go back to Wyvern Hall in the dead of night.

It was not an ideal way of proceeding, but when needs must… He would suggest to Warren that they have an early night. In fact, he would slip something into Warren's nightcap that would cause him to sleep heavily and not stir for some hours. When he was sure that Warren was sound asleep, he could slip out of The Priory and get over to Wyvern Hall. His first thought was that he would walk. It wasn't that far and it would avoid any mishaps with the Lagonda, but then it occurred to him that it might be handy for the Lagonda to be seen parked in front of the Hall rather than for him to encounter some local on foot and to try to pretend that he was on a midnight ramble.

He might even manage to get some sleep before Warren was back in the land of the living. He could then hotfoot it back to London and triumphantly hand over the dossier to Rafferty. He might even get a bit of a disembodied pat on the back from Nightshade or Moscow. Encouraged by his own ingenuity and already deciding that the Mother Goose dossier was in his grasp, Smallwood's mood improved considerably and he felt ready to withstand a few more hours of Warren's witless conversation.

At The Fox, the evening session was well under way. Richard and Smallwood had finished their supper and were contentedly observing the antics of the local drinkers from their corner table and dithering about whether to have another drink, when a tall, white-haired gentleman approached their table.

'Warren, fancy seeing you in here!'

Richard looked uncomfortable. This was not a good moment for their conversation to be interrupted, but he composed himself and retorted with as much levity as he could muster, 'Ho ho! Sage, I could say much the same about you.'

'Quite, dear boy. Did you have the steak and kidney? First class, I thought.'

'We did. Allow me to introduce my companion. Tony Smallwood, Professor John Sage. Tony and I were contemporaries at St Rad's. Tony's spending a few days with me, respite from the turmoil of Whitehall or something.'

Sage acknowledged Smallwood, inclining his head with understated courtliness. 'You are most welcome to our small community, Mr Smallwood. I trust you have some pleasant excursions planned. And if you are staying at The Priory, you are privileged indeed, one of the finest houses in the county.'

'Thank you, Professor Sage. I am of course aware of your work. I had no idea that you had retired to this pleasant backwater.'

'I'm flattered, Smallwood, but I hope you're not confusing me with my cousin who goes by exactly the same name and is also a professor of philosophy.'

'Well, I hope I am talking to the Sage who was Wittgenstein's collaborator, rather than the one who worked with Popper.'

'You are indeed. I am pleased to see that the British civil service continues to employ men of considerable acumen.'

Smallwood laughed. 'I'm not sure you would like to hear my unvarnished opinion on that matter.'

Sage joined in the laughter. 'Spoken like a true mandarin. But if you will excuse me, I must be toddling along.'

Sage doffed his invisible hat and made his way to the exit.

Before Smallwood could offer a deft observation on the improbability of meeting in a small market town a philosopher of distinction who, if not one of the greatest, had certainly traded syllogisms with the greatest, Richard said, 'He's a nice old cove, but apparently a bit of a red, often quoting Karl Marx. I've also heard him say in this very bar that the reason why the Nazis were defeated was not the pluck of this country or the economic might of the Yanks, but the huge sacrifices made by the people of the Soviet Union.'

Smallwood laughed. 'Well, he has a point, but the bar of The Fox in Fordham Market is probably not the best place to expound such views.'

Richard indicated a couple of less distinguished-looking men at the bar.

'Warren, what am I looking at now? More fugitives from our alma mater? The discoverers of some new astrophysical phenomenon, perhaps?'

'No, don't be such a smart alec. You see those two at the bar? The one on the barstool is Fred, the local butcher.'

'Now, I am impressed. I shall go and congratulate him on his viands. They are his, I presume?'

'They are, but it's the other chap, the one he's talking to, with the rolled-down Wellington boots and the ill-fitting suit.'

'I must admit, there is little one can do to enhance such a suit, not even Wellington boots, which in nearly all circumstances constitute a sartorial solecism, but one does not expect Jermyn Street standards in the snug of The Fox.'

'Smallwood, stop being such an idiot. The chap with the bad suit and the wellies is my nemesis.'

'I can well imagine.'

Richard could see that the alcohol had exposed Smallwood's inveterate facetiousness. 'The reason I'm pointing him out, is that *that* is Nippy, Cuthbert's former factotum.'

'Ah, I see. And is he, too, a regular in The Fox?'

'As you may have noticed, it's the only pub in the village. If one wants to get away from assorted former tenants and employees and their offspring, one needs to travel to The Brewery Tap in Standon.'

'How tiresome! But never fear. I am sure we can deal with Mr Nippy and his expectations. Even so we should keep our conversation as meaningless as possible. And I know you have form in this respect.'

'Smallwood, I'm beginning to regret having asked you to stay.'

'But you will bless me when you come into your own.'

Richard hoped that would indeed come to pass.

Smallwood was craning to get a better view of the couple at the bar. 'Before we go, I would like to get a closer look at Mr Nippy. One for the road?'

'Don't mind if I do.'

Smallwood went across to the bar and ordered two more large whiskies. While he was waiting for them, he introduced himself to Fred Hammond, the butcher.

'I am staying with my old friend Richard Warren at The Priory. We have just had the steak and kidney pie, for which he tells me you supplied the meat. May I congratulate you on the high quality of your kidneys?'

'Why, thank you, sir, though I fancy the congratulation should be more properly addressed to Vi Proctor, the landlady of The Fox, who does all the cooking.'

'Team effort, then. I look forward to future menu specials.'

He then turned to address Fred's drinking companion. 'And you must be Nippy?'

Nippy grunted, already certain that he did not like this oleaginous intruder, who was sitting with Richard Warren, the man who had evicted him from his billet. Smallwood ignored Nippy's unenthusiastic response. 'Mr Warren showed me over Wyvern Hall earlier this evening. I believe you have been the custodian until recently.'

'If you mean that I used to live there, you're right. And I should be living there still. That's what the Master said would happen.'

'Mr Warren mentioned something of the sort. It sounds as if a heart attack carried Mr Warren senior off before he could get around to communicating his wishes formally. But I believe that Mr Warren has provided you with a very nice estate cottage and granted you access to the machine you are building in the barn.'

'Yes, but the Master intended more than that.'

'Perhaps he did, Mr Nippy, but you know how it is. If these things aren't written down, it causes all sorts of misunderstandings. But I am sure that things will work out satisfactorily in the end.'

Smallwood picked up his drinks and returned to the table.

Fred was chuckling. 'Never had you down as a custodian, Nippy. Careful, I reckon he's after the secret of your perpetual motion machine.'

'I don't know what he's after, but I'll warrant he's up to no good.'

Smallwood downed his drink without sitting down again and signalled that they should go. Richard knocked back his own drink and they exited the pub.

It was a beautiful evening. Richard suggested they return to The Priory via the cricket field. Smallwood was happy to oblige. 'This really is a lovely spot, Warren. And with a bit of moolah in the old bank account, life will be blissful.'

The two men turned from the metalled footpath and set off around the perimeter of the cricket field. Smallwood inhaled the fragrant air, humming contentedly to himself. A thought occurred to him. 'Is the local cricket team up to much?'

'Not these days, but Fred, who you were speaking to just now, runs the youth team. And one of the lads, who happens to be a bit of a stunner, is also very handy with the bat.'

'What a delightful combination! Is he obliging?'

'I'm afraid not.'

'What a pity.'

'Anyway, I have enough troubles at the moment without outraging the *hoi polloi*. I have to go further afield for those purposes.'

'Very wise.'

As they approached the cricket pavilion, Richard touched Smallwood on the arm and said under his breath, 'I do believe that the young Adonis I just mentioned is sitting on the bench on the other side of the pavilion.'

Smallwood peered in the direction that Richard was indicating. 'With a female companion, it would seem.'

'Unfortunately, yes. He used to squire the dreadful termagant, Terri Hammond, daughter of the purveyor of kidneys. But she seems to have had her head turned by the young man whom Flo Hodges was meeting off the train. Adonis has therefore transferred his affections to Jacqui, a girl from the neighbouring village, who is probably more accommodating than the termagant.'

'Shall we acknowledge them? You are, as it were, the local squire.'

'If you wish, as long as they're not doing anything too unseemly. You know what youngsters are like these days. No restraint whatsoever.'

'Not like in our day!' observed Smallwood with, if Richard could have seen it, a raised eyebrow.

At the approach of the effete college chums, the young couple on the bench unwound themselves from each other and adjusted their clothing. The girl was the first to speak. 'Hello, Richard.'

'Hello, Jacqui, Mike. What are you two up to?'

Mike wasn't sure what to say and left it to Jacqui to explain. She always knew how to deal with situations. 'Nothing, really. Just enjoying the evening air.'

Richard wasn't going to let her get away with that. 'Isn't the vicar spinning discs in the church hall tonight?'

'No, the youth club is on Tuesdays and Thursdays.'

Richard turned his attention to Jacqui's bashful beau.

'And what about you, Mike, how's the cricket coming on?'

'Not too bad, thank you Mr. Warren. We're hoping for another good result against Standon this year.'

Richard nodded. 'I bumped into Miss Hodges at the station. She was picking up her great-nephew. He's staying with her for the summer holidays. Tall chap. I seem to recall he turned out for the village side last year and put in a good spell of bowling.'

'Pete did help us out last year. Standon were not used to his kind of spin. But he's not a real cricketer.'

'I think I get your drift, Mike. I'm sure you count for two or three ordinary players.'

'Thank you, Mr. Warren, I do my best.'

'I'm sure you do, Mike, and I will be cheering you on in this year's match as you smite Standon hip and thigh, resplendent in your whites.'

Mike murmured something inaudible, clearly embarrassed, unsure exactly what he meant. Richard liked the way Mike blushed when he wasn't quite sure what was expected of him.

'I was just telling my friend here, Mr Smallwood, what a fine cricketer you are. He's quite a dedicated follower of cricket himself. On first name terms with Ted Dexter and Colin Cowdrey, I shouldn't wonder. Maybe we'll come and watch you in the nets.'

This was too much for Jacqui, who didn't like seeing her hunk of a boyfriend being teased in this way. 'And then you could come to the youth club afterwards, and help the vicar with the records.'

She really was a bit of a spitfire. The best Richard could manage by way of riposte was, 'Well, if you fancy a bit of Doris Day's "Secret Love", then I'm your man. But I doubt the Reverend Heale has such things in his record case.'

Jacqui wasn't impressed and settled for staring Richard out in the fading light.

Richard decided to throw in the towel. Having to deal with the little hussy really took the shine off coaxing blushes from Mike. 'Well, we'll be getting back to The Priory. Be good, you two and if you can't be good, be discreet.'

The two men walked on. When they were almost out of earshot, Jacqui thought she heard the one called Smallwood say, 'I see what you mean.'

She waited for a few more moments, until they had almost disappeared into the gloaming before turning to Mike and saying, 'Weirdos.'

Mike was surprised. From his perspective, they were both upper-class adults, and, despite or more likely because of their curious way of talking, he was quite prepared to accord them due defer-ence, especially since they had been so complimentary about his cricketing skills.

'They seemed okay to me.'

Jacqui scoffed. 'They're a couple of nancy-boys and they were trying to get a reaction from you.'

This didn't make much sense to Mike. He knew some men were homos, but it was much more likely that Jacqui was irritated by the attention they had paid to his cricketing prowess, rather than compliment her on some aspect of her appearance. Mike had already worked out that saying something nice about a girl's hair or skin was the quickest way to get in her good books. Even so, he had a healthy respect for Jacqui's acumen.

'How can you tell?'

'The way they talk.'

'But don't all toffs talk like that?'

'Richard's father didn't, nor his uncle.'

It was true that he sometimes felt that there was another meaning to Richard Warren's quips and comments. But, right now, he preferred not to try and fathom the implications of Jacqui's assertion. He'd rather return to his none too subtle attempts to get his hand under her tee shirt. He put his arm, which he had withdrawn at the approach of the men, around her shoulder as nonchalantly as he could and pulled her towards him. But Jacqui had had enough of being pawed for one evening and pushed him away.

AFTER A PLEASANT SUPPER, Flo went next door with a small whisky and settled down in an armchair with her bad leg up on a footstool. She opened her book and started reading, but soon nodded off. Peter and Terri did the washing up. When they'd put everything away, Peter called out, 'Flo, I'm just walking Terri home. Don't wait up for me. I'll switch all the lights off when I get back.'

As they got ready to go, Terri whispered that they might need a torch. Peter found one in the utility room. Outside he said, 'Let's go across the meadow. No one's going to be around at this time of night.'

They slipped through the back gate of The Croft into the Wyvern meadows. There was still a glow in the sky, but it was likely to be quite dark by the time they got to the Hall itself. As they were crossing the big meadow in front of the lake, Peter said, 'So what's this secret way into the Hall?'

'The Hall has lattice windows, small pieces of diamond-shaped glass divided by strips of lead. On the other side of the building just behind the conservatory, one of the diamonds is hinged. You can lever it open with a penknife. Then you reach your hand in, open the window and climb in.'

'And you have your penknife?'

'Of course I do.'

It wasn't every girl that could be relied on to have a penknife about her person. Why had Peter even doubted it? 'You've done this before?'

'Well, not exactly…'

They circled the house by the outbuildings at the back, so that they couldn't be seen from the drive. Terri pointed to a small window that was to one side of the door into the conservatory. She located the hinged pane without trouble and levered it open with her penknife, but it was clear that in order to reach down to the catch she would have to get onto the windowsill.

'You're going to have to give me a bunk up.'

Peter thought it would probably be better if he were the one to open the window, but calculated that Terri would not welcome the suggestion and resigned himself to helping her up onto the windowsill. In the event though, his assistance was impaired by a certain reticence about firm contact with Terri's bottom and she slipped. As she picked herself up to try again, she said, 'Oh, for goodness' sake. I'll be very annoyed if I hurt myself because you're too shy to hold me properly.'

Peter apologised and said he'd do better this time.

Soon Terri was balanced on the windowsill with Peter keeping her stable by sustained pressure on her bottom. But no matter how much she strained, her arm wasn't long enough to reach the catch. Eventually she gave up and said, 'You'll have to try. Help me down.'

They swapped places. Peter didn't really need Terri to hold him up, but submitted to her help, partly so as not to hurt her feelings, but mainly because of the erotic element in the manoeuvre. After a bit of unnecessary rigmarole reaching down for the catch, he opened the window, swung his legs through and dropped down.

Terri said, 'The back door is round to the right. It's bolted top and bottom. I'll go and wait outside it.'

Peter did as she suggested. He then located the back door, drew the bolts back and opened it. Terri slipped in, shut the door behind her and said, 'Did you close the window?'

Peter nodded. Although there was still some light in the sky outside, it was extremely gloomy in the passage that led from the back door. Terri turned back to Peter and said, 'I think it's better if we don't put the lights on, just in case someone's watching the house.'

Terri led the way up to Cuthbert's study on the first floor. Once inside she said, 'There are some filing cabinets to the right of the desk. Maybe you can put the torch on, if you keep it low.'

Peter swept the beam across the room to get a better feel for the layout of the room. He picked out the filing cabinets, but then the beam of his torch fell on the folder that Smallwood had left on the desk. He stepped towards the desk and focussed the beam on the folder. It took him a moment to realise that the folder bore the single word WILL on its cover. He flipped it open and looked through the sheets of paper that it contained.

He waved Terri over. 'We're too late. They must have found it before they went to the pub. Look, the folder says WILL, but there's nothing that looks like a will in it.'

'What has it got in it then?' Terri asked.

'I don't know how to describe it exactly. It says it's secret. Here you take a look.'

He handed her the folder and held the torch while she leafed through the pages. On top was a single sheet of typewritten paper with the words MOST SECRET at the head of the page and beneath that a line which read HELIOS DECRYPTS – FIRST RUN. There was then a line of three words in capitals: LARK-SPUR, HEMLOCK, NIGHTSHADE. Underneath that were twenty or so lines starting with one or more of the initial letters of the three words at the top of the page, followed by dates and locations, some of which were addresses, some the names of hotels or restaurants. The sheet of paper was attached to several pages of closely printed text, in no language that either of them knew. The odd thing was that each *word* in the strange language was exactly five letters long.

Terri said, 'None of this looks as if it has anything to do with the will.'

Suddenly they were both startled by a beam of light sweeping across the windows of the study, illuminating them for a moment or two. Peter turned off the torch and they both dropped down below the level of the window frame. It was apparent from the sound that a car had just come up the drive and halted in front of the house. A few moments later, they heard the slam of a car door and footsteps crunching across the gravel.

Peter whispered to Terri, 'That looked like Richard's car. Maybe they've come back to finish the job.'

Terri said, 'We'd better hide. I wonder if there's room in the closet. I'll check.'

She opened the door and, switching the torch on for a moment, looked inside. 'It'll be a tight fit, but it should be okay unless they try to check every nook and cranny.'

At that moment, they heard the front door open and someone enter.

'Quick. Let's get inside.'

Terri went first and stood at one end of the closet. Peter stepped in after her and pulled the door behind him. It clicked shut. It was profoundly dark. Even though he was pressed up against Terri, he couldn't see her. He put out his hand cautiously, using his sense of touch to establish their mutual orientation. Terri took his hand in her own left hand and squeezed it. Fortunately, the closet had louvred panels, so not only was it not as stuffy as it might otherwise have been, but it was also possible to hear something of what was transpiring in the room.

A moment later Smallwood came through the study door. He too eschewed the overhead electric light, scanning the room instead with a powerful torch. He went over to the desk and was slightly surprised to find the folder that he had left on the desk was now open. He felt certain that he had closed it before leaving with Warren. He swept the beam of his torch around the room again to see if there were any other signs of change to the room since earlier in the evening. Reassured that it looked exactly as it had when he'd been there earlier, he sat down at the desk, lit a cigarette and perused the contents of the folder. After some minutes, Peter and Terri heard him let out a low whistle and say to himself, 'Well, bless my soul, this really is the Mother Goose dossier. Nightshade will be pleased.'

But the pleasure that he had felt earlier in the evening at having completed his assignment so easily was now replaced by the realisation that Mother Goose really had cracked the network and that it must only be a matter of time before they were all arrested. He studied the material closely. The top sheet listed all the code names of the network and what looked like the dates and locations of meetings. The rest of the material looked as if it was the encrypted material from which the decrypts had been derived. This was serious. The only slightly reassuring detail was that it didn't look as if a complete decrypt had been achieved at the point at which the top sheet had been produced. And in particular the actual identities of the three double agents hadn't been revealed. Which was just as well, since his own name would have been one of them.

It would seem that Mother Goose's heart attack had been arranged none too soon. On the other hand, it must be assumed that whoever ran Helios was planning to make further attempts to identify the individuals. The question was, which branch was conducting the operation? He certainly wasn't aware of a computer called Helios at Cheltenham. Whatever the case, he needed to get the file into Rafferty's hands as soon as possible. He would travel back to London first thing the next morning and deposit the material in the dead letter box that he and Rafferty used. He put the documents back in the folder and, tucking it under his arm, went back to the car.

As soon as they heard the sound of a car starting up and pulling off across the gravel, Terri said, 'Let's get out of here. I've got pins and needles in my legs.'

The two of them tumbled out of the closet. Terri rubbed her leg and stamped her foot a few times, trying to get the circulation going again. Peter went across to the table to retrieve the folder, only to find that it was no longer there. 'Oh, no, the folder's gone.'

'Richard must have taken it just now.'

'I don't think that was Richard.'

Terri was puzzled. 'But it looked like Richard's car.'

'It was Richard's car, but the tobacco that person was smoking was the strange old socks stuff that Smallwood was smoking on the other side of the hedge. So I think it was Smallwood.'

'What do you think he was doing? He wasn't here long.'

Peter was trying to make sense of what had just happened. 'I don't know, but it's almost as if he was after that folder.'

'Why didn't they take it earlier?'

'Perhaps they forgot it. Or perhaps Smallwood doesn't want Richard to know he's taken it and so he came back on his own. He'd left it out on the desk, so he didn't have to spend time looking for it.'

Terri thought that Peter might be onto something. 'Let's try and write down as much as we can remember of the top page while it's still fresh in our minds.'

Peter found a sheet of paper and a pencil and asked Terri to hold the torch so he could see what he was writing.

'Right, at the head of the page, it said TOP SECRET.'

'MOST SECRET,' corrected Terri.

'Yeah. And then it said something like HELIOS DECRYPTS.'

'Yes. HELIOS was in there and the word FIRST, I think. What's a decrypt?'

'Another word for decoding.'

'Okay. And then there was a list of words. Can you remember any?'

'They were all plants. I can remember two of them, LARK-SPUR and NIGHTSHADE, but I can't remember the third one.'

'It was HEMLOCK, because I remember thinking that was the poison that Socrates took. What do you think HELIOS means?'

'I haven't got the faintest idea.'

That was as far as they could get for the moment.

Peter was thoughtful. 'What do we think the other pages contained?'

'It looked like it was some kind of code. If it'd been a real language, the words would have been different lengths.'

Peter nodded. 'Good point. And did you hear what he said? He muttered something under his breath.'

'It sounded to me like Mother Goose.'

'Yes, Mother Goose dossier.'

'What's that mean? Mother Goose is something to do with nursery rhymes or pantomimes. And a dossier is a report. It feels like one of Cuthbert's puzzles. And there was something about Nightshade being pleased with the dossier.'

Peter laughed. 'Yes, shall I add that to the notes?'

'Might as well.'

Peter wrote down the words they thought they'd heard Small-wood utter. None of what he'd written down made much sense, but they could puzzle it out later. He folded the sheet of paper and put it in his back pocket. 'Okay, what now?'

'Let's get back before our absence is noticed.'

They were soon out of the house, making sure to bolt the back door from the inside, before Peter climbed out through the window. Half an hour later, Peter was back at The Croft, having first accompanied Terri to her house. He was relieved to hear Flo's gentle snores and slipped into his bed with considerable relief.

NIPPY

PETER GOT UP LATER than he had intended the next morning. The excitement of the previous day, the fresh air and the quietness of a country district at night, to which, as a city boy, he was unused, meant that he had slept more soundly than usual. He hurriedly washed and dressed and went downstairs to the kitchen, where Flo was sitting in a Windsor chair by the window with a cup of tea in her hand and listening to the Light Programme on the radio.

'Ah, there you are, dear. Did you sleep well?'

'Yes, thank you, Flo. Like a log. I'm sorry I'm up so late.'

'It's the summer holidays. You can get up when you want. What would you like for breakfast?'

'Just a bowl of cereal, please. I promised Terri I'd meet her at ten-thirty. We're going to see Nippy today.'

'Young man, I'm not going to let you go out without a decent breakfast. At least have a couple of slices of toast and marmalade.'

Peter bowed to Flo's wishes and sat down at the kitchen table. Flo poured him a big mug of tea and put it in front of him. While she toasted a couple of slices of bread, he demolished a large bowl of cornflakes. By the time he left the house, it was already ten twenty-five. If he went into the village, up through the allotments and along the railway cutting, it would take him a good deal longer than five minutes. He knew it was against the new rules about access to the Wyvern estate, but he decided to slip through The

44

Croft's back gate, which led directly into the meadow in front of the lake. If he kept to the dried-up bed of the drainage channel that ran beneath the huge elms and oaks fringing the western boundary of the estate, he was unlikely to be seen. Once he got to the lake he jogged across the top meadow up to the bench and crawled through the hole in the hedge. He was not entirely surprised to find that Terri was nowhere to be seen. He threw himself on the ground to catch his breath and looked up at the clear blue sky. He still hadn't readjusted to the delicious fragrance of the air and the riotous birdsong. He wished he could identify the different birds from their songs, in the same way that he could identify the instruments in a piece of music. He wondered how you would go about learning such a thing.

At that moment, he saw Terri coming up the slope of the railway cutting. She was wearing a pair of lime-coloured shorts, a white tee shirt and a pair of white plimsolls, all of which set off her lightly tanned skin to perfection. He might have been in very close proximity to her the previous day, but he hadn't really taken in how she looked from a distance. Now that he was able to watch her as she approached the level area in front of the hedge den, he was not disappointed in the figure she cut in the brilliant morning sunshine. When she reached the flat area at the top, she sat down beside him and pecked him on the cheek.

'Hello, you. I'm sorry I'm late. Mum made me have a *proper* breakfast.'

'Flo did the same to me.'

'Mum said that she supposed I'd be having supper at The Croft again.'

'I got up so late that I didn't have time to discuss it with Flo, but I'm sure she wouldn't mind.'

'Are you in the same room you were in last year?'

'Yes, in the guest room – the one with old paintings on the walls and weird books in the bookcase, most of them not in English, and a desk in front of the window.'

'Do you think Flo would let me stay over?'

Peter was nonplussed. 'I know she's pretty easy-going, but I don't think she'd let you stay with me in my room.'

Terri laughed. 'No, I meant in the other room. There's a third bedroom, isn't there?'

'Yes, but surely it's more about what your parents think.'

'I think they'd be okay as long as they knew that Flo was there and had agreed. Then you wouldn't have to walk me home all the time.'

Peter was doubtful. 'I'd rather not ask Flo until I've been back a bit longer.'

'I'm just thinking out loud. It's so much nicer at Flo's and my parents are driving me crazy. They treat me like a kid. They don't seem to realise that I'm seventeen now and I'll be off to university next year.'

'Yeah, I know what you mean. I don't think my mum realises that I'll be in the second year sixth next term.'

'How are you feeling about A-levels next year?'

'Okay, I realise, rather late perhaps, that I have chosen three subjects that require a lot of reading.'

'But you're good at languages.'

'Maybe not as good as I thought I was. I sometimes wonder whether I should have done maths and physics instead.'

'Well, I'm struggling a bit with the maths. But I love the Latin and French.'

'I don't think I would have been allowed to do that combination at my school. It's either science or arts. No mixing allowed.'

'That seems a very narrow approach.'

'I don't think it's particularly for our benefit; it's more about how teachers' time is allocated.'

Terri switched back to the arrangements on the upper floor of The Croft. 'Is there a radio in your room?'

'No, but I brought my transistor radio. I also brought my guitar.'

'Fab. How are you getting on with the lessons?'

'So-so. The Bert Weedon book is really good, but it's hard to get my fingers onto some of the chords. I try to do a bit each day.'

'You must play for me.'

'I'm not really confident enough to play in public.'

'I'm not public.'

Peter laughed. 'No, that's true. Maybe I will, but I'm not promising.'

'What kind of stuff do you play?'

'Well, I know it sounds ridiculous, but I'm trying to play Beatles songs.'

'Wow! Which ones are you doing?'

'"Love Me Do" and "Please Please Me".'

'I've got the singles of both those.'

'Brilliant. I remember you said in one of your letters that your dad had bought a record player.'

'Yeah, it's a Dansette. Trouble is it's kept in the living room, so I can't really listen to my singles properly. He keeps telling me to turn that rubbish down. But he turns up the volume when it's a matter of playing his LP of *South Pacific*. I don't suppose Flo has a record player?'

'Well, she's got a big old radiogram, but I don't know if it plays 45s.'

'If it did, I could bring my singles over on one of the days she goes down to London and we could play them really loud.'

'Yeah, I'll check later to see if it can play singles.'

Terri stood up. 'Let's go and find Nippy.'

Peter was all for that. They set off along the railway cutting in the opposite direction to that from which Terri had arrived until they came to the lane that led to Standon, where they turned right and walked towards a row of cottages. Terri pointed to the end-of-terrace cottage nearest them. 'That's his new place.'

Peter was impressed. 'It looks pretty good.'

'Yeah. I'm sure he could have had one of the estate cottages years ago, if he'd wanted. But he preferred to stay close to Cuthbert. He said that it was his job to look after the Master. He was his batman during the war, whatever that means. But now he feels he let him down.'

'You can't really protect someone against a heart attack. Well, not in that way.'

'Quite, but he seems to blame himself for the fact that Cuthbert's no longer with us. Also he misses the Hall and his dratted machine, of course.'

'But, Flo says that he can still go to the barn and work on the machine.'

'True, but it's not quite as convenient as it was for him. For some reason, he often works on it at night. And he's not getting any younger.'

Peter was thoughtful. 'What does he actually do when he's working on the machine?'

'I haven't got the foggiest idea. I seem to recall from O-level physics that you can't have a perpetual motion machine. It would break the second law of thermodynamics.'

Peter nodded. 'Something to do with friction.'

'I didn't really understand the explanation. And anyway all you can really see is the big flywheel.'

PETER WAS NOT THE only person rising late on this sunny Fordham morning. Richard did not wake until eleven-thirty. He was conscious of having a rather heavy head, which was strange since neither he nor Smallwood had drunk excessively the previous night. He went down to the kitchen to make himself a strong cup of coffee in the hope of pepping himself up a bit, only to find that Smallwood had left a note propped against the kettle saying that he had had to return to London unexpectedly. A small crisis had blown up, which he needed to deal with. He apologised, but was reassured that with the other copy of the will out of circulation, Richard could now get on with applying for the grant of probate. He was vaguely irritated by the peremptory phrasing of Smallwood's note, as if he were leaving instructions for a subordinate, but reflected that this had always been his supercilious friend's way and at least he had had to cut short his stay.

As Richard carried his coffee through to the drawing room by way of the central lobby, he saw a small pile of letters lying on the doormat. He stooped down to pick up the mail and noticed at a glance that they were all bills or formal communications. He carried them through to the drawing room and sat in an armchair with a view over the lawn. Sipping his coffee, he cursed himself for being so spineless about the matter of the will. Smallwood was right; he should just go ahead and obtain the grant of probate, then, as executor, he would have access to Cuthbert's funds for the purposes of keeping the estate going until the original will was proved. He had no idea how much the old boy had salted away, but he had been a canny operator and was probably pretty well-heeled. And after all, regardless of the details of the life interest, Richard was still Cuthbert's heir. So whatever he siphoned off now to deal with his personal cash-flow crisis was only an advance on what would come his way in due course. He resolved to fill in the form that very morning.

Already feeling considerably more positive, he went through the mail and was relieved to discover that the only item demanding money was the quarterly electricity bill for The Priory, which, because it was now midsummer, was not as painful as it had been earlier in the year and certainly nowhere near as large as the electricity bills at Wyvern Hall. He recalled Smallwood's throwaway remark when they had been going through Cuthbert's papers that the large electricity bills at Wyvern's just showed that Nippy's perpetual motion machine was a hoax. If Nippy really was pulling the wool over people's eyes and Richard could prove it, then Nippy's reputation in the locality would suffer a serious blow, making people less inclined to believe his claims about there being a revised will. The question was, though, what was the best way of exposing Nippy's fraudulent behaviour? He'd think about it while he was completing the probate form.

TERRI KNOCKED ON THE back door of Nippy's cottage. Receiving no answer, she tried the handle, and finding the door unlocked, pushed it open and called out, 'Nippy, are you there?'

She stepped inside and said, 'Let's wait for him in his kitchen. He's probably just gone to the shop.'

Peter felt a little uncomfortable about going into someone's house uninvited, but he presumed that Terri had done it before. After all, she knew Nippy much better than he did. Terri got them each a glass of water and they sat down at the kitchen table. Peter looked around. The room was simply furnished and noticeably short of mod cons, but it was beautifully cool on this warm morning. He noticed that there were three framed photographs hanging from the picture rail. One showed a young man in military uniform. Peter wondered if it was a picture of Nippy as a young soldier. Another picture showed a group of two men and a woman in front of a large country house and the final picture was of a large electronic machine with two men standing in front of it. One of the men was in a lab coat and looked as if he was the uniformed man a few years later.

Peter pointed to the photos. 'Do you think that's Nippy during the war?'

Terri studied the photos. 'Yeah, and I think the other man in front of the machine is Cuthbert when he was much younger. And do you know what? I think the tall woman in the picture is Flo.'

Peter took a closer look. 'Gosh, I think you're right. My mum did say that Flo and Cuthbert were sweethearts during the war.'

Terri was thoughtful. 'Why do you think they didn't get married?'

Peter was reluctant to express a view on the subject. 'Do you think they were trying to build a perpetual motion machine back then?'

'Maybe, but the machine in the picture hasn't got a flywheel. It looks more like something electronic. And, anyway, what use would a perpetual motion machine be in a war?'

'I don't know. If you could get more energy out of it than you put in, that might be useful.'

Terri wasn't convinced. 'But that's precisely what my teacher said you can't do.'

Just then the back door opened and Nippy came in and dropped his shopping onto the dresser at the back of the kitchen.

'I wondered when I'd be seeing you two. Welcome back to Fordham, Master Peter.'

'Hello, Nippy. It's great to see you again, but I'm so sorry about Cuthbert. It's terribly sad news. I was looking forward to playing more games of chess with him and to swimming parties in the lake.'

'He went before his time, right enough.'

Peter thought he'd talk about more positive things. 'Terri tells me that you've made a lot of progress with your machine and that

Richard Warren has allowed you access to the barn so that you can continue to work on it.'

Nippy harrumphed. 'He has, but by rights I'm meant to be able to stay at the Hall for the rest of my life.'

Peter was sympathetic. 'Of course, I'm sure that's what everyone thinks, but this does seem to be a nice house. You've got plenty of space and a nice garden.'

Nippy was not convinced. 'But I need to be at the Hall. I can't keep an eye on the Master's things from here.'

'You told me, when I helped you move in,' Terri said, 'that you have a good view down to the main drive of the Hall from the back bedroom.'

'That's true. And I saw Richard and his smarmy friend arriving in that ridiculous car yesterday. I don't like the idea of them poking through the Master's things. That's not what the Master intended.'

Terri was itching to tell Nippy about the conversation between Richard and Smallwood that she and Peter had overheard, but she thought it better not to mention it until they had found the copy of the will that the two men had been talking about.

Peter, guessing what she was thinking, and afraid that she might not be able to resist the temptation, said, 'What are you doing today, Nippy?'

Nippy was noncommittal. 'Same as most days. Working on the machine. I want to complete it before Richard decides I can't go to the barn any more. Or, even worse, sells the entire estate. Which, I hear, is what he's hoping to do.'

This was exactly what Terri feared too. 'Can we come with you? It'd be nice to see the machine in action.'

'I'm not sure that would be a good idea. If Richard saw us all trooping across the East Meadow, he might say that I'd broken the arrangement and ban me from going again.'

Terri, as was her wont, was not to be put off. 'Pete and I could go around by the railway cutting and walk down to the barn from the lookout bench. That path is not visible from the Hall itself. The barn gets in the way of a clear view.'

Nippy, who found it hard to resist Terri, agreed to the plan and said, 'Alright, but make sure that you spend as little time in the open as possible. And you can't stay all day. I've got a lot of work to get on with.'

Half an hour later, Terri and Peter knocked on the wicket door of the barn. A few moments later the door swung open and Nippy ushered them in. It was a hot day and it was a relief to step into the cool interior of the barn with its soaring height, almost like a cathedral made of huge wooden beams. Peter had been in the barn once or twice the previous year, but there had been considerable changes since then. The space was now dominated by a huge flywheel and various other wheels and gears. The flywheel was spinning and a low hum emanated from the contraption.

'Wow! Nippy, that's impressive. Is it actually working?' Peter hadn't meant to offer a backhanded compliment and Nippy took jocular exception to his comment.

'What's it look like?'

'Yes, but I meant without using energy.'

'Don't be daft. It has to use energy. What do they teach you at school these days? The question is whether it outputs more energy than you put into it.'

'And does it?'

'Well, let's just say we're not quite there yet. But this wheel will keep spinning for hours without the machine needing more energy being supplied.'

'Has it been spinning all night?'

'No, I started it a few minutes ago, so you two could see it in action.'

'And what do you start it with?'

'There *is* a small starter motor, but that's all I'm telling you.'

Terri had a question. 'Does the hum come from the machine or from something else?'

'What hum? I can't hear anything.'

Terri laughed. 'That's because you're as deaf as a post.'

Peter had been wondering about the hum too. 'It sounds like mains hum to me. I get it on my guitar amplifier. We discussed it in physics at school. The mains current alternates at 50 cycles per second and it makes the transformer vibrate at that frequency and its overtones.'

Nippy smiled at Peter. 'Oh, so you fancy yourself as a bit of an electronics expert, do you, Master Peter?'

'No, Nippy, I was just trying to remember what we learned when I did O-level physics.'

'You learned well. Let's just say that the hum *is* from a transformer, which the contraption needs for various reasons I don't want to go into now. And I'm swearing you to secrecy on that point. You're not allowed to mention it to anyone else. It will spoil the illusion. Do you promise me?'

Peter gulped. 'Yes, of course, Nippy.'

'And you, Miss Hammond?'

'Yes, Nippy.'

'If you can both keep your mouths shut for a week or two, I will explain everything.'

As Peter and Terri were walking back up to the railway cutting, Terri said, 'I didn't know you'd played chess with Cuthbert.'

'It was at the beginning of last summer before I'd got to know you. Flo mentioned to him that I was in the school chess team and he insisted on putting me to the test.'

'Did you beat him?'

'No, he was really good.'

'Will you teach me?'

'Yes, of course. I'll see if Flo has a set.'

Terri slipped her arm through his and said, 'Thank you. I wish I could teach you something.'

Peter patted her hand, but didn't reply. They continued walking in silence, both reflecting on the conversation with Nippy. Just before they got to the hedge, Terri said, 'So the machine's an illusion.'

Peter nodded. 'It's not like Nippy to want to pull the wool over people's eyes. There must be something else to it.'

'Yes, I wonder what.'

TOWARDS THE END OF the week, Smallwood was on the usual bench waiting for Rafferty. Soon he saw him approaching.

Rafferty sat down at the other end of the bench, opened his copy of The Times and said *sotto voce*, 'Moscow has had a close look at the material you found. The encrypted material is genuine. The brief abstract, so far as it goes, is an accurate decryption of certain details in the encrypted transcripts. But they are puzzled at the partial nature of the decrypts, in particular the fact that Mother Goose has not been able to match identities to codenames. They are not aware of the significance of the codename Helios. If it is a person, then perhaps he has been able to use a crib to get at some of the encrypted material, but not all of it. That would be reassuring. If it is a new computer system, we are not aware of it. That would be more alarming. But it seems unlikely that Mother Goose would have had access to Cheltenham's latest toys, especially since he left the service under something of a cloud. The feeling is that he could not have managed these decrypts working on his own.'

'Why not? He was one of the geniuses at Bletchley, wasn't he?'

'That was many years ago and involved a big team. Mother Goose was a fluent Russian speaker and a talented code-breaker of the old school, but he wasn't a boffin. Other people provided the technological magic later in the war. We believe that he must have had a collaborator or collaborators to decrypt the signals in question.'

'Isn't it possible that what we have here is the unfinished product of a retirement project? I glanced at those dates and they are not particularly contemporary. For someone like Mother Goose, code breaking is the equivalent of The Times cryptic crossword for the rest of us. He was whiling away his twilight years trying to crack some signals that he should have returned to the Registry, in a belated attempt to justify the failures that led to his being put out to grass and that was as far as he got.'

'That is not Moscow's view, nor, I might add, Nightshade's. And we want you to find out whether there is a collaborator and who he might be. We can then decide what is to be done about him.'

'How am I supposed to do that?'

'You will have to go back to Fordham and investigate.'

'Rafferty, I can't keep going back to Fordham and snooping around Mother Goose's place. Someone's bound to smell a rat.'

'I don't see why. You and Richard Warren are not only old college chums, but you also share an unconventional interest.'

'Oh, come off it, Rafferty. I think we queers are not as unusual as you seem to be implying, even in a backwater like Fordham.'

'Please don't bandy words with me. I am just telling you what you need to do and why it will be of little remark if you were to visit your old friend for another few days.'

'It is also being noticed in my department that I have been taking quite a lot of time off recently.'

'Well, perhaps I can help there.'

Smallwood shrugged. 'Alright, I'll get down there as soon as I can. But as far as I've been able to ascertain, the only collaborator Mother Goose has is a village idiot who goes by the name of Nippy.'

'Smallwood, I need hardly remind you that idiots can be useful and often have unexpected talents.'

Smallwood flinched. He felt the truism was unfairly directed at him. 'Yes, I suppose so.'

Rafferty folded his newspaper and walked away.

OVER THE NEXT FEW days, Terri and Peter went on several long bike rides into the surrounding countryside. On one particularly fine day they cycled to Standon, which had a small outdoor swimming pool, spending more time sprawled on the grass applying sun cream to each other than they spent in the freezing water. When they got back to Fordham, Terri finally persuaded Peter to overcome his reserve and play his guitar for her. He was gratified by her response. She asked if he'd show her how to finger one or two simple chords. He said he'd be happy to, but she shouldn't be too disappointed if she found it difficult to place her fingers accurately. If she kept at it, she would eventually make progress. Having delivered this warning, he was therefore somewhat perturbed to find that she seemed to have a natural gift and was playing those chords without a hitch by the end of the afternoon, a feat that had taken him several weeks.

A day or two later, the mild dismay he'd felt at her facility in playing the guitar was offset to a degree by her subsequent lack of aptitude at picking up the rules of chess. Peter had found a set of wooden chess pieces and a handsome inlaid chessboard in Flo's dining room following their visit to Nippy's, and he spent an afternoon showing Terri the moves of the different pieces. But she seemed to have difficulty memorising them and became despondent. Peter said that it had taken him months to master the moves too. This wasn't strictly true, but it enabled them to put the set away and return to the guitar with a certain amount of relief on both sides.

Terri was now taking quite a few of her meals at The Croft, but Flo seemed entirely happy with the arrangement. She had something on her mind and it saved her from having to think of ways to entertain Peter. One evening towards the end of the week, as Terri and Peter were washing up and putting the supper things away, Flo said that she would be going down to London the next day and wouldn't be home until late. Peter remembered that on a number of occasions the previous summer, Flo had had to go to town. She never explained what it was that she did in London, whether she was meeting old friends for dinner or going to the theatre.

The next morning after breakfast, as Flo got herself ready to drive to the station to catch the train to London, she said, 'Well, at least this year, I don't have to worry about leaving you on your own. I am sure Miss Hammond will be here before long and Beatles songs will be pouring forth. I am afraid you will have to fend for yourselves so far as lunch and supper are concerned, but you are welcome to anything you can find in the fridge. Or maybe Doreen Hammond will take pity on you and invite you to supper there.'

Flo had hardly gone more than five minutes when Terri appeared at the back door and said, 'All clear?'

Peter nodded. Terri whooped. 'Yippee, a day of unchaperoned fun.'

It was a glorious day, the sun shining brightly in the sky and already very warm. Terri had brought her singles and the first thing they did was put them on the radiogram and turn the volume up. When they had exhausted Terri's small collection of singles, Peter suggested that they cycle to the swimming pool again. He had found the sight of Terri in a bikini on their previous visit a thrilling corrective to the impression created by her normal boyish attire. But Terri protested that it was already too hot for cycling. They would be dripping with sweat by the time they got back.

Peter conceded the point, but couldn't help feeling disappointed not to be able to spend an hour or two admiring her in her bikini. Suddenly morose, he said, 'This is the kind of weather that Cuthbert had the lake dredged for.'

Terri sat up. 'Yes, you're right. Why don't we swim in the lake? Smallwood has gone back to London, we haven't seen Richard for several days and Flo is also away. Who will be any the wiser?'

'Nippy?'

'Maybe. He might tell us off, but he's not going to sneak on us.'

Peter wasn't sure, but Terri knew Nippy a good deal better than Peter did. It certainly appealed on this sweltering day.

'I don't know …'

'Come on, Pete. We probably won't get another chance like this. It'd be too risky to try it with Flo around or once Richard is back snooping around the Hall.'

'Okay, let's go to your place and get your swimming togs.'

'I don't want my mum poking her nose into what we're doing. Not only will she ask lots of questions, but she'll probably ask us to pick up some shopping in Standon, like she did the other day.'

'Well, what will you do then?'

'I'll swim in my underwear.'

Peter was both appalled and delighted at the prospect, but felt unable to express himself on the subject. He just looked at her to see if she was serious.

Finally, he said as evenly as he could, 'Okay, I'll go and get a couple of towels.'

Fifteen minutes later, they were at the side of the lake furthest from the Hall and its outbuildings. The willow trees on the little island meant that they were not visible from the barn, which, if Nippy was around, was where he was most likely to be. Nor was the little baked clay beach that they were sitting on to take off their sandals visible from the bench at the top of the hill. Only someone coming down the dry drainage channel from the back of The Croft or approaching the lake directly from the big meadow in front of it which stretched to the road boundary would be able to see them.

Peter had brought his swimming trunks and struggled into them demurely. Terri laughed at his contortions and started to remove her jeans and tee shirt. Peter, somewhat unnecessarily since she was only removing her outer garments, turned his back to give her some privacy. When he turned around he realised that actually there was not much difference in terms of decency between the bikini she had been wearing previously at the pool in Standon and the bra and pants that she was now treating as a swimming costume.

Terri was in an elated mood. 'Come on, then. Last one in is a sissy.'

She rushed into the water and, once the water was up to her knees, dived below the surface. Peter thought this was a bit reckless since they had no idea how deep the lake was, but she surfaced a moment later and said, 'It's lovely.'

Peter waded into the water much more cautiously and eventually sank his shoulders beneath the surface and swam sedately towards Terri, whereupon she turned and struck out across the lake with a very efficient front crawl stroke. Peter followed her with his somewhat more inelegant breaststroke. When he reached her, she threw her arms around his neck and gave him a hug. 'Looks like I'm going to have to give you some swimming lessons in exchange for the guitar lessons.'

'I don't think I'll make such quick progress as you have on the guitar. I've never really got the hang of the crawl.'

'It's all about breathing, but you also have to get flatter in the water. Don't let your legs drop down. Let's get back to the shallower part and I'll show you.'

She let him go and glided smoothly back to where she could put her feet on the bottom. She then demonstrated with a few lazy strokes what she meant. Peter tried to copy her, but only succeeded in swallowing a mouthful of lake water. Terri laughed. 'Just let yourself float and then turn your head and shoulders to one side and take a breath. If you don't turn the top part of your body, you won't be able to breathe. And don't keep your head tilted up. Look down as if you were trying to see the bottom.'

Peter tried again, this time with a little more success. Twenty minutes later, his crawl was already much better. Terri was proud of her efforts. 'The next thing would be to extend the distance, but perhaps we shouldn't try and cross the lake, just in case we're noticed.'

Peter agreed. In any case he wasn't sure that he could make it all the way across without having to revert to breaststroke. Terri spun over on her back and stared up into the clear blue sky. 'This is dreamy, isn't it? It's a pity that we can't do this every day. I bet it would be fun even in the rain.'

Peter followed suit and floated on his back. It certainly was amazing, swimming in a natural lake with this beautiful girl. They had brought a bottle of diluted barley water and a couple of packets of crisps with them. Terri had turned onto her front and said, 'Let's have a drink and sunbathe for a bit.'

Getting out of the water, Terri became tangled up in some duckweed and emerged from the lake with strands of it draped over her head. Peter couldn't help laughing, which prompted Terri to scoop up a handful of the weed and throw it at him. During this passage of horseplay it was only too apparent to Peter that if there had not been much difference between Terri's bikini and her underclothes when they were dry, there was a considerable differ-ence now that those same underclothes were wet. The thinner fabric of her wet bra and pants clung to her body and had become all but transparent.

She noticed the direction of his gaze and, looking down at her torso, said, 'These things are soaking. I think I'd better lay them out in the sun to dry.'

Without more ado, she slipped off her bra and, knotting a towel over her breasts, slipped off her pants. Freed from the wet under-garments, she did a little pirouette and then hung them on the branch of a tree to dry.

Peter, still in his wet swimming trunks, lying propped on one elbow on his own towel, followed every moment of the perform-ance closely. But now Terri stood over him with her hands on her hips. 'Well, I'm glad you enjoyed that. Your turn now. Your swim-mers are soaking wet. You need to let them dry.'

Peter shrugged. 'I'll be okay.'

'I don't know what you're worried about, Pete. It's easier for you. You can just wrap your towel around your waist and take them off.'

Peter reluctantly did as she suggested and hung his swimming trunks alongside her underwear on the branch of the tree.

They lay in the sunshine for the next hour, talking quietly, until they had finished the bottle of barley water and the packets of crisps. Terri then jumped up to see whether her things were dry enough to put on again. Deciding that they were, she wriggled back into her bra and pants, a little more carefully than she had removed them. Only at that point did she remove the towel and pull on her jeans and tee shirt.

Now, respectably attired once again, she said, 'C'mon, Pete. I'm starving. Let's go back and get some lunch.'

Peter struggled back into his own clothes and soon they were heading back to The Croft.

Back at The Croft, they tucked into large hunks of bread from Hart's, some tangy Cheddar and thick slices of ham from Hatch-ett's, followed by a bowl each of Flo's homemade apple crumble and cream. Both of them drank two or three cups of tea. Re-freshed and refuelled, they washed up and put the lunch things away, then went into Flo's dining room to continue work on one of Cuthbert's jigsaw puzzles that they had started earlier in the week. This one was a view of Fordham High Street showing Terri's father's shop and the three neighbouring shops.

Each puzzle was unique. From time to time people in the village would receive one in thanks for some act of kindness or to celeb-rate a significant birthday or life event. A number of individuals had been the recipient of a puzzle more than once and there had been a certain amount of local rivalry as to who had been most favoured in this respect. Any accolade, though, was for the position of runner-up, because it was acknowledged that Flo's collection was more extensive than any but Cuthbert's own.

Peter and Terri had got all the edge pieces assembled. This had turned out not to be as easy as it was with the shop-bought puzzles with which Peter was familiar, in which the shapes of the pieces followed a fairly regular pattern—most being roughly square, with mortices and tenons (or "lugs and slots," as Peter called them) opposite or adjacent to each other. Rarer were the pieces that had one lug and three slots or one slot and three lugs. But a number of the pieces in Cuthbert's puzzles were in the shape of birds, butter-flies and animals without any lugs or slots at all. This in turn meant that the pieces surrounding these zoomorphic shapes had an unconventional profile. It certainly added an extra level of diffi-culty to solving the puzzle, but it was clear that this was not the first time that Terri had assembled one of Cuthbert's jigsaw puzzles and they were now making good progress.

Shortly after seven o'clock, they heard the sound of Flo's Morris turning into the drive of The Croft. Peter and Terri went to the front door and greeted her. Peter said, 'What would you like for supper? Or would you prefer a cup of tea first?'

Flo hung her coat and hat up and said, 'Thank you, dear, I don't need anything to eat, but I think I need something a bit stronger than tea to drink. I've done too much walking and my leg is killing me. What you could do is bring me the bottle of Cutty Sark from the drinks cabinet in the sitting room.'

When Peter got back with the bottle, Flo had taken off her shoes and she had her bad leg up on a chair.

'There's a tray of ice cubes in the top compartment of the fridge. Plop a couple in a glass, please.'

Peter did as he was asked and Flo poured herself a large Scotch. She took a mouthful and then said, 'I can't drink on my own. What are you young 'uns having? The whisky is excellent.'

Neither Peter nor Terri had ever drunk whisky before and Peter wasn't sure now was the best time to start, but Terri was keen to experiment.

Flo said, 'Just a drop, mind. And maybe with a splash of soda water. Or I'll have Fred giving me a piece of his mind.'

Flo could see that Peter didn't know how to fix the drinks and gave him brief instructions. A few minutes later, all three of them clinked glasses and Flo said, 'Bottoms up.'

Peter sipped his drink and was pleasantly surprised by the fiery liquor. Terri's reaction was not so positive. Instead of sipping it, she took a gulp and ended up spluttering.

Flo laughed. 'Take it easy, girl. Try sipping to begin with.'

Once Terri's coughing had abated, she declared in a spirit of bravado that it was lovely.

Flo was already feeling more relaxed and said, 'So, what did you two get up to today? I don't want to know all the details...' – at which point she winked at them theatrically – '...just the main points.'

They gave her a condensed account of their day and told her that they had spent the evening doing Cuthbert's jigsaw puzzle, on which they had made good progress. Another two or three days and they might have completed it.

Flo was impressed. 'Those puzzles are by no means easy.'

She took another sip of her whisky. 'But you didn't play Beatles singles at top volume all day long then?'

Peter admitted that they had played them, but not all day long, because they only had a few singles.

Flo said, 'I imagine you could do with something else to listen to then. Would you mind passing me my bag, dear?'

Peter handed Flo her bag, from which a moment later she withdrew a copy of the Beatles' *Please Please Me* LP. 'So I hope this might come in handy.'

She passed the LP to Peter, who looked at her wide-eyed in amazement. It took him a moment to recover his wits. 'Thank you, Flo. That's amazing.'

Flo laughed. 'I may come to regret this. The only stipulation I make is that we save the first play through until tomorrow. I need to get to bed and you need to walk Miss Hammond home.'

Half an hour later, as Peter and Terri reached her door, Terri said, 'Wow, old Flo is an amazing person. I can't wait until tomorrow. Thank you, Pete. It's been a lovely day.'

She leaned forward and kissed him on the cheek and then disappeared into the house.

BY THE END OF the week Richard had plucked up the courage to quiz Nippy about the Wyvern electricity bills. He sat in the Lagonda until he spotted him trudging across the east meadow and then through the orchard on his way to the barn. Richard jumped out of the car and intercepted him just as he was about to open the wicket door to the barn.

Affecting a nonchalant manner, he said, 'Good morning, Nippy. And a fine one it is, too.'

Nippy was immediately wary. Affability was not Richard Warren's normal mode. 'Good morning, sir.'

'How are you settling into your new accommodation? I've been meaning to come around, but I've had a lot on my plate.'

Nippy found that hard to believe. 'I imagine you're relieved that your guest has returned to the Great Wen, sir.'

'Ah, been at the old Cobbett again, eh, Nippy?'

'No, sir. It was a saying of the Master's.'

'Well, of course. And you are not wrong about the chore of having house guests. Anyway, I don't expect to be seeing Mr Smallwood again for some time. We were only slight acquaintances. He is an amateur architectural historian and wanted to see an unmodernised but well-preserved Elizabethan manor house in all its glory.'

'I hope he was impressed, sir.'

'He was indeed.'

'He should have had a look at the barn. It is even older than the house.'

'I had no idea. But it was not the barn that I wanted to talk to you about. It was to do with the house.'

Nippy didn't like the sound of this. 'Yes, sir.'

'I've started going through my uncle's accounts for the purposes of probate and I noticed that the Wyvern's electricity bills are very high.'

'It was a bitter winter, sir, you may remember, and the Master liked to keep the whole house warm. These old buildings can get terrible damp in the winter and then they start to crumble.'

'Well, yes, I know that. But here's the thing, the Wyvern's electricity bills are three or four times as high as those for The Priory, which is quite a lot bigger, and they have been so for more than eighteen months. What do you think might explain that?'

'I have no idea, sir.'

'I hope you don't mind me saying that I wondered whether it might have something to do with your machine.'

Nippy looked uncomfortable. 'Well, sir, the machine does draw a small amount of power, but just to start it. And of course there is electricity in the barn for lighting and for the equipment that we used to actually build the machine.'

'We, Nippy?'

'I mean the things I used, of course. Though the Master used to drop in to see how I was getting on.'

'So, one would expect to see the electricity usage lower when the next quarter's bill drops on the doormat?'

'I expect so, sir. All the running costs were dealt with by the Master. I had no idea that my machine might be costing him so much. He never mentioned it.'

'Well, that is a measure of the man. Never one to stint when it came to making sure that a loyal servant was justly rewarded.'

'He was one of the best, sir.'

'Indeed, Nippy. I wonder if you would care to give me a demonstration of your machine in the next few days. I feel that I have been neglecting a project that my uncle took great pleasure in supporting.'

'Certainly, sir. The machine is not working at the moment. I am making some modifications. I will let you know when it's back in working order.'

SMALLWOOD SAT IN HIS poky, Paddington flat, smoking furiously. He was uncertain as to how best to invite himself back to The Priory. It had been obvious on his previous visits that Warren had been far from delighted by his presence, but at least he had had a plausible excuse on both occasions. Now, thanks to Smallwood's intervention, Warren was actively engaged in the probate of the estate and would market the property as soon as he was able. Once the property was sold, Warren's financial difficulties would evaporate together with his readiness to tolerate his old college friend. Furthermore, access to Wyvern Hall would become considerably more difficult once there was a new owner.

He was rather irritated that Moscow had not accepted that what he had found was the end of the matter. He supposed that it was possible that there was a safe somewhere on the premises that Warren was unaware of. But he could hardly suggest such a thing to Warren. Certainly, he could put up at an inn in a neighbouring village and break into the house at night. However, not only was there a high chance of his being recognised in the locality, but there was also the risk that, if he were to encounter Warren or one of the other locals, explanations would be tricky. Rafferty should really have found someone else to do the job, someone who was not a familiar face in Fordham Market.

So it seemed that if Smallwood was to do Moscow's bidding and re-engage with Warren without calling into question the reasons for his earlier visits to The Priory, he was going to have to come up with something not just plausible but persuasive. It did not take a lot of insight into Warren's psychology to see that an appeal to his baser instincts would be the way to go. Smallwood doubted that there was anything of a sufficiently novel or reliably sexual nature that he could arrange, so filthy lucre might be a better bet. If there were a way to speed up Warren's access to the money that he desperately needed to stave off his creditors, or at least to make him believe that to be the case, then he might be prepared to tolerate Smallwood's presence for a while longer. Not that Smallwood had any idea how to do that right now.

He reviewed the short list of wealthy people in his network of acquaintances who might be persuaded to consider buying a country estate, especially if they could acquire it at a knockdown price with a view to selling it on almost immediately, in the process pocketing a healthy premium. Of course, it would be vital to keep the nature of the arbitrage from Warren. The more he thought about it, the more the idea appealed, particularly since Smallwood would then be in a good position to extract a success fee from the intermediate buyer. The fly in the ointment was that setting up a deal like that would take time and effort, and time was inevitably short.

He paced around the room, turning the idea over in his mind when it suddenly occurred to him that in such cases it was immaterial whether the buyer existed or not. What was more important was the extent to which the dupe wanted to believe in the outcome of the proposal. Warren desperately needed the money and he was also timid and lazy, a perfect combination of predispositions. All Smallwood needed to do was to create a convincing illusion that he had a buyer waiting in the wings. But who?

And then it came to him. *He* could be the buyer. And the beauty of his pretending to be the buyer was that it would give him a good reason to make a thorough survey of Wyvern Hall and its curtilage. Warren would be bound to ask where he expected to get the funds for the purchase. Tricky. Maybe he could say that he was the beneficiary of a family trust. He could claim that all he needed to do was convince the trustees, the most influential of whom was a doting uncle, of the advantages of the investment. There was something pleasing about the creation of a rival uncle *ex nihilo*, as a solution to the difficulties that Mother Goose had created for Smallwood. Then, as soon as he had satisfied Moscow's absurd demands, he could find some impediment to the purchase and withdraw from the deal.

Smallwood knocked back his Scotch and headed off to bed in a much better frame of mind than he had been in for several days.

Richard and Smallwood were once again sitting on the terrace of The Priory in Fordham Market, enjoying the first snifter of the evening, although in all honesty neither of them was particularly relaxed. Richard was feeling distinctly irritated with Smallwood for having insisted on coming to stay again so soon. He didn't entirely believe that he really had something to tell him that couldn't equally well be conveyed in a phone call. At the same time, Smallwood was doubtful that Warren would take the bait that he was about to offer him.

Richard sipped his Scotch. 'Smallwood, people are going to start talking.'

Smallwood snapped into action. 'I'm sure they were talking long before I ever set foot in Fordham. My dear chap, I would advise against looking a gift horse in the mouth. I am here to make a proposal that will not only take the heat off you but will also solve your immediate financial problems.'

'In that case I'm all ears, Smallwood.'

'I have found a buyer for Wyvern Hall.'

'You have? But surely you could have told me the name of the sap on the phone.'

'You might regret those words somewhat when you learn of the identity of this person.'

'Oh, come on, Smallwood. Why all the coyness?'

'Because I am the buyer.'

'You! But how? I did not know that you had access to such sums.'

'Well, not day-to-day, otherwise I would have turned my badge in long ago. But I am one of the beneficiaries of a family trust and the most influential of the trustees is a doting uncle. I have already sounded him out and he is, in principle, well-disposed. He just needs a little more information.'

'This is unexpected, Smallwood. It did not strike me when we were undergraduates that there was wealth in your background.'

'One doesn't like to trumpet these things, and in those days the trustees were a much more conservative bunch.'

'And he is not deterred by the price I am asking.'

'Not in the slightest. He will pay the asking price.'

Richard was surprised. He had had a tussle with the agent who had thought that his expectations were a little on the speculative side. Maybe he had actually set the asking price too low, seeing that Smallwood seemed uninterested in haggling. Perhaps that was the inevitable result of it being trust money rather than his own hard-earned cash.

'So what kind of information does he need beyond what is contained in the agent's particulars?'

'He is a little infirm and would rather not travel without good reason, so he would like me to take some photographs. Those in the agent's particulars do not give a good impression.'

'And you are a competent photographer and have the right equipment?'

'I do indeed. I have come equipped with my Leica, several rolls of film and a sturdy tape measure. If it is alright with you, I propose to start work first thing tomorrow morning. I will not need your assistance. I don't see why it should take more than a couple of days. And I would be delighted to stand you dinner in The Fox for the time that I am here. Of course, if in the meantime you receive a better offer, you are at liberty to accept it. Whether I could persuade the trustees to increase their offer is another matter.'

'Be my guest, Smallwood. I will give you the key and you can snap away to your heart's content. You will forgive me if I do not join you.'

'I will get on much faster on my own.'

As they strolled to The Fox, Richard said, 'I hope you don't mind me saying that I will find it very strange if your uncle decides to proceed with the purchase and you become a neighbour, particularly in a house that has been in the Warren family for many years.'

'You have nothing to fear, my dear chap. I have no desire to usurp the position of the Warren family in the local community. I will acknowledge your standing as lord of the manor and do my best not to embarrass you. Of course, there may be advantages too. It is not impossible that I can attract some of the disapproval that until now has attached to you.'

'Disapproval?'

'Well, I imagine that life in the countryside can be a challenge for those with our proclivities.'

'You can say that again. I just worry that you might be a little less discreet than me.'

'Impossible, dear boy. I have my position at the department to think of.'

HELIOS

EARLY THE NEXT MORNING, Smallwood strolled through the village jingling the keys to Wyvern Hall in his pocket. Over his shoulder was slung a leather case for his Leica. It was a beautiful morning and Fordham basked in the bright sunshine. Smallwood really was coming to like the place. It seemed a pity to have to import the vile shenanigans of the Cold War into this little paradise. But that was the mess he had got himself into and there was really nothing else he could do other than follow orders. He certainly had no desire to have to beat a hasty retreat to Moscow. He doubted that he would be welcomed as a conquering hero. But the truth was that Smallwood was not confident of satisfying Moscow on the matter of Mother Goose's supposed collaborator, nor what they would accept as evidence to the contrary.

He reached the front door of Wyvern Hall and let himself in. He really had no desire to go through the whole business of photographing the house and its interiors, but it was just possible that Warren would ask for copies. Best to get that side of things out of the way first. He thought that he'd start with the attic and work his way down. He climbed up the creaky stairs and started work. Smallwood knew that Nippy had had three rooms in the attic. Smallwood, who was a fastidious man, flinched at the primitive kitchen and bathroom arrangements, but in the spirit of the subterfuge that he was involved in, he dutifully snapped them. He then moved on to Nippy's living quarters. These were not much more prepossessing and it was clear that Nippy had failed to remove all his effects to his new accommodation. There were still a number of pictures hanging on the wall. They looked as if they dated from the war. One was of two individuals in uniform. Another was of the same people in civilian dress in some kind of scientific installation. But it was not photographs that Smallwood was after. It was material related to the Mother Goose dossier. He quickly took a couple of snaps of the room and then moved on.

Two hours later he had nearly completed the ground floor and was standing in the back hall of the house, contemplating taking his lunch at The Fox. There were only two other doors he hadn't peered into. He tried the one nearest to him, which proved to be some kind of broom cupboard. Quickly shutting that door, he then tried the door opposite, which turned out to be locked. It struck him as curious that this was the only internal door in the whole house that was locked. In the course of his survey of the ground floor, he'd noticed a bunch of keys in the utility room near the back door. Maybe one of the keys in the bunch might fit the locked door. As he passed the back door which led to the stable yard, he noticed through the grimy window Nippy leaving the barn by its rear door and heading across the meadows to his cottage. Smallwood laughed to himself. It was curious how no matter what the physics said, there were always those who thought it possible to get something from nothing. Truly, they were the modern day alchemists. Smallwood wondered whether Nippy was deceiving himself or just the citizenry of Fordham. He'd like to have a close look at the machine, preferably without Nippy in attendance. Still, that was not the top priority at that moment.

He located the bunch of keys and noticed that each key had a fob with a label. He glanced through them and found one labelled CELLAR. Well, he certainly hadn't yet found the cellar. Perhaps that was what lay behind the locked door. He detached the cellar key from the bunch and noticed that it was linked with another key, the fob of which said BARN. This was a happy coincidence. Once he had checked the cellar, he could have a quick snoop around the barn in Nippy's absence. And if Nippy returned whilst he was doing so, his cover story would serve to explain his presence. As a prospective buyer of the estate, he was well within his rights to look over one of the larger outbuildings.

He returned to the locked door in the servants' passage and inserted the key. It turned easily and the door swung open. A dank, musty odour assailed his nostrils. He felt around inside the door and was relieved to find a light switch only lightly encumbered with dust and cobwebs. A short flight of steps led down to the lower level. He descended the steps carefully and looked around. Apart from an electricity meter fixed to the wall at the bottom of the stairs, there was very little in the cellar, although its further reaches were lost in the shadows. He was little minded to stumble around in this Stygian gloom in the vain hope of finding a clue to Mother Goose's supposed collaborator.

He was about to return to the ground floor, when he stopped and cocked an ear. There was a decided hum, in fact an electrical hum, which he'd not been aware of in the rest of the house. He remembered Warren's comments about the Wyvern Hall electricity bill. He studied the meter. Clearly the supply was still connected otherwise there would be no electric light to see by. But it did seem to him that the silver disc was spinning very rapidly indeed.

He wondered whether he should mention it to Warren. He stood there for a few moments lost in thought. No, he had other fish to fry. His Soviet masters would not be amused by the idea of his putting his mission on hold while he helped his old college friend solve the mystery of the exorbitant electricity bills. He was starting to believe in his own cover story. It was time for a refreshing pint and a pork pie in The Fox, but not before he'd had a quick shufti around the barn. He exited the house by the front door, with the cellar and the barn keys in his pocket. He could return them later when he'd finished his survey.

He went around to the front of the barn and, trying the key in the lock, let himself into the barn. The sight that presented him really was rather surreal. In the middle of what was probably a mediaeval building, all massive arching beams of wood, was something out of a Heath Robinson drawing, a huge flywheel, twice as high as a man. The bottom third of the wheel was recessed into a trench so that the cast iron struts which supported the wheel's axle could be set low. In front of the strut nearest Smallwood was a small control panel. The wheel was spinning slowly. The electrical hum that Smallwood had heard in the cellar of the house was also evident and seemed to be coming from below the flywheel.

Smallwood walked around to the other side of the flywheel and saw a trapdoor in the floor. He pulled the metal loop and the trapdoor opened on well-oiled hinges. Smallwood peered into the void. There was a sturdy ladder leading down into the space beneath the flywheel. He looked around, not sure if what he was about to do was entirely wise. But his curiosity had now been piqued. He climbed carefully down the ladder and found himself in a room with a number of grey metal cabinets connected by cables. It was clear that the hum was coming from one of the cabinets. Smallwood knew enough electronics to guess that the cabinets were transformers or voltage stabilisers.

Beyond the cabinets was another door. Smallwood was intrigued. He tried the door. It was unlocked. He pushed it open and felt inside the door for a light switch. Immediately, the room beyond was flooded with bright light. Inside was what could only be described as a spacious control room. To one side was a large electronic machine. In front of it was a console with a kind of electric typewriter on it. On the other side of the room was a sofa and several wooden chairs. On the far side of the room was a curtained off area. Smallwood pulled back the curtain and saw a small kitchen with yet another door on the other side. He tried that door, but it was locked.

He went back into the main control room and took his Leica out of its leather case. He was glad of the strip lights. It would mean he could get some good pictures. He took several close-ups of the electronic machine and the typewriter device and as he did so noticed that there was a badge on the front of the machine bearing the word HELIOS in embossed letters. After switching the light off and shutting the door, he went out to the machine room under the flywheel and took a further series of pictures. Finally he went back up the ladder to the main body of the barn and finished off with a couple of shots of the flywheel. Putting the Leica back in its case, he went outside and pulled the wicket door of the barn shut behind him. He looked around and felt reasonably certain that he had been unobserved.

BUT IN THIS REGARD Smallwood was in error. His movements in and out of the barn had not in fact gone unnoticed. Peter and Terri were back on the little baked clay beach by the lake talking about this and that. Peter was saying, 'I'm not sure we should come here when Flo's at home.'

Terri was unimpressed. 'You can't see this part of the lake from The Croft and Flo's not one for walks these days. I don't think she'd even notice if we went in for a swim.'

Peter was about to prevent that apparently stray remark from turning into a concrete proposal when Terri put her hand on his arm and shushed him. She pointed across the lake in the direction of the barn.

'That's Smallwood. He must have come back to Fordham. And he's going into the barn.'

'Maybe he's arranged to meet Nippy there.'

'I don't think so. Nippy told me he was going to the doctor in Standon this afternoon.'

As they watched Smallwood, they saw him step through the wicket door.

Peter said, 'He must have a key.'

'Yeah, I don't think Nippy would forget to lock the barn. That machine is his pride and joy.'

'What are we going to do?'

'We'll just stay here and watch how long he's in there and what he does when he comes out.'

They hadn't had long to wait until they saw Smallwood emerge from the wicket door and lock it behind him. He took a few steps away from the barn and then raised a camera to his eye and took some shots of the barn and the back of the Hall. He then sauntered towards the main gate.

Once they were sure that he was out of sight, they relaxed a little.

Peter said, 'What do you think he was up to?'

'I don't know, but we'd better let Nippy know that he's been snooping around. We'll go and wait for him at the cottage.'

It took them fifteen minutes to get to Nippy's by the long route along the railway cutting and then along the Standon Road. Even so, they had an hour to wait until Nippy reappeared. Peter was feeling uncomfortable that he hadn't let Flo know that he wouldn't be back for lunch and was also feeling hungry, but Terri was determined that they should let Nippy know that Smallwood had been snooping around and that he had got into the barn. When Nippy got back, however, and they told him what they'd seen, he didn't seem in the least put out.

Terri was outraged. 'He was taking photographs.'

Nippy ignored what she was saying and said, 'Have you young 'uns had any lunch?'

Peter said, 'No, we came straight here.'

'Well, let me make us all some cheese sandwiches. I've got a fresh loaf of crusty bread here and some good cheddar.'

Even Terri realised that a bit of lunch was a good idea and sat down at Nippy's kitchen table. Ten minutes later, Nippy had assembled a pile of sandwiches and made a big pot of tea. As they sat around the table and munched their sandwiches, he said, 'I bumped into Richard Warren in Standon and he said that his friend Smallwood was hoping to get his uncle to buy Wyvern Hall for him.'

Terri was aghast. 'But that's terrible.'

Nippy seemed to be in a philosophical mood. 'It's better than it being sold to a property developer who'll just knock everything down and build rabbit hutches on the estate.'

Terri wasn't about to concede that having Smallwood as the owner of Wyvern Hall was a good thing. 'That's exactly what that creep Smallwood will do.'

Nippy slurped his tea. 'Maybe. But as I understand it, the will business, what they call probate, hasn't been sorted out yet, so they can't do anything irreversible yet.'

Peter swallowed a mouthful of sandwich and said, 'Does that mean that you still hope to find the real will?'

'Of course, I'm sure that the Master would have put it somewhere safe. He probably told me, but in a kind of riddle.' He looked at Terri. 'You know what he was like, a great one for puzzles.'

Terri nodded, but she had something else on her mind. 'How did Smallwood know you weren't there and how did he get into the barn without your being there?'

'I daresay that he used a key. That's the usual way of getting through a locked door.'

'But where did he get a key from?'

'I should think that he found it with all the other keys in the utility room. Richard gave him permission to get into the house to take photographs.'

Terri said, 'I didn't know there was a bunch of keys there.'

'Well, daughter of the dragon, you don't know everything, at least not yet.'

Peter couldn't help laughing. He could learn a thing or two from Nippy in how to deal with Terri when she was in an imperious mood.

Terri gave Peter a withering look. He was going to pay for that brief chortle.

AT THE FOX, SMALLWOOD found Richard in his usual corner. A few minutes later, over their beers, Richard said, 'How did you get on?'

'Pretty well, actually. I think I got everything I need. My uncle will be able to get a better idea of the property once I've had the photographs developed.'

'It's a pity he can't come and see it for himself.'

'It's not impossible, if he is reassured by what he sees, that he might come down. If we get to that stage, it will mean that he's seriously considering the proposition.'

Richard took a sip of his beer. 'Did you take a look in the barn?'

Smallwood nodded. 'The barn is magnificent. I wouldn't be surprised if it's older than the house. To be quite honest, Nippy's machine is a travesty and not just because it's a con, although I have to admit that it is much more impressive than I was expecting. Unfortunately, it disfigures that marvellous building.'

Richard shifted uncomfortably in his seat. 'Well, I'm rather glad it'll be you rather than me to tell him that it's got to be dismantled.'

ON THE WAY BACK to The Croft, Peter said, 'Nippy seems to have had a change of heart. He didn't seem in the least concerned that Smallwood was poking around the Hall and, more particularly, the barn.'

Terri agreed. 'There's something going on here. It's like when you can't find a piece for one of Cuthbert's puzzles.'

Peter thought that was exactly what it was like. 'Even Nippy thinks that Cuthbert probably told him where he put the will, but wrapped up in a riddle.'

'But we know where he put it. And we know that Richard and Smallwood have got the will now.'

Peter was thoughtful. 'Yes, they probably have, but we don't know that for sure, because we never saw a copy of the will ourselves. What we did see was all that Helios code stuff. Maybe that was the riddle.'

Terri wasn't convinced. 'If he was trying to keep the will safe, the last place to put it was in a folder marked 'WILL'. Not much of a riddle there.'

But Peter had had an intuition. 'Supposing that the thing that Cuthbert wanted someone to find was not the will but the Helios stuff.'

'Why would he want Richard to find the Helios stuff?'

'I don't know. And actually we don't know whether Richard actually knows about the Helios documents. After all, it was Smallwood who took the folder.'

'But he would have given it to Richard.'

'Would he? He might have his own reasons for wanting it.'

'Like what?'

'Maybe he's a spy.'

Terri burst out laughing. 'Smallwood? He's no James Bond. He's too poncy.'

'But that might be exactly what would make him a good spy.'

'But Bond's a British agent. And if Smallwood is a British agent, why is he after the Helios stuff?'

'Well, maybe it was Cuthbert who was the spy and Smallwood's trying to find out what he was up to before he died.'

Terri's eyes blazed. 'Cuthbert was never a spy.'

Peter tried to calm her down. 'I think maybe he was, but one of ours. I'm just trying to think why Smallwood was so interested in what was in the WILL folder that he took the whole thing. Maybe he really works for the other side.'

'So you think Smallwood is a double agent?'

'Maybe.'

'That would mean that Richard is one as well. I don't buy that. He's as thick as two short planks. And anyway, he hardly ever leaves Fordham Market. He can't have been doing much spying here.'

Terri had made a good point. 'Perhaps Richard doesn't realise what Smallwood is up to. And Smallwood is using the will business as cover for finding something out about Cuthbert. What did Cuthbert do before he retired?'

'I don't know. He has just been the kind old gentleman who owned Wyvern Hall for as long as I can remember. I bet Flo knows what he did. We could ask her.'

Peter was hesitant. 'I'm not sure. Cuthbert's death has really upset her. I don't want her to think that we're poking our noses in where they don't belong. But to judge from Nippy's photos, they all worked on something together during the war. And maybe it was top secret.'

'But the war's been over for years and, anyway, that was against the Nazis.'

'Yeah, but now we're in a Cold War and the enemy is the Soviet Union.'

Terri laughed bitterly. 'If the Russians are trying to bring our democracy down, they're going about it the wrong way by recruiting upper-class twits like Smallwood.'

BACK AT THE PRIORY after their lunch, the two men repaired to their rooms for a siesta. But Smallwood did not sleep. His brain was working busily. He had planned to make a further close inspection of the papers in Mother Goose's study to find evidence of his collaborator; however, he was beginning to think that he now knew who the collaborator was. But would Rafferty buy into the proposition that it was Nippy, the village idiot, who was, if not the builder of the decryption device that was concealed beneath the perpetual motion machine, then at least its operator? And as far as Smallwood could tell, Nippy was still running the machine, despite Mother Goose's demise. And that could only mean that Nippy, improbable though it might seem, was still working on decrypting the signals intelligence that Mother Goose had purloined from the firm.

It suddenly occurred to Smallwood, lying on the bed in one of The Priory guest rooms, that not only were the keys to the cellar and the barn of Wyvern Hall still in his jacket pocket, but the framed photographs in what had been Nippy's quarters might be more relevant than he had at first supposed. If the two figures in the photographs could be identified as Mother Goose and Nippy in their heyday, then Rafferty, and therefore Moscow, might be more convinced. He would have to go back and take close-ups of both photographs and at the same time return the keys to their hook in the utility room. The bad news was that he would have to do without a siesta; the good news was that he could now return to London first thing the next morning.

PETER AND TERRI HAD now reached The Croft and thought it better to suspend their speculations. They went through to the kitchen and Peter apologised to Flo for not having let her know that he wouldn't be in for lunch.

Flo dismissed his apologies. 'You must be starving. I can get you something now.'

Peter said, 'Thank you, but we had plenty at Nippy's.'

'I'm so pleased you're spending time with him. It will make the cottage seem more like his real home. I must pay him a visit soon to see how he's fitted all his things in.'

Terri said, 'It's really nice. He's got all his old photographs and pictures up on the walls.'

Peter was horrified that Terri appeared to be blundering into a subject that only a few minutes before he'd suggested they treat with caution. But Flo seemed happy to talk about them. 'Ah, so he's let you see the mugshots of the old gang.'

Peter thought that it would be more honest to admit that they had looked at them before Nippy had returned, but Terri was not to be deterred. 'You wore a terribly smart uniform in those days.'

Flo laughed. 'Thank you, dear. I was in the Wrens, but I never went to sea. I was thought to be useful for my skill in languages.'

'Is that what you did when the war finished?'

'For a while, but eventually I was just a plain old civil servant moving from department to department.'

'Was that what Cuthbert did too?'

'I'm afraid I can't really tell you what he did, because it's still secret, but mainly because I didn't really understand it myself.'

'And what about Nippy?'

Flo raised an eyebrow. 'Terri, what is this all about?'

Terri's eyes flashed. 'I just don't want Nippy to be thrown out of Wyvern Hall and his machine smashed up. We saw Smallwood coming out of the barn this morning and he was taking photographs. We went and told Nippy, but he didn't seem to be too bothered.'

Flo wrinkled her brow. 'I am sure Mr Smallwood got permission from Mr Warren. But I assume that, to have seen Mr Smallwood going into the barn, you must have been on Wyvern land yourselves.'

Terri now realised that she had said more than she had intended. 'Well, yes, we were just lying in the grass by the lake. We were hoping to see Nippy so that he could explain more about his machine. He said he would.'

Flo seemed surprised. 'Really?'

Terri tried to clarify the position. 'He didn't say when exactly. But we hadn't seen him for a few days. We weren't doing any harm. And then when we did go to Nippy's, we went the long way round.'

Flo said, 'I suppose I should tell you off, but I happen to think the ban on people walking in the meadows is a bit excessive. I would just like you to exercise some discretion if you do so. I know you have had the run of them since you were a little girl and they do look so splendid at this time of year.'

Terri was crestfallen. 'I'm sorry. We're just so worried about what's going on.'

Flo pounced on Terri's apology. 'And what is going on? I think perhaps you're not telling me the whole story.'

Terri writhed in embarrassment. 'Cuthbert's will and everything.'

Flo stood up and smoothed her skirt down. 'Well, yes, the will business is annoying. Let's hope that it all gets sorted out soon. But I'm wondering what the *everything* is.'

'Nippy said that Cuthbert had probably told him where the will was, but in a kind of riddle. We thought we might be able to help solve the riddle.'

'Ah, I see. So it is Nippy who is being a little indiscreet.'

Peter and Terri sat in silence, hoping desperately that they hadn't got Nippy into trouble.

Flo noticed the looks that they exchanged and said, 'I think it's time we all had a cup of tea.'

As Flo was making the tea, she caught Peter's eye and flashed him a little smile, as if to say that she wasn't really annoyed.

PETER AND TERRI HAD arranged to meet at the recreation ground the next morning. Peter got there early. He sat on a bench and enjoyed the sleepy quietness of the Fordham rush hour, so much nicer than the bustle of London. As he sat there waiting for Terri, he saw Richard Warren's Lagonda sweep out of the gates of The Priory and roar towards the high street. Smallwood was sitting in the front passenger seat, with a self-satisfied look on his face. Peter supposed that Richard was giving him a lift to the station for the next London train.

Some minutes later, Terri appeared and waved at him. Peter was slightly shocked. She was wearing a short skirt and a blouse. This was not her usual jeans and tee shirt outfit. He wondered whether she was going out somewhere with her mother and had forgotten to mention it. She joined him on the bench and gave him a little kiss on the cheek.

Peter said, 'Have you got to go out today?'

'No, why?'

'You don't normally wear a skirt.'

'Don't you like it?'

'Of course. You look fantastic.'

'I thought maybe I should get the sun on my legs.'

This wasn't a convincing explanation as far as Peter was concerned. She often wore shorts, which were equally good for getting a tan on her legs, but he was not about to point this out. She had a great pair of legs whether in shorts or a skirt, but the skirt was definitely more attractive. She seemed to be enjoying the effect her new outfit was having on him and kept crossing and uncrossing her legs as they sat there.

Eventually he said, 'So what are we going to do today?'

'We're going to find out what Smallwood was taking pictures of.'

'And how are we going to do that?'

'We're going to get into the barn.'

'So we're going to go around to Nippy's again?'

'No, Nippy's away again today according to my dad.'

'So how are we going to get into the barn?'

'Well, didn't Nippy say that there was a key to the barn in the utility room of Wyvern Hall?'

'Terri, I don't think we should be breaking into the Hall again.'

'Nippy's away. I saw Richard taking that creep Smallwood to the station. This is a perfect time. If we get a move on, we'll be in and out before Richard gets back.'

She stood up and said, 'Come on, then.'

Peter knew it was futile to argue.

Peter was starting to get used to getting into Wyvern Hall through the window by the conservatory. He went around to the back door and let Terri in. They went to the utility room and soon located the keys to the cellar and the barn. As they were exiting the room Terri noticed a torch on a shelf. She picked it up and pressed the switch. The beam came on strongly. 'We might need this.'

A few minutes later they were in front of the wicket door on the lakeside of the barn. They let themselves in and shut the door behind them. Terri switched the torch on and said, 'I can't believe that Smallwood was just taking photos of the big wheel, unless he's some kind of engineering nut. I think there's something else here, something that Nippy didn't want us to see and which Smallwood knows about or has discovered. I noticed a trap door on the other side of the wheel when we were here last week. If you ask me that's where we need to look.'

They walked around to the other side of the wheel and Terri scraped away with her foot the straw that covered the ground. 'Thought so. There's a ring in it. I'll hold the torch and you pull it up.'

The trapdoor opened easily revealing a ladder leading down to a basement room. Peter offered to go first. He turned around and climbed down into the same space that Smallwood had explored the previous day. Once he was at the bottom, he called up. 'Throw me the torch and I'll hold it while you come down.'

He caught the torch and shone it up towards the trapdoor. His intention was to ensure that she could see where she was putting her feet, but the result was that for a brief period, as she reached up to pull the trapdoor shut behind her, he had a good view of her bottom. A short skirt was not the most sensible of garments for such a manoeuvre, but he was not complaining. When she got to the foot of the ladder, having first pulled the trapdoor shut, she noticed the amused expression on his face. 'Enjoyed that, did you?'

'I didn't want you to slip.'

'I wouldn't mind betting I've climbed more trees than you.'

'You probably have, but not in that skirt. But seriously do you think it was wise to close the trapdoor?'

'Well, if someone did come in, they'd notice the open trapdoor almost immediately.'

Peter didn't like the idea of being closed in underground, but Terri was looking around the room. 'So these big grey cabinets are what really drive the big wheel.'

Peter looked closely at them. 'Possibly, but perhaps they do something else. I certainly don't think we should touch them.'

He swung the torch around the room and brought the beam to rest on the door in the wall furthest from the ladder. Terri, as determined as ever, said, 'Let's see what's in there.'

She tried the handle and, finding the door unlocked, stepped into the room beyond. Peter followed her with the torch, but Terri had already found a light switch. She pointed at the same large electronic installation that Smallwood had photographed and said, 'Well, that's Helios.'

Peter was doubtful. 'What makes you say that?'

Terri pointed scornfully at a badge on the electronic keyboard of the desk.

Peter bent down and picked something up from the floor. 'And Smallwood was standing exactly here and probably taking photographs.'

'What makes *you* say that?'

Peter pointed to the cigarette butt he had picked up. 'It says Balkan Sobranie on the wrapper.'

'That was careless of him.'

'I can't imagine how many cigarettes he must smoke a day.'

But Terri wasn't listening. 'So, Helios is a computer.'

She picked up a sheaf of typewritten pages from the desk. 'This is where the decoding, no, the decryption gets done.'

'But who works down here?'

'Nippy, presumably. Or Cuthbert when he was alive.'

'So it *does* look as if they are spies.'

Terri became angry. 'I don't believe they're traitors. There has to be another explanation.'

But Peter was pursuing his train of thought. 'And it looks as if they're being investigated by Smallwood.'

Terri was outraged. 'If anyone's a traitor, that creep is. He's just pretending that he wants to buy Wyvern Hall. He's using it as an excuse to snoop around.'

'What's he trying to find?'

'The Helios of course. And now he's gone back to London to tell his boss and show him the photos.'

'And then what? They can't arrest Cuthbert because he's dead.'

'But they can arrest Nippy. We've got to tell him.'

'Hang on a moment. We've got to think this through. If Nippy is a traitor and we warn him, then we'll probably get into trouble too.'

Terri was defiant. 'I don't care. Anyway I refuse to believe he's a traitor.'

Peter tried to stay calm. 'Okay, let's say that he's doing something legitimate, or at least morally sound, then who are the people who are hunting him?'

'The Soviet agents, of course. That's why we've got to warn him.'

'So you're saying that Smallwood is a Soviet agent. But supposing we're wrong and Nippy really is a Soviet agent and we tell him what we know about Smallwood, he'd probably have to kill us.'

'Don't be ridiculous. Nippy's known me all my life. He's not going to kill me.'

Peter had to admit that in the time he'd known Nippy, he'd only known him to be a lovely man. But what was the explanation for a secret computer installation in a cellar under a barn in the depths of the Hertfordshire countryside? It wasn't as spacious as Dr. No's bunker in the recent James Bond film, but computers were not everyday objects. And why was a member of the security services investigating that same installation? If that was what Smallwood was.

Peter noticed that beside the pile of papers was a small cardboard box about the size of a paperback book. He lifted the lid off to reveal a pocket chess set, with small peg-type pieces in white and red plastic that slotted into a small hole in the centre of each square on the board. The disposition of the pieces looked as if things had been paused mid-game. Peter studied the board. 'I think white has the upper hand.'

Terri said, 'What are you talking about?'

'Whoever worked down here also played chess.'

'Cuthbert, of course. You played several games against him yourself.'

'Yes, but many people play chess. It might have been someone else.'

'I don't see Nippy as a chess player. Anyway, can you play against yourself?'

'Not really. You can study positions. Or follow famous games move by move.'

But Terri had lost interest in the chess set and had now turned her attention to the curtained off area at the end of the room. She ignored the basic kitchen arrangements and tried the door on the further wall. She noticed the key hanging to one side of the door, but on an impulse tried the key marked CELLAR on the keys they'd picked up in the utility room. The door swung open smoothly to reveal a dark space beyond.

'Pete, give me the torch.'

Peter handed her the torch and she shone it into the dank and musty passage. 'This must be the tunnel to the cellar under Wyvern Hall. Nippy mentioned it to me years ago as an old legend. I bet this is how Nippy and Cuthbert got to the Helios machine without drawing attention to themselves and the real reason that Nippy didn't want to vacate the Hall. I think we should see what's at the other end.'

As far as Peter was concerned, they were already far enough underground. He had no desire to enter the narrow passage. If they wanted to go back to the Hall, they could simply go back up the ladder and leave by the wicket door of the barn. But the matter was taken out of their hands by the sound of footsteps overhead and the trapdoor being raised. Terri gestured to Peter to draw the curtain that separated the kitchen area from the main body of the Helios room. As he did so, he realised that the light was still on in that room, but it was too late to do anything about it. He rejoined Terri by the door into the tunnel. She extinguished the torch and they stood side by side on the threshold of the tunnel.

A moment later they heard Nippy muttering to himself, 'I'm sure I switched the lights off.'

Then they heard the sound of Nippy bustling around and an electronic machine starting up, presumably the Helios.

Terri whispered in Peter's ear, 'We'd better get into the tunnel. He might come in here to make a coffee.'

They stepped into the tunnel and Terri pushed the door shut quietly, saying, 'I suppose I'd better lock it.'

She fished the keys out of her pocket and locked the door.

Peter was unenthusiastic about the idea of shutting themselves in the tunnel. It was dark and cold in the tunnel. Almost immediately, he started to feel a rising sense of panic. 'Why are we hiding, when you were so certain a few minutes ago that Nippy was not a Soviet agent? Why don't we just let him know we're here, even if it does get us into trouble?'

'Because I'm not sure any more.'

'So what are we going to do then? We could be here for hours and it's rather cold in here.'

'Pete, I'm the one in the short skirt. You've got jeans on.'

'Terri, it's not really the temperature. I'm feeling a bit claustrophobic. I've always hated confined spaces.'

Terri's mood softened. 'Oh, Pete, I'm sorry. You should have told me. It'll be alright. Here, put your arms around me.'

The two young people embraced, their bodies pressed close together. A moment later they were kissing passionately and caressing each other. Peter's sense of panic was now supplanted by a much more positive emotion. He'd been wanting to hold Terri and kiss her since his return to Fordham. But he had started to doubt that he would ever find the courage to do so. It was a little ironic, therefore, that it had taken one of his panic attacks, something of which he had always been a little ashamed, to bring about this new level of intimacy.

After some moments, Terri said, 'Oh, Pete, that's lovely. I've been wanting to do this since you got back.'

Peter said shyly, 'Me too.'

'I thought maybe you didn't want to.'

'It's all I think about.'

'Well, when we get out of here, we'll have to work out what happens next.'

She released him and straightened her blouse. 'But now let's try and find our way through to the Wyvern Hall cellar. I'll go first.'

She switched the torch on. 'With a bit of luck, this'll be very straightforward. It can't be that difficult, if Nippy used it regularly, let alone Cuthbert.'

It didn't take them long to reach another door.

'Let's hope this key works all the locks down here.'

She was not mistaken in her supposition and the next moment they found themselves in a much larger space.

'I'm pretty sure this is the cellar under the Hall. If I'm right, there should be a short flight of steps on the other side leading up to the servants' passage at the back of the house.'

Once again Terri's intuition was borne out and it was not long before they had returned the keys to the utility room and exited the house in the usual way, making sure that the back door was bolted. Peter was relieved to be back in the sunshine. Terri could see that he was still looking pallid.

'Let's go up to the railway cutting and warm up in the sunshine. We'll go straight up the track between the lake and the barn. Too bad, if anyone sees us.'

As they passed the barn, they were both aware of the hum coming from its interior.

Terri shook her head. 'So now we know what makes the hum. It's nothing to do with the perpetual motion machine. It's Helios working.'

Up at the top of the railway cutting, they threw themselves on the ground, relishing the warmth and the light of a summer after-noon, pleased to be out of the gloom and dankness. Soon the colour had returned to Peter's face. Emboldened by Terri's patent cure for his panic attack in the tunnel, he rolled over and, putting his arm around Terri, drew her towards him. 'Thank you for not mocking my claustrophobia in the tunnel.'

Terri laughed. 'I was glad to be able to take things into my own hands.'

She looked at him sideways and Peter laughed nervously, trying to work out whether the innuendo was accidental or not. Without waiting for his response, she jumped up, brushing the dried grass off her skirt and smoothing it down. 'And I think there's some beer left in the box.'

She disappeared into the hedge and returned a little later with two bottles of Pelham Pale Ale and a bottle opener. They flipped the caps off and clinked the bottles. The beer wasn't particularly cold, but it was delicious. After a few moments of quiet contempla-tion, Terri said, 'So, what do we think is going on?'

Peter said, 'I'm not sure. You know all these people better than me.'

'Flo's your great aunt.'

'But until last year I hardly knew her. And anyway I don't think she's involved.'

'She was in one of Nippy's photos.'

'But that was years ago. It doesn't mean she's involved in this Helios business. Anyway, she told us she was a civil servant after the war. And there is absolutely no way she could get down that ladder or through the tunnel.'

'Okay, maybe that's going a bit far, but on one side we've got Nippy and, when he was alive, Cuthbert. And on the other side Smallwood and Warren. I know who I think the good guys are.'

'But you have to admit that whatever Nippy is doing is pretty weird and very secret.'

'Not so secret any more. If you're right about that cigarette end, it means that Smallwood has been down there.'

Peter nodded. 'Yeah, and he's immediately rushed back to London.'

Terri was thoughtful. 'Let's try and get this in some kind of perspective. Nippy and Cuthbert have been at work on building and operating Helios for some time. Let's say since Nippy started building the perpetual motion machine. They have some secret material that they are trying to decipher. Why are they trying to do this? Is it so they can give it to the Soviet Union or is it so they can hand it over to the British security services? I'd suggest that it's the latter.'

Peter agreed. 'Yes, based on what we know of the people involved.'

Terri continued with her line of thought. 'But then why don't they just give MI5 what they've got now? And that brings us to Smallwood. How is it that he turned up here? Most people in Fordham, if they give it any thought, just think he's one of Richard's fey friends. And dimwitted Richard thinks Smallwood's helping him diddle Nippy out of being able to live at Wyvern Hall. But you and I are pretty sure that he was really after the Helios documents, which for some reason he calls the Mother Goose dossier. It's almost as if he knew they were here before he ever got to Fordham. But what he didn't seem to know about was the Helios itself. Or at least know where it was. He does now, of course.'

Peter was impressed with Terri's analysis. 'That all makes sense, but it still leaves us with more questions than answers. You know what? I wouldn't mind betting that the Helios folder and the Mother Goose dossier are the same thing.'

Terri jumped up. 'Yes, that's it. Nippy and Cuthbert called that stuff the Helios decrypts. But some other people already knew about the material and called it the Mother Goose dossier. That's what Smallwood was really looking for. He didn't know that Helios was involved until yesterday. Who are those other people?'

'They must be people who Smallwood knows or works for.'

'Yes, but are they our people or people who work for the Soviets?'

Suddenly the issue crystallised for Peter. 'Both.'

Terri didn't see what Peter was getting at. 'How can it be both?'

'Because whoever Smallwood works for on the Soviet side, let's call him Mr X, is either also his boss in MI5 or in one of the other branches.'

'Yes, of course. You're brilliant, Pete.'

'It was you who analysed it all. I just put two and two together from what you were saying.'

'So Mr X got wind of what Cuthbert was up to and told Smallwood to look into it more closely. The question is how did Mr X find out about it?'

It seemed obvious to Peter. 'Cuthbert told him. Or, at least, Cuthbert let someone know what he was working on and that person got the information back to Mr X.'

'Yes, yes, yes. But he died before he could provide all the information. So Smallwood was given the task of getting the rest.'

'It could be even worse than that. Perhaps Mr X realised that if Cuthbert completed his project, then he, Mr X, would be unmasked. So Cuthbert had to be stopped and the dossier destroyed.'

Terri could see where he was heading with this now. 'But fortunately for Mr X, Cuthbert died of a heart attack before he was able to identify him.'

Peter suddenly had a chilling thought. 'Or maybe Cuthbert was murdered, rather than died of a heart attack. It was just made to look like a heart attack.'

Terri was aghast. 'Oh, no. I've got a terrible feeling you may be right. You don't think it was Smallwood who killed him, do you?'

'He might have done, but if Cuthbert was killed, it was more likely someone else who did it.'

'Well, in that case Mr X has succeeded. Cuthbert is dead and they've got the dossier.'

'Maybe, but perhaps they didn't realise there was some kind of computer involved. So as long as the Helios exists, they're not safe. The obvious thing then would be to destroy the Helios.'

'So that means they'll be back.'

'Yes.'

'What about Nippy? Is he in danger?'

'Yes, I suppose so.'

They both fell silent, not daring to think about the implications of everything they had been saying. Suddenly, Peter said, 'Cuthbert is Mother Goose.'

Terri said, 'I don't get what you're saying.'

'Mother Goose is a codename. As are those other words we tried to remember. I bet you one of them is Mr X. And I bet another is Smallwood.'

Terri jumped on Peter and gave him a big hug. 'Pete, you're brilliant.'

Peter blushed, happy to be in Terri's arms once again. '*We're* brilliant.'

She kissed him hard on the mouth. 'We are,' she said with passion.

A little later when they had finished taking things as far as they could go without going too far, they rolled away from each other and adjusted their clothing.

As they got up to walk to The Croft, Terri said, 'I'm glad you've got the hang of kissing. We're starting to make progress. Have you got any Durex?'

As so often Terri's directness wrong-footed Peter. In fact he did have a small blister pack of condoms in his wallet. But if he said he'd already equipped himself with some, it might look as though he was being presumptuous. On the other hand if he denied the fact, then it might suggest that he was less ardent than he actually was. Eventually, he managed to say, 'Yes, I think I do.'

Terri screamed with laughter. 'You think you do! No doubt you get through them at a rate of knots.'

Peter thought that there was little point trying to explain himself and decided to let Terri enjoy the moment.

SIR JAMES MILNE

SMALLWOOD AND RAFFERTY SAT on a park bench in the usual way.

Rafferty was the first to speak. 'Good work, Smallwood. Moscow is pleased, but of course in a worried sort of way.'

It wasn't often that one got approbation, even qualified approbation from Moscow. Smallwood glowed with pride.

But Rafferty saw no reason to overdo the praise. 'The problem is that before we decide what to do with the Helios machine, we need to try and get some more information about its capabilities and the technology that it's employing. I appreciate that this is not your forte, but it is mine. So we need to work out a way of your getting me into the installation as discreetly as possible. And we think Mother Goose's collaborator is the other individual in the wartime photographs you provided, a certain Neville Smith, who worked with Mother Goose during the war and built some of the devices that cracked the Nazi ciphers. You, of course, may know the gentleman in question as Nippy.'

Smallwood nodded. 'That was the conclusion I came to, although to all intents and purposes he is the village idiot.'

'As I think I remarked before, idiots can have their uses. But we happen to think he is not such an idiot. If possible, it would be useful for us to have a talk with Mr Smith before we deal with him.'

'What do you have in mind?'

'Another heart attack at Wyvern Hall might arouse suspicions. I will give the matter some thought. As for your friend, he has no inkling of these matters?'

'None at all. He is a complete nincompoop.'

'And he now thinks of you as a potential buyer of the estate, which will be acquired by a family trust controlled by your doting uncle.'

'Yes, more or less.'

'Good, I have decided that I will pose as your uncle, and we will pay a visit to Fordham together. It would be embarrassing if I were to be recognised by someone from my circle of acquaintance, unlikely in such an insignificant place, I know, but one can't be too careful, especially when one is incognito. I think you'd better arrange for us to stay at your friend's house.'

Smallwood was far from certain that Warren would welcome yet another visit, especially with the doting uncle. Rafferty sensed his hesitation. 'Is there some problem?'

'Well, to be honest, Warren has not really welcomed my visits.'

'Tell him I am delighted with the photos of the house and that I want to see it myself and then we will make a formal offer.'

Smallwood reluctantly agreed. 'What identity will you be going under?'

'I think it's time to revive Sir James Milne. I have some rather nice calling cards in that persona.'

Smallwood said he would make the arrangements, and the two men parted. Smallwood walked back to the office deep in thought. He wasn't sure that what Rafferty was suggesting was a good idea. It seemed to go against all the rules of tradecraft. It was true that he himself was ill-equipped to make a technical assessment of the Helios machine, but surely there was someone else in the network with those skills. On the other hand, it was true that Smallwood was the only person who had a plausible reason to revisit Fordham and Wyvern Hall, and Rafferty was of the right age and demeanour to pose as his rich uncle. Smallwood also felt distinctly uncomfortable about having to spend an entire weekend with Rafferty. What would they talk about for goodness' sake?

RICHARD WAS SITTING IN The Fox and starting the evening with a large one. It looked like things were going well with Smallwood's plan to get the trust fund of which he was a beneficiary to buy Wyvern Hall. The trustees were not quibbling over the price, and the doting uncle had even decided to take a look at the property. That could only be good news. But there was one small fly in the ointment: Agatha, his childhood playmate and distant cousin several times removed, had invited herself to The Priory for the weekend too, which meant that he would have to make up a third guest room. He did wish people would stop inviting themselves. Yes, he did have a large and beautiful house, but he had no staff and very limited financial resources. Fortunately, things in that regard had also taken a turn for the better. The bank had accepted that he was the executor of Cuthbert's will and that he would need access to Cuthbert's account to deal with bills falling due on Wyvern Hall and for a certain amount of cash in hand, a sizeable chunk of which now nestled in his back pocket. Otherwise, he would have been in a very bad mood indeed.

He was expecting Agatha to appear in the bar of The Fox at any moment. He had tried to put her off until the Saturday, but she had insisted. He was fond of Agatha, but her manner could be disconcertingly brisk. He wondered what it was that brought her to these parts. Her normal hunting grounds were the Cotswolds, as she migrated from country house to country house with the change of the seasons.

It was not Agatha, however, who came through the door of The Fox at that moment, but Professor Sage.

'Warren, you've beaten me to it this evening.'

'I've been hard at it all day, Professor. I was in dire need of a snifter.'

'I know exactly what you mean. But I thought you were a man of leisure.'

'This probate business is a bit of a slog.'

'I can well imagine, but at least you are a qualified solicitor and, as I understand it, have previous form in such matters.'

'This is true, but in all honesty when it comes to form I am more of an aficionado of the *Sporting Life*.'

'As indeed am I. And if I am not mistaken, you have the look of a man who has done well in the July Cup at Newmarket.'

'As a matter of fact, over the years I *have* done rather well in the July Cup, but as you know August is a rather barren month for those of us with equestrian interests. But that is not the reason for my present contentment. It looks as if I have a buyer for Wyvern Hall.'

'Well, that is good news. Congratulations. Is the buyer local?'

'No, it is my old college friend, Tony Smallwood. He is the beneficiary of a trust fund and the trustees are minded to buy the estate.'

'Smallwood? Is he the chap who was in here with you a couple of weeks ago?'

'Indeed. He seemed to be familiar with your work.'

'Always flattering, Warren, to be recognised, even if the name is a bit of a giveaway. So when do you hope to complete?'

'We're not at that stage yet, but Smallwood's uncle, Sir James Milne, who is one of the trustees, is coming down this weekend to look at the property. You may know of him. I believe he is quite eminent.'

'No, I'm afraid the name doesn't ring a bell, but then I have been out of circulation for many years now.'

'Well, I have booked a table here for my guests tomorrow evening, so it is not impossible that I will be able to introduce you.'

'I look forward to that, Warren. Enjoy your supper. I'd better go and claim my favourite table before the bar fills up.'

Sage could be irritatingly patronising, but he was a nice old cove really. When he had first moved to the village, Richard, in an attempt to inform himself of Sage's work and as a fellow Cantabrigian, had bought one of his books, *Certitude and Dubiety*, but had closed it after only a couple of pages and had never opened it again. Nevertheless, Sage had seemed to be flattered by the gesture when Richard mentioned the fact that he'd bought the book, and seemed to have little expectation that anyone would actually read it, let alone understand it.

Richard went to the bar and ordered another large Scotch. If the first one had been a snifter, this was most certainly a stiffener, to help him deal with the imminent arrival of his robust cousin. The door of the bar opened almost as soon as Richard was back in his seat, but instead of the willowy figure of Agatha, the somewhat more Junoesque frame of Flo Hodges appeared in the doorway. She spotted Richard and came over to his table.

'Good evening, Richard. How lovely to see you. I gather Mr Smallwood is considering buying Wyvern Hall himself.'

'Yes, indeed. News does travel fast.'

'It's very hard to keep things secret in a place like Fordham.'

Richard moved uneasily in his seat. 'Fortunately, I have no secrets to hide.'

Flo smiled. 'Much the best policy.'

Richard half-rose to his feet. 'May I buy you a drink?'

'That's very kind of you, Richard, but I'm joining the professor this evening and I think I see him in his customary seat. Of course, you would be very welcome to join us.'

'Nothing I'd like better, but I am awaiting the arrival of a distant cousin, who is staying with me for the weekend.'

'I'm glad to hear that you have company. I sometimes worry about you, moping around on your own in that huge pile.'

'I can assure you, Flo, that I mope but seldom. My cousin, Agatha, is not the kind of girl to tolerate a chap indulging in a spot of moping. She is one of those people who is resolutely cheerful and optimistic.'

'Much the best way. I presume she has therefore not inherited the infamous Warren melancholy.'

'When I say cousin, I use it in a very loose sense. We are several times removed.'

Flo raised her eyebrows and said, 'I see.'

Richard was a little perturbed that Flo might think there was some romantic dimension to the meeting. 'Oh, nothing like that, I can assure you.'

'But you must admit that The Priory could do with a woman's touch.'

'You may well be right, Flo, but I have no reason to think that this is what the reunion is about. We were childhood playmates, but that, most decidedly, is as far as things went or indeed go.'

'I'm sorry, Richard, it's none of my business. Have a lovely weekend. I will now go and join the professor.'

Richard was irritated. It was certainly no business of Miss Hodges. She was hardly one to lecture him on what might be a suitable attachment. But he had no time to savour his irritation, because at that moment Agatha Ponsonby burst through the door of The Fox and fell upon his bosom.

'Oh, Dicky, how lovely to see you again, it's been too long.'

'I'm sorry, Aggie. The last couple of years have been rather odd.'

'I know. Poor Cuthbert, so soon after your parents. And incidentally, why didn't Cuthbert have a proper funeral?'

'Those were his wishes.'

'Well, it was jolly thoughtless of him.'

'I think he thought he was being *thoughtful*. Sparing the family another bout of obsequies.'

'Yes, I suppose so. Are there plans for a memorial service?'

'Once I've sorted out probate and certain problems to do with Wyvern Hall.'

Agatha wanted to know what those problems were. Richard gave her a highly skewed version of the situation, before realising that he hadn't yet offered Agatha any refreshment.

'What are you drinking, old thing? You must be exhausted.'

'Oh, a G&T, please, Dicky. A large one.'

Richard returned with the drinks and the menu card and said, 'The food here is terribly good. All local produce.'

As Agatha was perusing the menu, having first taken a hefty slug of her G&T, Richard said, 'I say, old thing, would you mind not calling me Dicky when other people are around? I am sort of the lord of the manor now.'

'Of course, Dicky. What shall I call you?'

'Well, Richard. And I'll call you Agatha, rather than Aggie.'

'Well, alright. It does seem strange to be so formal with you.'

'I know, but only when we're in public.'

Agatha chose the ham, egg and chips and Richard chose bangers and mash.

When they had finished their meal, Richard said, 'Did you go back to The Priory first?'

Agatha shook her head. 'No, I parked the car right outside the pub.'

Richard laughed. 'Well, it'll save us a bit of a walk and then we can have a nice chat on the terrace. It's a beautiful evening.'

Outside the pub was a bright red Triumph TR3 with the hood down, which was drawing admiring looks from a knot of boys.

Richard was impressed. 'I say, Aggie, what a spiffing little car.'

Agatha glowed with pride. She threw him the keys. 'Here, you drive.'

They climbed in. Richard started the engine and revved it experimentally, basking in its well-mannered roar. He released the handbrake and they shot off on the short trip to The Priory. A few minutes later he pulled up outside the *porte cochère* of The Priory and said, 'Right, that's settled. I'm getting rid of the Lagonda. This is much more fun.'

Agatha laughed. 'It is, but you won't get your golf clubs in the back.'

'Can't stand the game.'

His enthusiasm waned a little as he helped her put the hood up. It was a fiddle pushing the studs home. He showed her to her room. She was delighted. 'Oh, it's my old room.'

Richard nodded. 'Of course.'

He forbore to mention that most recently it had been Small-wood's room.

'I'll leave you to powder your nose and see you on the terrace. No hurry.'

A short while later, when Agatha had freshened herself up, she joined Richard downstairs. It was a beautiful evening. In the gloaming, even the unkempt grounds looked romantic.

'Oh, Dicky – I may call you Dicky now, mayn't I? – It's lovely to be back at The Priory. But don't you find it a little lonely on your own?'

'Oh, I have friends down from time to time. It's not so much that I get lonely. The Fox is not far away and Fordham is a friendly place, but the truth of the matter is that I can't afford to heat the place or even to employ staff. The old boy's financial affairs were in a terrible state when he died. I have been at my wits' end.'

'Oh, you poor love. You're really an orphan now, aren't you? You need someone to look after you.'

'Well, you know how it is, Aggie. I just haven't met the right chap. And even if I had, I don't know whether I could import a boy here without scandalising the spinsters of the parish.'

'Well, you have made things difficult for yourself in that respect.'

'It's not what I've chosen, Ag. It's the way I am.'

'You need a disguise.'

'I don't think a false moustache and a pair of heavy glasses are going to deceive the gimlet-eyed biddies of the village.'

'No, I don't mean disguise in that sense. I mean an arrangement in which you could give full rein, or perhaps it would be better to say, some rein to your inclinations, while presenting an impeccable façade to the world.'

'That's easier said than done, old thing. How would I do that?'

'By getting married.'

Richard laughed. 'What girl is going to have me on those conditions?'

'Me.'

Richard looked at Agatha in stunned silence. 'Aggie, it's not nice to joke in this way.'

'I'm not joking, Richard Warren. I'm absolutely serious.'

'Of course, we're old friends and very fond of each other, but not in that way.'

'Look, Dicky, I'm not trying to *cure* you. I could provide you with cover for your activities and help you get The Priory shipshape.'

Richard's mind, never the fastest at grasping complex matters, was moving particularly slowly. 'What would be in it for you, if you don't mind me putting it that way?'

'I could have a child.'

'I'm not sure I could give you one.'

'Of course you could. I'm not asking you to make it a regular occurrence. Just enough intimate congress to get the process going for one.'

'Steady on, old thing. I'm sure there are better bets than me, if that's your aim.'

'Yes, there probably are, if I wanted to be in love, but I'm in a hurry.'

'Well, I know these things are difficult for women of a certain age.'

'There is that, but that's not the reason for the hurry. If I marry and have a child, I will come into a lot of money.'

Things weren't getting any easier for Richard to understand. 'Eventually?' he said nervously.

'No, immediately, well, after nine months or so.'

'How does that work?'

'It's the terms of a family trust. It's only recently that I realised that because of a narrowing of the field, let us say, that I stood to gain a good deal of money if I married and had a child. It has never been anything that I really wanted to do. But then I thought if I were to have a marriage of convenience, *un mariage* presque *blanc*, who would be a suitable candidate? Who could I bear? Who could I trust? And all the answers spelt Richard Warren.'

Richard was still finding it difficult to process the information. The uppermost thought in his mind was that Aggie and Flo Hodges must be in cahoots. Eventually he found his tongue and said, 'Aggie, this is all a bit of a stunner. I need a bit of time to think it through.'

'Of course.'

'How much time do I have?'

'Until tomorrow.'

Richard gulped and turned white. 'I see. Another brandy?'

'I'd love one.'

RICHARD FOUND IT DIFFICULT to get off to sleep that night. What Agatha was suggesting was preposterous. And yet, perhaps it wasn't. Of course, he didn't much fancy the icky business that seemed to be an essential part of the plan. On the other hand, he and Agatha were old friends and while they had never been intimate in that way, Agatha's no-nonsense approach to the body and its functions and his own biddability meant that they were closer to each other than persons of the opposite gender with divergent sexual orientations might otherwise be. In short, neither was entirely unfamiliar with the other's unclothed body. But it was one thing to be comfortable with a woman *en déshabillé*, quite another to generate a sufficiency of the inseminating material on demand. But surely he was overthinking this. There were time-honoured ways of achieving the desired state and if the counterpart was as broad-minded and co-operative as Agatha was sure to be, it would probably go off rather smoothly. Richard was not particularly well-informed about the mysteries of ovulation and conception, but he was sure that Agatha knew what she was doing in that regard and would arrange things to minimise the number of sessions required to quicken her womb.

The other side of the coin, if he could be forgiven being quite so mercenary, was whether her assessment of what would come her way if she met the requirements of the trust fund was accurate. The windfall would have to be ten thousand pounds at least and preferably closer to twenty or thirty thousand. Would it be too mercenary to ask her to be more specific? He thought not.

That brought him to the matter of Wyvern Hall and the impending visit of Smallwood and the doting uncle. How was it that the Warrens had managed not to set up a trust fund with which to make straight the current heir's financial way, when many another family seemed to have done so? The financial acumen of the founders of the Warren dynasty who had built Wyvern Hall and The Priory had clearly deserted its more recent generations. But perhaps here was his opportunity to reverse that tendency, even if indirectly. The Warren ascendancy in Fordham Market would be maintained and, if Agatha had her way, he and she would provide their little kingdom with an heir. And even better, if their progeny were male, the Warren name would live on. That would be one in the eye for Smallwood. Richard had thought the tone of his remarks about the unlikelihood of Richard continuing the line had been in bad taste.

Ah, yes, the blasted Smallwood. The truth was they had not been particularly close at college and the relationship had withered with the passing of the years. So it had been something of a surprise when, just after Cuthbert's death, Smallwood had got in touch and acted as if he and Richard were bosom buddies. It was true that

Smallwood was a bit of a loner and might have few, or indeed no, friends, but something didn't feel right about how assiduous he was now being in the matter of Wyvern Hall. What was he really up to? And was it a serious proposition?

Things might become clearer when he met the uncle. Because it was hard to believe that a man, whose horizons for many years had extended little further than a mile from the Athenaeum, actually wanted to live in a house that was forever sinking into the loam. But perhaps Smallwood was now tiring of the cosmopolitan round. And if he, or his trust fund, was indeed prepared to pay the asking price, then it would give Richard the means with which to call off his creditors. But the loss of Wyvern Hall would be a mortal blow to his *amour propre* and in the locality the family name would undoubtedly be mud for some considerable time. The alternative, which seemed scarcely less credible, was to accept Agatha's proposal. But on balance and leaving aside the physical mechanics of what was involved, he preferred the idea of being yoked to Agatha in sensible connubial accommodation to the idea of having Smallwood as a neighbour and master of Wyvern Hall. And if it meant the restoration of his financial position and the retention in the family of the Warrens' hereditary seat, so much the better. He was steadily coming to the view that Agatha's proposal had much to recommend it. Her opinion of Smallwood and Sir James Milne would be extremely useful too. She was no one's fool.

Next morning over a simple breakfast, Agatha said, 'So, who are these people you're expecting today?'

Richard explained the situation, without going into the matter of the suppression of the amended will. He emphasised the financial chaos that his father and uncle had bequeathed him and how the best way of dealing with the mess was the sale of the Wyvern estate, once probate had been granted. Agatha knew Wyvern Hall from the time she had spent in Fordham as a girl, but she hadn't visited in recent years.

'I am afraid that Cuthbert let the place go. I haven't got to the bottom of his financial affairs yet, but it looks as though there is not enough in savings to put the place to rights.'

As Agatha was clearing away the breakfast things, she said, 'What time are your guests arriving?'

'Not until this afternoon. I thought that we could have drinks on the terrace and then eat at The Fox.'

'Dicky, we ate there last night.'

'Well, to be honest, old thing. I eat there most nights. I never really got the hang of cooking.'

'What happened to Mrs Entwhistle?'

'Mother and Father had to let her go, a couple of years ago, after the failure of the old boy's, ultimately as it turned out, ill-advised investment. Mother took over. She was a dab hand at the old eggs and bacon. But the era of Mrs E's sumptuous repasts was over. At first I started taking my meals at The Fox as a bit of change from Mother's limited repertoire, but I then discovered that Vi Prosser, the landlady of The Fox, was almost the equal of Mrs E when it came to the preparation of victuals. There are a number of retired folk in the village, who do much the same, take their evening meal at The Fox, that is.'

'But you're not retired. Well, not of retirement age.'

'No, that's true. But they're a nice bunch on the whole and the conversation at The Fox is surprisingly elevated, really rather too intellectual and progressive for my liking at times.'

Agatha laughed. 'You're a born fuddy-duddy, Dicky.'

'And proud of it, Aggie.'

Agatha was thoughtful. 'I have a suggestion, but tell me to back off, if you feel I'm trying to take over.'

Richard had no idea what she had in mind, but he readied himself to shoot down anything too radical.

'After we have attended to our ablutions, let's go around to Wyvern Hall. I'll let you drive the TR3 again. Show me over the place. I'd like to remind myself of the layout and I'd like to look at this ridiculous machine. On the way back we'll stop off in the high street and pick up some supplies. I will prepare a meal for our guests and get some things in for breakfast tomorrow. I am not in Mrs E's class as a cook, but I can pull together a decent Boeuf Stroganoff with jam roly-poly and custard to follow.'

How could Richard refuse such a generous offer? He did take slight exception to the use of the word *our* in the context of the guests, but it would be churlish to quibble.

Agatha was already scribbling down a shopping list. 'What is the state of The Priory wine cellar?'

'Sadly reduced, I'm afraid, but there are still a few bottles of decent claret and one or two bottles of port.'

'That should do. Any champagne left?'

'One bottle.'

'I see. Things really have reached a pretty pass. Still, one bottle is all we need right now. Before we leave for our tour of Wyvern Hall, please make sure it is transferred to the refrigerator.'

Richard felt distinctly uncomfortable. It was not pleasant having one's wine cellar scrutinised nor being given menial tasks, but he knew that Agatha's motives were well-intentioned.

Later, as they were sitting over cooling drinks in the garden of The Fox, Richard was starting to allow himself to think that maybe his salvation was at hand. Agatha had not been too fazed by the state of disrepair into which Cuthbert had allowed Wyvern Hall to slide. She thought it was fixable. Clearly the fields, meadows and orchard needed proper management too, but that aspect of things was not quite so pressing.

Then as they had strolled around the outbuildings, Agatha sticking her head into horse boxes and tack rooms, the very thing that Richard had been dreading, came to pass. They bumped into Nippy. But the truculence that Richard had been expecting from Nippy never materialised. He remembered Agatha with affection, considered it a good sign that she had appeared on the scene and even professed himself pleased with his new accommodation. It was just his machine that he was worried about. Agatha had asked to see the contraption and had made approbative, if vague, noises, but done enough to put Nippy's mind at rest.

Then Richard and Agatha had had a happy half hour in the shops that lined Fordham High Street buying enough supplies to feed an army, which they packed into the tiny boot of the Triumph before seeking shade and refreshment in the garden of The Fox.

Richard took a deep draught of his glass of ale. 'Aggie, I'm not sure I share your optimism about how easy it will be to put the Hall to rights. I have had a few quotes for things like fixing the roof and I have to say that it will cost many hundreds of pounds.'

'Dicky, perhaps you weren't paying attention when I said that on the production of a marriage certificate and then some months later the production of a squalling infant, specifically one from my own loins and those of the other name on the marriage lines, I will find a sum only a little short of one hundred *thousand* pounds deposited into my bank account.'

Richard choked on his Pelham ale. When he had regained his composure he said, 'I was paying attention, but you didn't mention a figure. I was thinking in terms of a few hundred, or maybe a couple of thousand, quid.'

'Does that make you feel any better disposed towards the proposal?'

'Would you be very upset with me if I said that it does make me feel much better disposed?'

'Not at all. I would be relieved that you weren't out of your tiny mind. If I am to produce a child, I would rather not give birth to one that was at risk of inheriting premature softening of the brain.'

Richard couldn't work out whether that was an insult or not. 'Of course, I can see all the advantages, but I hope you don't mind if I say I can see a few disadvantages too.'

'Dicky, that goes for both of us. We might have to draw up a code of conduct and an enforceable agreement about what happens if we decide that we really can't live with each other at some point in the future.'

Richard was suddenly worried. 'Is there a risk that I might lose my ancestral home?'

'If I am not mistaken that risk already exists and is currently rather high. A better way of looking at it might be that I will take care of many of the things that you find tedious or difficult and you will be free to indulge in the usual pursuits of a man of your background and station in life, some of which are not so conventional. You will of course grant me the same latitude in terms of the latter.'

'Of course, dear thing. What's sauce for the goose is sauce for the gander.'

'In this case, I think the old saying should be the other way round.'

Richard was beginning to think that the moves were being put on him in a rather brutal way. It might be as well to make some attempt at playing hard to get.

'I know you said that I need to make a decision today, but Small-wood and uncle are due in a couple of hours. They are going to want to tie down the details of their purchase of Wyvern Hall. I am not trying to play you off against them, but it would be terribly impolite to bring them down here only to inform them that the deal is off the table. Would you mind if we went along with the pretence? They will be leaving tomorrow morning and then I can concentrate on your proposal and give you a firm answer tomorrow.'

'Alright, Dicky. You have until tomorrow. And now we'd better get back to The Priory so that I can get on with preparing this evening's meal. I would appreciate some help in the kitchen. Nothing complex. Mainly a bit of kitchen portering. Perhaps a quick trip to the general stores, if I find I have forgotten something vital to the recipe.'

Richard had been looking forward to a siesta, but bowing to Agatha's wishes, postponed it for an hour or so.

As it turned out, there was to be no siesta for Richard that day. Agatha managed to find a steady stream of tasks for him. He was becoming progressively more irritated, but suddenly at four-thirty everything was ready and they still had half an hour or so before Smallwood was expected.

'Right, time for us to tidy ourselves up before showtime,' Agatha said, briskly.

It was as if this was her event, not Richard's. He was about to protest mildly, but decided that there was nothing to be gained by it. He went up to his room and stripped off his casual togs and ran himself a bath in the adjoining bathroom. A few minutes later he was luxuriating in the hot water, when there was a peremptory knock on the door of the bathroom.

'Dicky, may I come in?'

Without waiting for a reply Agatha strode in dressed in her slip.

'I say, old girl, we need to come to some understanding about privacy.'

'Fiddlesticks, Dicky. Whatever you're up to in your bath is not going to shock me.'

'I was actually thinking about how to deal with Smallwood.'

'Don't worry about that. I'll handle everything. But I find that I have not brought the right clothes for a dinner party. I was wondering whether you had disposed of your parents' wardrobes.'

'No, I haven't touched a thing in their rooms since they died.'

'I thought that might be the case. Would you mind if I had a look through Gloria's wardrobe for a blouse that might fit me?'

Richard wasn't sure what he thought about Agatha going through his mother's clothes, but couldn't think of a way of expressing his reservations. In any case Agatha wasn't interested in his reservations. As far as she was concerned, hesitation was consent.

'Don't worry, I will observe all the proprieties.'

She swept out of the room and Richard heard her padding down the stairs to what had been his parents' quarters. Richard climbed out of the bath and dried himself. He went into his bedroom and selected his Austin Reed double-breasted navy blue blazer, a light blue shirt and grey slacks from the wardrobe. Was he going to wear a tie? He thought not. But if he was going to wear the blazer, he'd better have something around his neck. He selected a red silk paisley cravat which would contrast nicely with the shirt and blazer. Grey socks and a pair of Loake's loafers completed the ensemble. He studied himself in the cheval mirror. Not bad. Smart, but not too formal. He went downstairs to the lobby to wait for Agatha to descend, taking a seat in the alcove to one side of the front door, so that he could also keep an eye on the drive as it curved up to the house from the main gates.

The clacking of Agatha's heels on the first floor alerted him to her imminent arrival in the lobby. He raised his eyes to see her standing at the top of the stairs. She was wearing a short-sleeved green dress with a full skirt and a nipped-in waist. At her neck was a string of pearls. She was also wearing high heels. He couldn't remember ever having seen her dressed like that before. She looked magnificent, but somewhat worryingly, she also looked like his mother. She joined him in the alcove.

'What do you think? I was just looking for a blouse, but I realised that some of Gloria's older things were very close to my size. Nothing that couldn't be fixed by the judicious use of a couple of safety pins. This dress must be nearly twenty years old. The cut is perhaps a little old-fashioned, but it's beautifully made.'

Richard was looking at her open-mouthed. He felt like he'd seen a ghost.

'Dicky, are you alright?'

'Yes, yes. It's just a bit of a shock seeing you in one of Mother's dresses. I remember that one very well, not that she'd worn it in recent years. Gosh, I must still have been at school the last time I saw her in it.'

'Oh, Dicky, I'm sorry. I'll go and take it off, if it's upsetting.'

'No, no. It's fine. You look spiffing. I just wasn't expecting it. I'm more used to seeing you in jodhpurs or a tweed skirt and brogues.'

'Well, if I may say so, you brush up very well too.'

This moment of mutual sartorial appreciation was interrupted by the sight of a long grey car sweeping up the drive. Richard whistled. 'A Bentley drophead coupé. Smallwood's uncle really must be loaded.'

Agatha was not impressed. 'We shall see. Let's go and greet them.'

They stepped out onto the portico and watched the Bentley draw to a halt. Smallwood climbed out of the front passenger seat and waved cheerily to Richard. A moment later an older man got out of the driver's seat and bowed slightly in Richard and Agatha's direction. Smallwood bounded up the three steps and said 'Hello, Warren. I didn't know you had other guests. I hope we are not *de trop*.'

'Smallwood, this is my cousin Agatha Ponsonby.'

Smallwood and Agatha shook hands. 'Mr Smallwood, I imagine you have a first name.'

'Yes, of course. Please call me Tony.'

A gentle cough indicated that Smallwood's uncle had reached the top of the steps and was expecting to be introduced.

'Uncle, this is Richard Warren and his cousin Agatha Ponsonby.'

Smallwood turned back to Richard and Agatha. 'Please allow me to introduce my uncle, Sir James Milne.'

Richard said, 'You are welcome, Sir James. Agatha will show you to your rooms and Smallwood and I will bring up the bags. I am afraid it is a long time since we had staff here.'

'Not at all, Warren.'

'Please call me Richard.'

Sir James pointedly ignored Richard's attempt to put relations on a more informal footing and followed Agatha into the lobby.

As Richard and Smallwood were getting the bags from the back of the Bentley, Smallwood said, 'You didn't tell me about the cousin.'

'I didn't know myself until the day before yesterday. She rather invited herself. People do, you know. But Agatha and I go back a long way, childhood chums. She's a jolly good sort. And it also means that we'll be eating here tonight. She has prepared a magnificent repast.'

'Well, that sounds excellent, although I had rather built up the cuisine at The Fox for Uncle James.'

'I think you'll find that Agatha is quite a formidable cook herself.'

'But does that mean we'll have to mind what we say on the matter of Wyvern Hall?'

'Oh, no. I have no secrets from Agatha.'

'None?'

'Well, not many.'

'The boys?'

'Of course. She knew about that almost from the start. The one thing I haven't mentioned is the little matter of the amended will, but she knows all about your own interest in Wyvern Hall.'

'So, we can talk freely.'

'Certainly.'

'I must say she looks very regal, almost as if she were the chatelaine of The Priory.'

'Some people just have that sense of entitlement.'

'Not like you and me, eh, Warren?'

Richard didn't reply, but led the way inside the house.

Fifteen minutes later the party was gathered on the terrace and Richard was struggling with a bottle of Pol Roger. Eventually he managed to open the bottle without losing too much of it. A toast was drunk and everyone started to relax.

Sir James leaned back in his chair and said, 'What a splendid house The Priory is, Warren. I can see why you are keen to sell Wyvern Hall. With the proceeds you will be able to restore The Priory to its former glory. I have had good reports from Tony about the potential of Wyvern Hall as an investment and as somewhere for him to live. In principle, I am well-disposed towards the idea, but I need to assure myself that the trust will not be acquiring a white elephant. We plan to have a close look at the estate tomorrow, if that is convenient for you.'

Richard sipped his champagne. 'Most certainly.'

Sir James turned towards Agatha. 'And what do you do, Miss Ponsonby?'

'Well, at the moment, I'm looking for a husband.'

'And do you have anyone in mind?'

'I do as a matter of fact, Mr Warren.'

Sir James looked startled. 'But I believe you are cousins.'

'Only in a manner of speaking. People of the better sort all turn out to be related to each other if you go back far enough. We may even be related to you. I seem to recall that there was a Milne branch of the family who had estates in Rutland. Is that where your people come from, Sir James?'

'Oh, no. My people come from Hampshire.'

'So, you must be related to Bunty and Reginald Milne?'

'Ah, no. But let us not delve too deeply into genealogies, fascinating though it is, otherwise we'll never get off the subject. What I meant, when I asked what you did, was what your line of work was.'

'I'm afraid I don't have one. I've never seen the point.'

'But then how do you make ends meet?'

'My dear sir, I have no need to work. I too am the beneficiary of a family trust. I am sure this must come as little surprise to someone who is himself a trustee of a similar arrangement.'

Sir James laughed. 'In that case I imagine that you will have little problem in persuading Mr Warren to enter into the holy state of matrimony.'

'You may well be right, Sir James. But we should perhaps let Richard speak for himself.'

Richard was feeling none too comfortable with the direction the conversation had taken. 'Agatha, I don't think we should go into our personal relations at this stage in proceedings.'

'Oh, I don't agree on that score. The fact is that the matter of Wyvern Hall affects me too and I think it may be premature for us to consider selling the property.'

Sir James laughed again. 'I am beginning to see what you are playing at, Miss Ponsonby. I can't say that I blame you. No one likes to be perceived as a forced seller. Let me assure you that we are happy to pay the asking price. We will not seek to drive a hard bargain if the property is as promising as Tony has indicated. I should be able to give you a firm offer tomorrow when we have looked over the estate.'

Agatha brushed some invisible crumbs from Richard's mother's dress. 'I am glad to hear it, Sir James. If you will excuse us, we just have some things to do in the kitchen. We'll be back shortly and then we'll go through to the dining room. Richard, would you mind giving me a hand?'

When Richard and Agatha had gone to the kitchen, Rafferty said to Smallwood, 'You didn't tell me about the girl.'

'I didn't know about the girl. Girls and Warren is not something that makes any kind of sense.'

'Well, I would say she is the one who wears the trousers in that relationship.'

'It does rather look like it.'

'Do you think he's set this up?'

'Absolutely not. His mental powers are negligible.'

'So, you think she just happened along.'

'Does it really matter? It's not as if we really want to buy the property. It hardly matters if she thinks that she's seeing off a couple of carpetbaggers. It just lends credence to our cover.'

At that moment, Richard reappeared on the terrace. 'Sir James, another drop of Pol Roger?'

Richard divided what was left in the bottle between the three of them. He resumed his seat. 'Is the Bentley an S1 or S2?'

'It's an S2, V8 engine, power steering, air-conditioning.'

'It's a magnificent beast.'

'Thank you, Warren. It's one of the fruits of many years of hard work.'

Richard snorted. 'That's no doubt why I drive a Lagonda. No fruits to speak of.'

Sir James adopted a consolatory tone. 'Nothing wrong with a Lagonda, a fine vehicle.'

'With mine, everything that can go wrong, does. I'm lucky if it gets me to Puttenham Junction, if I need to go down to London.'

'Well, Warren, if this deal goes through, you may be in a position to acquire something a little more reliable. You'll need it for the honeymoon.'

'Oh, it's a bit premature for all that. Agatha acts on impulse. Next week she'll be setting her cap at some other hapless chap.'

'Of course, I've only just met the both of you, but I'd wager she tends to get what she wants.'

Richard drained his glass. 'Please come through.'

The supper was a success. Agatha's Boeuf Stroganoff was a triumph and as for the jam roly-poly, well… All the men agreed that they hadn't had a better one since they'd been at school. Sir James asserted that the only place you'd likely get a better one was in the House of Lords' dining room. The cheese board was decent and the port superb.

Sir James grew expansive. 'What a delightful evening. Thank you both.'

Richard beamed with pride. Agatha had done an incredible job. The tucker had been a revelation. Maybe domestic life with her would have its compensations. He could put up with being bossed around, if the catering was that good. Before bedtime, arrangements were made for the following morning. Sir James was confident that they wouldn't need much time at Wyvern Hall and they'd aim to be on their way before lunchtime.

By the time he crawled into bed, Richard was feeling rather pleased with the recent turn of events. Under the influence of the three glasses of port he'd drunk, he fell into a deep slumber, dead to the world until he was roused by someone shaking him by the shoulder.

'Dicky, wake up.'

Richard opened his eyes slowly. To judge by the light it must still be very early. 'What time is it?'

'It's five-thirty.'

'Aggie, it's far too early for breakfast.'

It occurred to him she might have decided that he should make an immediate start on begetting a child. 'Or for anything else.'

Agatha sighed. 'Don't be an idiot, Dicky. I'm not asking you to service me now.'

'Thank goodness. I mean, well, I'm not feeling too good. I feel like I've been hit over the head with a mallet.'

'I think perhaps you have, a chemical mallet.'

'I don't follow you old thing. I say, would you mind not hovering there like an avenging angel. Sit down on the bed. You can soothe my fevered brow. And that's not an invitation to climb in with me.'

Agatha perched on the side of the bed and placed her hand on Richard's forehead. 'You're not running a fever. You've been drugged.'

'You've lost me again.'

'Smallwood and Milne gave you a Mickey Finn. They tried to give me one too, but I didn't drink any of the digestifs. I fed them to the cheese plant.'

'Why would they do that?'

'So we wouldn't be aware of what they were up to during the night.'

'You're not suggesting that they were indulging in a bit of hanky-panky? For goodness sake, they're uncle and nephew.'

'Well, I'm not so sure they are. But no, so they could leave The Priory under cover of dark and return without our noticing.'

'And what makes you think they did that?'

'I saw them go out at three o'clock and come back half an hour ago.'

'Really?'

'Yes, and what's more, they took your car.'

'Aggie, it seems to me that you're the one who's acting as though you're drugged. Why would they slip off in the middle of the night? This isn't Mayfair. There's nothing to do at night in Fordham.'

'They went to Wyvern Hall.'

'How do you know?'

'They sat in the dining room for a while when they came back and talked. I slipped downstairs and went into the kitchen. I could hear some of what they were saying through the serving hatch.'

'I say, eavesdropping on one's guests is not really very seemly.'

'Nor is drugging one's hosts.'

'And why would they want to go to Wyvern Hall in the middle of the night when we are all going there in a few hours anyway?'

'So they could look at something without us.'

'Like what?'

'The barn.'

'I might have known. They're probably concerned about Nippy's machine.'

'They're worried about something. Is Nippy's machine called Helios?'

'I don't think it has a name.'

'They definitely used the word Helios. He was the sun god, wasn't he?'

'Yes, but I can't see Nippy naming his machine after a figure from Greek mythology.'

'Well, they're very concerned and were discussing what should be done about it. It needs to be destroyed but not until someone properly qualified has had a look at it and interrogated the people responsible.'

'I say that's a bit extreme. I'm no fan of Nippy's machine. I'm pretty sure it's a fraud, but there's no call to talk in terms of interrogation.'

'Do you know what Smallwood does for a living?'

'No idea, some kind of minor mandarin, I think.'

'They didn't sound like the kind of people who are considering the pros and cons of buying a down-at-heel estate. Nor did they sound like close relatives of each other. I would say that Sir James is actually Smallwood's boss, although I don't think his name is Sir James Milne anyway. Smallwood called him Larkspur at one point.'

'Sir James Larkspur?'

'No, just Larkspur. And then Sir James said, "Do I call you Hemlock? No! So please refrain from addressing me as such even when we are alone."'

'Aggie, this is getting more and more preposterous. I'm not even sure I understood what you just said. But before you explain, would you mind standing up for a moment? I need to spend a penny.'

Agatha let Richard out to use the WC. When he came back she was under the covers on the other side of the bed fast asleep. Richard shrugged and got in beside her and was soon asleep too.

The visit to Wyvern Hall after breakfast went off without incident. Sir James made only the most cursory inspection of the house and no mention of the barn was made at all. What he did say, however, was that there was some concern about whether the house and barn might in fact be prone to subsidence and Sir James would like to get a structural surveyor to take a look. He would contact Richard to arrange a convenient time for the surveyor to attend. He would need access to the house and its cellar, if it had one, and to the barn. Tony might well accompany the surveyor to speed things up. Richard said he would be happy to make the arrangements and invited the two men to lunch at The Fox, but they declined saying they wanted to make an early start back to London. If they allowed themselves to have a leisurely lunch in the pub, they would be vying with the other weekenders on their way back to the metropolis. And so shortly after the visit to Wyvern Hall, Richard and Agatha stood under the portico of The Priory and waved their guests off.

A little while later, Richard and Agatha were sitting on the terrace enjoying a nice cup of tea. Richard was feeling more pleased with life than for many months.

'Well, there was no mention of the machine, let alone Helios. And it seems the concern is about subsidence.'

Agatha was not convinced. 'I don't believe it. They must know that buildings of that age don't have what we would consider conventional foundations.'

'Really? I had no idea. But they do seem serious if they're going to bring in a surveyor.'

'Perhaps, but that brings us to the nitty-gritty. Do you really need to do this deal if you are going to throw in your lot with me? Come on, Dicky, it's time to make your mind up. Even if you found a boy who was your perfect life partner, it's not as if it's particularly easy to live as a couple in that kind of relationship, especially in a small place like Fordham. But if you and I were married, we could have long-term house guests. Tongues might wag, but they'd find it hard to prove anything. And you know yourself that neither of us is likely to find that special person that would suit until sundered by death, whereas we both get on very well together. What you call the icky side of things need not detain us long, just long enough to produce an heir to the Warren estates. And I think we might be a good team. We could restore the Warren finances to something more appropriate to an ancient county family.'

When put like that, what was not to like?

'Okay, Aggie, let's do it. Let's be man and wife, just as long as we don't have to fall in love.'

'Dicky, we've always been in love, just in a different way from the normal run of things. Shall we kiss to mark the occasion?'

'Of course, old thing, but no tickling.'

The couple kissed chastely and then returned to their cups of tea. Agatha looked thoughtful.

'Right, no backsliding, Dicky, because there are a number of things I need to do in the light of our decision. I will return to the Cotswolds. I need to make some arrangements and notify a number of people about our decision. I will pack a couple of suitcases and return here in a few days. Would you mind if I took the Lagonda? It will have more space for my cases. I'll leave the TR with you. When I return, we will then have a serious chat about your finances. I enjoyed preparing the Boeuf Stroganoff yesterday, but I don't want to have day-to-day kitchen duties. We need to find a cook, a cleaner and a gardener, maybe two of the latter.'

'Aggie, that's the sort of thing that terrifies me. I do have access to Cuthbert's funds to pay the Wyvern bills, but I'm not sure if I can divert to The Priory account the sums that your staffing requirements imply.'

'Don't worry. Leave it to me. I will take full responsibility for that kind of thing. I will just leave you to arrange the wedding. Where shall we spend our honeymoon?'

'Ooh, I say. Menton? Cap Ferrat?'

'Oh, yes, splendid. Start making some enquiries. Do you want to have a preliminary bash at making a baby?'

Richard turned pale. 'Well, okay, but you'll have to be gentle with me.'

'Of course, I am not expecting abandon. We will both regard it as an act of civic responsibility. Would you like to go and get ready and I will join you when you are about to reach boiling point. Which way up would you like me?'

'Would you mind rear entry, I mean entry from the rear, until I am more confident in my ability?'

'Not at all. Eminently sensible. Anyway there are certain advantages from my point of view and it's common belief that what you have in mind is a more reliable way of conceiving.'

Richard finished his tea and nervously repaired to his bedchamber to prepare himself for his first session with Agatha.

IN THE BENTLEY ON the journey back to London, Rafferty seemed preoccupied. Smallwood sat meekly in the front passenger seat, forbearing to interrupt Rafferty's cogitations.

They were almost halfway back to London before he said anything of substance.

'Things are more serious than I thought. We will need to get someone involved who is an expert in computing. That means we'll probably have to use one of the attachés from the embassy. They won't like it, but I think they'll see that it's the only way to get a proper idea of what's involved here. Since the person will obviously be Russian, you'll have to make sure that he doesn't find himself in a position where he is required to speak to any of the locals. But if you make an early start, you should be able to get down there and back to London in a single day. You, of course, could stay with your friends, but that's entirely up to you. And we'll have to devise a way of getting Nippy out of the way.'

'That shouldn't be too difficult.'

'Well, I leave that to you to work out. But then at some point not too long after that, you and I will have to return to Fordham incognito to interrogate and liquidate Nippy.'

'Fordham is a small place; it will be difficult for us to maintain our incognito.'

'That's a fair point. We will have to treat it as an active service operation. We'll take a vehicle we can sleep in and some provisions. We'll park up some distance from the Hall and wait for Nippy. We'll extract as much information as possible from him and then set incendiary devices to go off once we are clear of the site.'

Smallwood didn't like the sound of what was being proposed. How had what had originally started as an arrangement by which he passed snippets of information to the Soviets in return for fairly modest backhanders turned into his operating as a Soviet executioner?

ENGAGEMENT PARTY

AGATHA WAS BACK AT The Priory barely three days later. The Lagonda was loaded to the gunwales. Strictly speaking, there were only two suitcases, but there were quite a few other things too. Richard was amazed that the car had made it back without breaking down. He seldom took it on long runs, because it overheated so easily. When he mentioned with some pride how surprised he was that the Lagonda had performed so well, she informed him that she had arranged for the car to have a complete service in the intervening time at a specialist garage where they had fixed what the mechanics assumed were bodges by a local Fordham garage.

'I think you'll find it runs much better now,' she said evenly.

Before she left for the Cotswolds, Agatha had given some thought to sleeping arrangements on her return. She had identified two bedrooms on the first floor that had an interconnecting door between them while also having separate bathrooms. This seemed ideal. But it meant Richard relocating from what had been his childhood bedroom. He'd had a momentary pang of regret at the prospect of leaving the room in which he had slept for so many years. Deciding that softly, softly was the best approach, he had in effect left nearly all his things in the old room and moved only a selection of his clothes to the wardrobe in the new room. The advantage of this approach was that if Agatha was getting a bit too demanding in her desire to conceive, he could slip up to his old room and lock the door. On the positive side, the view from the windows of the new room across the lawns to the front of the house was magnificent.

Agatha approved of the new arrangements, but said that in due course she would need a dressing room. However, there was one point that disturbed her. 'Dicky, where is your teddy bear?'

Richard looked shifty. 'I left him in the old room. He didn't want to move.'

'Poor Teddy. Do you think he's feeling a bit jealous?'

'I think maybe he is.'

'I believe I might have the same problem with Ursula. Why don't I go and put her with Teddy? Then they'll both have company and won't have to watch us going hammer and tongs.'

'Oh, Aggie, would you mind? I think that might be a very good solution.'

A few minutes later Agatha returned to Richard's room, having placed her own teddy bear beside Richard's. 'It went very well. They're going to get on fine.'

Richard sighed deeply. 'I'm so pleased. I hope you won't mind if I check on him from time to time.'

'Not at all. Might I ask if you've recovered from the other day?'

'Oh yes, I'd stopped trembling within twenty-four hours.'

'Are you ready for another bout? I don't want to get too technical about it, but there are about six days each month when I'm likely to conceive. We've only got today and tomorrow in this present cycle and then we're going to have to wait three weeks before I'm fertile again. So the bad news is we'd better try several times today and tomorrow and then you can have a break for three weeks, unless of course you want a bit of practice in between times.'

Richard gulped. 'You're not suggesting right now, are you?'

'Yes, I'm afraid I am.'

'Unfortunately, the old man is not very lively right at the moment.'

'Would you feel too disgusted if I helped to get him going?'

'That might work.'

'And why don't we do it with our clothes on? That might make it feel more like a knee-trembler in the jakes. Of course, I'll need to get my drawers off first and I'll need to get myself going a bit too.'

'Ooh, Aggie, not too many details please. Just do whatever you think is best.'

It didn't take Agatha long to get him to the point where he was gently simmering. As she climbed onto the bed and got on her hands and knees, Richard said, 'I say, Aggie, you're rather good at that.'

'I can assure you that any practice I've had is on rather smaller protuberances. Anyway enough chat, don't lose your momentum.'

She flipped her skirt over her bottom and guided Richard home. It didn't take him long to make his delivery and withdraw. Agatha turned over and stretched out on the bed and Richard collapsed beside her. She took his hand. 'There, that wasn't too bad, was it?'

'No, I must say I'm feeling rather proud of myself.'

'As should we both. After all, we're sacrificing our instinctive ways of getting pleasure in the interests of creating new life with the paradoxical result that we will also become very rich.'

'When you put it like that, I think I might be able to try again this evening.'

'Well, I'm very pleased to hear that, my darling.'

Whereupon they both drifted off to sleep.

That evening over a light supper of *omelette aux fines herbes*, a green salad and a glass of Chablis, Agatha outlined how she saw things developing. It might take them a while to get her with child, but there was no reason to delay the wedding. They should make arrangements with the vicar for the banns to be read as soon as possible. They should also put an announcement in the local paper and perhaps invite a few neighbours for a drink to celebrate their engagement.

Richard was puzzled. 'Are we engaged, Aggie?'

'Well, you haven't actually asked me to marry you and you haven't got me a ring, but those are mere details.'

'I'm awfully sorry, old thing. It's all happened so fast.'

'There's absolutely no need to apologise.'

But Richard had already got to his feet. 'I'll be right back.'

He returned a few minutes later, a sheepish look on his face. 'I wonder if this ring would be acceptable as an engagement ring?'

He handed her a platinum ring with a large solitaire diamond.

It was not often that Agatha was lost for words, but this was one of those occasions. 'Oh, Dicky, it's lovely. This wasn't Gloria's by any chance?'

'Yes, it was. Does that make it a bit difficult?'

'No, I would be honoured to have it.'

'It just seems that if we're going to have some people around to celebrate the event, it would be handy to have a stage prop.'

'This is hardly a prop. But it will make the plan seem more authentic to our neighbours.'

She tried it on. It fitted perfectly. Agatha admired the back of her hand and the scintillations from the sparkler on her finger.

'It's lovely, but I do feel a bit guilty about wearing your mother's ring.'

'To be quite honest, old thing, I was contemplating selling it, to get various urgent repairs done on The Priory. So you've saved me from feeling that I'd done something sacrilegious.'

'Dicky, there's no need to sell any more of the family silver. As I said the other day, I have funds enough to tide us over without our having to sell Wyvern Hall.'

Richard suddenly felt a great weight had been lifted from his shoulders. The only problem was that Smallwood and Sir James were going to be rather disappointed and might turn a bit nasty.

Agatha saw something in Richard's expression that betrayed his disquiet. 'Is that not a reason for rejoicing, poppet?'

'Yes, it is. Most certainly. I'm just wondering how Smallwood and Sir James will take it.'

'Oh, I wouldn't worry about them. Let's see if they get back to us with a request to bring their surveyor down. We can tell them then that the property is no longer on the market.'

Richard seemed doubtful. 'Alright. I'll be guided by you in these matters.'

'That is much the best thing, Dicky, as you know. But let me say right now that if for some reason we are unable to proceed with our plan or the arrangement appears not to be working, I will of course return the ring.'

Richard looked uncomfortable. 'I'll do my best, Aggie.'

'It won't necessarily be your failing, Dicky. It might be just one of those things.'

He felt only slightly reassured by this rationalisation. But Agatha hadn't finished itemising her plans.

'I would also like to put an advertisement in the local paper for a cook and a gardener. And I wonder if we could re-engage your old cleaner?'

'Of course.' Since Richard wouldn't be paying for the advertisement or the wages, he had no grounds for objections. He was less certain that Doreen would want to resume doing the cleaning at The Priory, but there was no harm in asking. There were few enough opportunities in rural communities for part-time employment.

'Good.' Agatha looked pleased. 'So, who should we invite to our engagement drinks?'

Richard named a small group of people, mainly owners of some of the bigger houses in the locality. Agatha jotted their names down on her pad. 'What about the vicar?'

Richard found him a bit of a queer fish, but conceded that since he would be marrying them, he'd better be at the engagement ceremony. But there was another local worthy, much more to his liking, to add to the list. 'We should ask Professor Sage. He's a good old stick.'

'The old boy at the corner table in the pub, sitting with Flo, Cuthbert's friend?'

'Yes.'

Agatha added him to the list. 'And what about her too?'

Richard stuttered. 'Flo Hodges?'

'Yes. She's almost one of the family, isn't she?'

'I'm not sure I'm in her good books now though.'

'Oh dear, do you think you'd better tell me about it?'

Richard wasn't sure how to answer. He had no actual evidence that Flo was annoyed with him, but he was terrified that there might be some mention of Nippy's assertion about Cuthbert's revised will.

Agatha could see the turmoil clouding his mind. 'Dicky, I think you'd better get whatever's troubling you off your chest.'

'Oh dear, Aggie, I think you might be rather annoyed with me.'

'All the more reason to make a clean breast of it then.'

Hesitantly at first, but with increasing confidence as he managed to minimise the degree of forethought involved, he told her about the copy of Cuthbert's revised will, witnessed by his mother and father, which he'd found in the library table drawer. His initial interpretation of the document had been that he would have to allow Nippy to remain in the Hall, which would in turn mean that not only could he not sell the estate, but he couldn't even let it. He had contacted the local solicitors who held a copy of Cuthbert's original will, but they were unaware of any codicils. While Richard was wrestling with whether to produce the amended will, Small-wood had appeared upon the scene and offered to help solve the problem.

They had searched Wyvern Hall together and found Cuthbert's copy of the will, which turned out to be identical to the one in the library at The Priory. Smallwood had suggested that since the family solicitors seemed to be unaware of the revised will, there was no real need to admit to its existence. He wondered whether there might be an estate cottage that could be made available to Nippy. As it happened, one of the cottages on the Standon Road had recently become vacant. Smallwood said that offering the cottage to Nippy would spike his guns. Richard would in effect be acting in the spirit of the codicil, without running the risk of the will being interpreted as granting Nippy the right to live in Wyvern Hall for the rest of his days. Once Smallwood had put it that way, it all seemed so obvious. That was probably what made him a good mandarin. But why he had been so keen to apply his brainpower to this particular issue was beyond Richard.

Nippy had gone to see Flo. He had complained that he was being hard done by. The Master had intended more than that. But what really upset him was the possibility that he might not be able to continue work on his machine in the barn. Flo sympathised. She, Cuthbert and Nippy had worked together at some hush-hush place during the war. After the war, even when she was working in London, she had continued to keep a matronly eye on the two men. Now that Cuthbert had passed away, her nurturing tenden-cies were focussed on Nippy. She came to see Richard and inter-ceded on Nippy's behalf. Wasn't Richard being a little harsh? Surely Nippy could be extended this favour. He had been a loyal servant of the Warren family. The village spinster exterior concealed a formidable advocate. Richard soon abandoned any attempt at resistance and agreed to let Nippy have access to the barn.

Agatha drew in a deep breath. 'I see. You do rather seem to have fallen under the sway of Mr Smallwood. The good thing is that if you are prepared to go through marrying me and producing an offspring, it will really not matter whether Nippy's life interest is in the Hall or in one of the cottages on the estate, because you and I will become very rich people courtesy of the trust of which I am a beneficiary.'

When Agatha put it like that, it became clear that Richard's scope for independent action was now limited. On the other hand, his chains would be luxurious ones.

Agatha had not finished. 'And that being so, we need have no fear of the consequences of the revised will coming to light in the course of the rearrangement of rooms consequent upon my arrival at The Priory, say. That kind of thing happens all the time in these situations. There need be no mention of deliberate suppression. So there should be little in the way of public opprobrium. The naughty part of what you were planning with Mr Smallwood was that, had you sold to his trust, you would not have been able to protect Nippy's interest. For that oversight, a modicum of punishment is unavoidable. But I don't see why it shouldn't be restricted to the private realm.'

Richard was suddenly all a-quiver. 'What do you have in mind?'

'Oh, the usual, six strokes on the bare bottom with a cane. I think you'll find that I thwack rather well. If we do it at bedtime, it might even help with the impregnation. And then first thing tomorrow we will let Mr Smallwood know that the Hall is no longer for sale.'

Richard had not realised that Agatha was an *aficionada* of the cane. Things really were looking up.

RICHARD AND AGATHA WERE standing in the large reception room of The Priory inspecting the arrangements for their engagement party. Agatha had insisted on hiring a firm of caterers, and

Richard was delighted by the waiting staff in their black waistcoats and starched white aprons. The fact that several of them were young women was to be regretted, but no doubt there would be those among their guests who would appreciate a pretty girl thus attired. The Priory silver and crystal looked magnificent against the countless yards of white napery that the caterers had brought with them or found in the further reaches of The Priory's storerooms. Agatha had also bought up the stock of all the florists in Standon and arranged the flowers throughout the public rooms. It was many years since The Priory had looked quite so splendid.

Agatha was sipping a gin and tonic, and Richard was swirling the ice cubes in his Scotch. 'I say, Aggie, I wish you hadn't invited those kids. Flo's one thing, but her great-nephew quite another. And then he asks to bring his girlfriend, the dreadful termagant.'

'Flo assured me that the boy is very well mannered. And the girl is *so* sweet…'

'But she is the daughter of the local butcher.'

'There's nothing wrong with that these days.'

'Well, yes. But I don't think it's a good idea to get the hots for the village maidens. Or at least not that one.'

'Dicky, I do believe that you're already jealous. I can assure you that I have no thoughts in that direction. At least not yet.'

'Aggie, I am not reassured by your words.'

'Let us not get in a tizz about it. Flo put me rather on the spot and the boy and the girl were in the next room and so could hear everything. I do not think they were delighted to have to come to what would be, from their point of view, a stuffy cocktail party. I think it was more that Flo needs a little help getting around these days. Didn't want to be tottering home on her own perhaps.'

'Well, she is fond of a drink…'

'Anyway, having a couple of teenagers at our betrothal is hardly as bad as having the dreadful Mr Smallwood in attendance.'

'Yes, well I'm sorry about that. At least he's not staying at The Priory this time. I said it was out of the question. It was one thing to accommodate his uncle, quite another to put up his surveyor. Since when was one expected to find lodgings for one's tradesmen?'

'Why didn't you just tell him that the deal was off? I thought that was what we had agreed last weekend.'

'It's been such a busy week with this engagement business that I still hadn't got around to it by the time he phoned yesterday and I'm afraid I didn't have the courage to give it to him straight. To be honest I'm pretty sure the surveyor will condemn the whole project. So, with luck, things will go no further.'

'You may be sure, one way or another, things in that regard will go no further. But we now have the prospect of an awkward encounter between Nippy and Smallwood.'

'But there you are. If we're talking about unsuitable guests, what on earth induced you to invite Nippy?'

'I strolled up to his cottage the other day. I thought I ought to reintroduce myself. He was delightful and said that he remembered me from when I was a girl and that the Master had had a soft spot for me. I told him that you and I were getting married and that Wyvern Hall was definitely not going to be sold. He looked so pleased that I felt mean not also inviting him to the party.'

'But what if he comes in his wellington boots?'

'I made a point of telling him that he needed to have a bath and put his best clothes on.'

'I don't think I've ever seen him not in wellies. No, I tell a lie. He didn't wear wellies to Cuthbert's funeral.'

'Well, thank goodness.'

'Instead he wore a gigantic pair of army boots. Kept calling them his daisy roots.'

'I didn't know he was a cockney.'

'He's not. I believe he got the phrase from a popular song.'

'Dicky, let's not come to blows. I am sure the evening will be a great success.'

At that moment the butler appeared in the doorway of the room and announced, 'Professor Sir John Sage and Lady Sage.'

Agatha and Richard crossed the room and introductions were made. A waiter approached with a laden salver. Lady Sage took a sweet sherry and the professor a glass of champagne. Toasts were offered and drunk, whereupon the professor, addressing Agatha, said, 'Miss Ponsonby, I can assure you that your appearance on the scene has met with unqualified approval in the locality. The fact that you have taken this young man in hand is even more to be welcomed. The Priory is looking splendid and will undoubtedly once again be the centre of refined social life in our little township.'

Agatha simpered unconvincingly and said, 'Sir John, anyone would think you were a professor of rhetoric, not of philosophy.'

Sage beamed. 'My dear, there is very little difference.'

Lady Sage was not one for beating about the bush and said, 'And do you have a date for the wedding?'

Agatha, seeing Richard's confusion, replied, 'Not yet, but the first banns will be read this Sunday.'

Lady Sage raised an eyebrow. 'So soon!'

Agatha smiled mischievously. 'Not a moment to lose.'

Lady Sage nodded. 'Oh, I see. Well, how exciting.'

'You might say that I made Richard an offer he couldn't refuse. Fair swept him off his feet.'

Richard winced and looked around the room wondering if he could invent something to attend to.

The professor noticed his discomfort. 'Warren, they're teasing you. Why wouldn't the master of The Priory and now Wyvern Hall be a good catch? But I am sure Miss Ponsonby has her own sterling qualities, indeed I believe the match will be a fine one.'

'Thank you, John. I do believe I'm a little out of my depth in these matters, but contrary to appearances, Agatha and I go back a long way.'

'I heard as much from Flo Hodges. Before my time in Fordham, of course.'

As if on cue, the butler announced, 'Miss Florence Hodges, Master Peter Marshall and Miss Teresa Hammond.'

Richard looked over at the little group that stood in the doorway of the room, Flo in the lead, the boy looming behind her and, bringing up the rear, as if not quite sure of herself in such a gathering, the termagant. The first shock was that, so far as he could make out, the termagant was demurely attired, wearing a dark, simply cut dress with long sleeves and a high neck. She had her hair up and was wearing a little eyeliner and light pink lipstick.

But as Flo hobbled towards him and he was able to take the girl in properly, it became apparent that the demureness of the upper part of her outfit was offset by the scandal of her hemline, certainly an inch or two above the knee. He shuddered to think what his mother might have said, had she still been alive. His father, on the other hand, would have been delighted and might have found it difficult to keep his hands to himself. The fact was that the termagant looked like a modern young woman and not the grubby tomboy who had haunted The Priory when his parents were still alive.

The boy by contrast still looked like a boy, not that there was anything wrong with that. He was in a brown corduroy jacket (ugh!) with grey trousers, a red shirt (ugh again!) with a soft collar and a knitted tie. All in all a regular student type, but one who might brush up quite well in a year or two. And Flo was in her usual tweeds and brogues. The only one of them who looked dressed for the occasion was the girl. He went over to the little group, conjuring up a well-practised bonhomie to mask his apprehension. 'Welcome, welcome. Flo, Terri and Peter. So pleased you could make it.'

He waved a waiter over. 'Flo, I know what your tipple is, but what can these two drink? I'm not sure we have any dandelion and burdock.'

Flo dismissed his cumbersome joke. 'Richard, they can drink whatever they want. They are not children.'

Soon drinks were chosen, white wine for Peter and Terri, and Flo, following Richard's lead, her usual Scotch on the rocks. The newcomers joined the Sages and their hosts in the middle of the room under the big chandelier. Introductions were made where necessary. Agatha enthused over Terri's dress and pale tights saying that she wished that she had the confidence to wear such a high hemline and what a clever idea tights were. The professor asked about the young people's academic ambitions. He said that if either of them had aspirations to study at Cambridge, he would be happy to show them around and put in a good word, if it were appropriate.

Flo took Agatha to one side. 'I can't tell you how pleased I am that you've persuaded Richard not to sell Wyvern Hall. I know these big houses are expensive to maintain, but I am sure there must be other ways of dealing with the situation. And I'm not saying that because The Croft abuts the Hall. I can only wonder how you have managed this feat, especially since Mr Smallwood seems particularly determined to snap up the Hall for his family trust.'

'I can't go into details here, Flo, but let us just say that in such cases one needs to fight fire with fire. We will have a thorough chinwag at a more appropriate moment.'

'I look forward to that. I do believe that Mr Smallwood is not a positive influence on Richard.'

'I couldn't agree more, but I'm afraid to say that he will be joining us this evening.'

'Oh, dear that's unfortunate. I wouldn't have suggested that you invite Nippy, had I known that.'

'I'm afraid the matter only arose yesterday. When Smallwood was last here he told us that he intended to retain a surveyor to produce a full structural report of the Hall and its outbuildings. He arrived this morning with the surveyor in tow, having given Dicky only twenty-four hours' notice of his arrival. To be fair he was not asking to stay at The Priory. He said that the surveyor would drive back to London at the end of the day's work and that he would put up at The Fox. But Richard was caught off guard by the phone call and was unable to pluck up the courage to tell him that the deal was off. Instead in his confusion he invited Smallwood to join us this evening. I can assure you that that is one relationship that will wither on the vine once I have established myself properly in Richard's life.'

'I am pleased to hear it. I just hope that Nippy behaves himself.'

'Me too. We must both be alert for any flare ups.'

'You can count on me.'

'Thank you, Flo. I look forward to being your friend and neighbour. I do believe we have certain things in common, but it may be that those things are easier for my generation than they were for yours.'

Flo nodded knowingly. 'I see. Well, good for you. Still Cuthbert and I didn't do too badly. But I *do* miss him.'

Agatha patted Flo's hand. 'Of course you do, dear. In the end friendship is much more important than the other thing.'

'Oh, I wish I'd had your assurance when I was your age.'

'Flo, it's all bluster.'

'Well, it's very convincing.'

In the meantime, the large reception room was starting to fill up. Richard had moved closer to the entrance to the room to intercept the knots of local worthies as they arrived. Agatha felt that it would not do to be thought to be neglecting her intended so early in the evening. Her place was at his side.

'Excuse me, Flo. I must go and stand by my man.'

'Of course. But I'm glad we had this little chat.'

Agatha crossed the room like a ship in full sail and slipped her arm through her fiancé's. Soon gales of laughter could be heard issuing from successive waves of new arrivals as they encountered their hosts.

Meanwhile Terri and Peter had spotted the buffet and had loaded two plates and were now making their way to a small table to one side of the room near a door that led to a cloakroom. As they worked their way through the canapés, they reflected on the events of the previous few days. They had been in the dining room at The Croft the day that Agatha had called on Flo to invite her and, at Flo's prompting, Peter and Terri to a party at The Priory to celebrate her engagement to Richard Warren. Peter had not been delighted at this prospect. He had not brought a set of smart clothes with him to Fordham. But Flo had said that his brown jacket and shirt and tie were perfectly acceptable. She herself had no intention of putting on a little cocktail dress. It would be tweeds and brogues for her as on any other day. Surprisingly, Terri had also been keen to accept the invitation. She said that she knew her way around The Priory and could show Peter some of the other public rooms and, if the weather was nice, the grounds too. It would also give her an opportunity to dress up for the occasion. Now that he'd seen what that entailed, Peter could only marvel at the transformation. The only problem was that she also now looked older and more sophisticated, making him feel even more uncomfortable in his casual clothes. But there was no point brooding.

Looking around the room, he said, 'I'd say that we are closer in age to Agatha than she is to virtually everyone else in the room.'

Terri didn't agree. 'What about Richard? He must be about the same age as Agatha.'

'But he dresses and behaves like someone twenty years older.'

'Well, Agatha must find that attractive.'

'And that's another oddity. He seems to be what my mother would call a confirmed bachelor.'

'I've heard those whispers too, but you know what people are like. Always ready to think the worst. You didn't like me at first.'

'That's not true. I thought you wouldn't be interested in someone like me. And I didn't know how to go about becoming friends with you. But I wanted to get to know you from the first moment I saw you.'

'What? In my scruffy jeans and tee shirt?'

'Particularly in your jeans and tee shirt.'

'You had a funny way of showing it. You seemed to ignore me.'

'I didn't want to stare. I didn't want to make you feel uncomfortable.'

'I think you ought to know that girls like to be liked at. Not by dirty old men who seem to be undressing you with their eyes, of course. But I wouldn't mind being undressed by you. Why do you think I put that miniskirt on the other day?'

Peter was shocked. 'Terri, shh. Someone might hear.'

Terri giggled. 'Ooh, this wine must be going to my head. So do you really prefer me in jeans?'

'Terri, you look beautiful. You always look so stylish, whatever you're wearing.'

'I don't imagine I looked particularly stylish in my wet underwear with pond weed in my hair when we were swimming in the Wyvern lake.'

Peter blushed. 'You looked incredibly sexy.'

'I wish I'd known then that you had some Durex …'

Peter didn't let her finish the sentence. 'Terri, this is not the right place for that …'

'Sorry, Pete. I'm just teasing. Anyway, to get back to Agatha, whatever is going on between her and Richard can only be a good thing from my point of view. If it's true that she's persuaded him not to sell the Hall, I will get down on my hands and knees and worship her.'

Terri giggled again. Peter was starting to worry that despite her demure apparel, Terri's tomboy nature had been freed by the alcohol. 'Terri, I really do think the drink has gone to your head.'

Terri pulled a face. 'Still, the one disappointing aspect, if it is the case, is that we won't find out what all that stuff about Helios, Larkspur and Hemlock is all about.'

'I don't see why not. Helios is still under the barn, even if we never find out what Larkspur and Hemlock mean.'

Just then they heard a gentle cough behind them and turned to see Agatha standing there, having just come out of the cloakroom. They hadn't seen her go in, but surmised that there was another door on the other side of the room. How long had she been standing there? Terri went pale beneath her already pale makeup.

But Agatha showed no signs of annoyance or irritation. 'May I join you for a few minutes? These heels are killing me. I wish I was wearing shoes like yours, Terri. Very smart, but possibly too trendy for me.'

Peter jumped up and offered his seat to Agatha, which she took with a slight inclination of the head. Peter remained standing, but Agatha said, 'Pull yourself up another chair, Peter. I'd like to have a discreet chat, so it might be better not to have you hovering a few feet above us.'

Peter was alarmed at what might be involved in a discreet chat, but did as he was asked.

Agatha smoothed her dress down and said, 'I don't make a habit of eavesdropping, but I couldn't help hearing something of what you were saying just now. In particular, I heard the words, *Helios*, *Larkspur* and *Hemlock*. Would you care to explain to me what those words mean, not in themselves, of course, but taken together? I mean one would not be surprised to find that they were all early nineteenth-century sailing ships. On the other hand one would be surprised to find a couple of twentieth-century teenagers discussing ships of the line in Nelson's navy at a cocktail party, rather than the latest Beatles LP, say.'

Peter and Terri looked at each other in alarm. Neither of them knew what to say.

Agatha was thoughtful. 'I see. I can assure you that I have no intention of getting you into trouble. Perhaps it would make it easier, if I were to tell you how I came to hear those words used in combination on a previous occasion. But I'd like you to promise me that you won't tell anyone else what I am about to tell you.'

Terri nodded vigorously and Peter said with a dry throat, 'Promise.'

Agatha took a moment to compose herself. 'I said that I don't usually eavesdrop, but the fact is that I did just that a few days ago and on that particular occasion I did so on purpose. Would it surprise you very much if I were to tell you that the person that I was eavesdropping on was a certain Mr Smallwood, who was a guest with his uncle, Sir James Milne, at The Priory?'

Terri and Peter exchanged nervous glances, unsure just where Agatha's account was heading.

'Without going into all the details, let's just say that I was in the kitchen here at The Priory in the small hours of the morning and Mr Smallwood and his uncle were sitting in the dining room talking. There is a serving hatch between the kitchen and the dining room and I was able to hear some of what they were saying. You may imagine that it was a somewhat uncomfortable situation, not least because I was standing there in my nightdress. Fortunately, they were unaware of my presence.

'It was apparent that they had left the house in the middle of the night and from their conversation I deduced that they had gone to Wyvern Hall. This was strange since there was a plan for us all to go to the Hall the following morning. They were talking about something called *Helios*. The uncle was of the opinion that it should be destroyed, but not until someone properly qualified had taken a look at it. My first thought was that they were talking about Nippy's machine, but it became clear that they were referring to something more like a computer. The other odd thing was that Mr Smallwood at one point called his uncle *Larkspur* and Sir James responded as if Mr Smallwood might in another context be called *Hemlock*.

'With all the arrangements for tonight's event and connected matters, I put the whole thing out of my mind, especially since Dicky and I have decided that we are not going to sell the Hall to Smallwood or anyone else.

'And then inadvertently I overhear you two talking about *Helios*, *Larkspur* and *Hemlock*. It seems too much of a coincidence to suppose that they are not in some way related to what I heard Sir

James and Mr Smallwood talking about. Would you care to help me in this regard?'

Terri and Peter were suddenly in uncharted territory. They had not had time to agree a response to such enquiries. Peter's mind was racing, but he could see no easy way of deflecting Agatha's question. Typically, Terri filled the breach.

'We were trying to find Cuthbert's copy of his revised will to prove that after his death Cuthbert wanted Nippy to be able to stay at Wyvern Hall for the rest of his life. We guessed that it might be in his study at the Hall. Years ago Nippy showed me a way to get into the Hall without a key. We found a folder labelled WILL quite quickly, but instead of a will it contained a document that didn't make much sense. It was called HELIOS DECRYPTS.'

'Hmm. That accounts for the word *Helios*. And what else did it say?'

'Unfortunately, at that point Smallwood came back to the Hall. We hid in a cupboard. When he had gone and we thought it was safe to come out, we found that he had taken the whole folder. We tried to remember some of the other words on the top sheet and wrote them down. That's where *Larkspur* and *Hemlock* came from. We also wrote down *Mother Goose*.'

Agatha frowned. 'Mother Goose?'

Peter had now found his voice. 'Smallwood seemed surprised when he opened the folder and said something like "It's the Mother Goose dossier."'

Agatha's eyes were glittering. 'Who was he talking to?'

'Himself presumably,' Peter replied, not entirely convincingly.

Something occurred to Agatha. 'If you were in the cupboard, how do you know it was Smallwood?'

More secure on this point, Peter said, 'From the kind of cigarettes he smokes.'

Agatha smiled. 'Yes, his ciggies really do pong a bit. So have you got any idea what he was referring to, what all this means?'

Terri took over. 'We think they are codenames.'

Agatha nodded. 'I think you may be right. And I think we now know who Larkspur and Hemlock are. It also seems that Helios is Nippy's machine...'

Peter was about to say that the perpetual motion machine was just a disguise for the electronic device beneath it, when Terri kicked him in the shin and said, 'And Mother Goose. Who's that?'

Agatha shook her head. 'No idea. What do you think?'

But before Terri or Peter could answer, there was a small commotion at the double doors to the reception room resulting in the butler announcing, 'Mr Anthony Smallwood.'

A familiar darkly brilliantined head appeared in the open doorway and scanned the room looking for his old chum and reluctant host.

Terri scowled, 'What's he doing here?'

Agatha put her hand on Terri's knee and said, 'I'm afraid my bonehead of a fiancé didn't have the courage to tell Mr Smallwood that the deal was off. Smallwood had made arrangements for a surveyor to come and make a structural survey of the Hall and its outbuildings. They have been at it all day. Dicky also invited Smallwood to join us tonight, but thank goodness had the good sense not to invite him to stay here. Mr Smallwood will be making do with a room at The Fox. Unfortunately, I must now go and make sure that Dicky doesn't allow himself to be talked into any other ill-advised schemes.'

Agatha rose from her chair, but before she went over to join Richard, she said, 'I don't think we have quite pooled all our evidence or aired our suspicions. Would you be able to come around for a cup of coffee at about eleven o'clock? Dicky will be out for a couple of hours, so we can continue this conversation without fear of anyone else overhearing us.'

Peter and Terri looked at each other and Terri said, 'Yes, we'd love to, Agatha. We may call you Agatha, mayn't we?'

'Of course. Actually my friends call me Aggie. I leave it to you.'

She rose, blew the couple a kiss and crossed the room to join Richard, who was already talking animatedly to Smallwood. Agatha greeted Smallwood brightly and slipped her arm through Richard's.

When she was out of earshot, Peter said, 'Do you think we told her too much?'

'I don't know. That's why I kicked you in the shins when you were going to tell her about the real Helios. She clearly doesn't know about it. Or was testing us to see what we knew.'

'Do you think she's one of them?'

'Perhaps. We need to tread carefully. I was prepared to believe her that the deal for the Hall was off, until Smallwood walked in.'

'Her explanation was plausible.'

'She might have made it up on the spot.'

'And what about tomorrow? Should we meet her as she suggests?'

'Yes, but we need to work out what we're going to say.'

Just then Flo came by on her way to the cloakroom. 'You two look rather serious. Has something happened?'

They hastened to assure her that everything was fine and that they were enjoying the party.

'I noticed that you were hugger-mugger with Agatha. I hope she wasn't being beastly to you.'

Terri said, 'Oh, no. She was very friendly. She has asked us to come around for coffee tomorrow.'

'Goodness me. But then I suppose she is closer to you two in age than she is to me. She does seem to have swept into Fordham like a whirlwind and wasted no time in persuading Richard that he would be better off married to her than skulking in this huge house on his own. And if she is able to keep him out of the clutches of charlatans like Tony Smallwood, so much the better. I am surprised he had the nerve to show his face here.'

Having delivered herself of these views, Flo continued on her way to the cloakroom.

Terri said, 'Phew! Flo doesn't miss much.'

Peter laughed. 'She's certainly got Smallwood's number. Let's hope she hasn't got ours.'

'It's too late to worry about that. I'm pretty sure she knows more than she's letting on.'

Just then the butler swung into action again and intoned, 'Mr Neville Smith.'

Terri jumped up. 'Nippy's come. That's brilliant. I wonder if he was invited or just decided to turn up. Blimey, I don't think I've ever seen him so smart. Come on let's go and talk to him.'

Terri set off across the room with Peter a pace or two behind. Nippy looked pleased to see them. 'Ah, daughter of the dragon…'

But Terri cut across him. 'Nippy, you're not wearing wellies and your suit looks as though it's been pressed.'

'Miss Agatha invited me, but said I had to dress smartly. Considering that she has persuaded Richard not to sell the Hall, I could hardly refuse. Anyway, I'm not the only one who is unusually dressed. What happened to the lower part of your dress?'

'It's a mini dress, Nippy. They're very fashionable at the moment.'

'It's indecent, if you ask me. I'm surprised that your parents let you out looking like that.'

'Nippy, you can go off people, you know. Actually, they weren't very happy about it. They made me wear a coat that came down below my knees…'

At that moment one of the waiters had returned with the glass of mild ale that Nippy had asked for when rejecting the glass of champagne that he had been offered. As Nippy took the glass and raised it to his lips, he caught sight of Smallwood on the other side of the room. 'What's he doing here? When I got back from Standon earlier, I found him snooping around the Hall with a chap he called his surveyor. Didn't look much like a surveyor to me. I'm starting to think that Miss Agatha might have been leading me up the garden path.'

Terri leapt to Agatha's defence. 'No, the deal is definitely off, but Richard chickened out of telling Smallwood. You can relax. He's wasting his time.'

Further speculation about the likelihood of Smallwood's success in acquiring Wyvern Hall was cut short by the butler banging one of the tables with a gavel and requesting silence for Mr Richard Warren. When the hubbub had died down, Richard cleared his throat nervously and said, 'Ladies and Gentlemen, thank you all for coming this evening to join with Agatha and me in celebrating our engagement. Agatha and I are old friends. In recent years our lives had taken different directions, but when we met again recently, it became clear that we were made for each other. We decided that at our stage in life, there was no point beating about the bush and decided to get married as soon as possible. I know that both sets of parents, were they still alive, would be delighted with this development. So I would like you to raise your glasses and drink a toast to the future Mrs Agatha Warren.'

The toast was drunk and then Agatha stepped forward. 'I know it is not traditional for the bride to speak at such moments, but times are changing and those of you who know me will also know that I like to have my say. On this occasion, however, I will keep it brief. I would just like to say that Richard and I intend to return The Priory to its former splendour. It is also our intention to keep Wyvern Hall in the possession of the Warren family. It will not be sold to a third party nor demolished for new housing nor developed in line with any of the other rumours that have been floating around. Mr Smallwood's presence here this evening is not as the future owner of Wyvern Hall, but as an old friend of Richard's. So I would ask you to raise your glasses to the linking of two ancient families the Ponsonbys of Moreton-in-Marsh and the Warrens of Fordham Market.'

Peter looked across the room to see how this news was received by Tony Smallwood. But Smallwood seemed remarkably unperturbed, notwithstanding the fact that he had spent a good deal of the day inspecting Wyvern Hall with his surveyor. In fact he looked rather pleased with himself. He did not look like a predator who had had his prey snatched from his jaws. No doubt Richard had already given him the bad news earlier and he had had time to put a brave face on matters.

AFTER THE PARTY

THE NEXT MORNING TERRI had reverted to her normal jeans and tee shirt. Clearly a good night's sleep had clarified things in her mind. As she and Peter met at the corner of the recreation ground to walk up to The Priory, she said, almost before they had even greeted each other, 'I think we have to trust her.'

'And tell her what the Helios really is?'

'Yes, probably, but I'm not sure. We'll have to take it step by step. I don't think she is a fan of Smallwood and she might welcome a reason to declare him persona non grata.'

Peter was apprehensive. He had a feeling that one question would lead to another. On the other hand Agatha seemed to have her own suspicions about Smallwood and his uncle. 'Okay,' he said doubtfully.

A few minutes later, they found Agatha already sitting on the terrace in the morning sunshine. She waved them over to join her. 'I hope you enjoyed the party last night. I'm sorry that there weren't others of your own age, but you both behaved impeccably.'

She poured some coffee and handed round a plate of biscuits.

'So, where were we? Ah, yes. I know that you're not sure whether to trust me or not. To a certain extent I have the same problem. I'm pretty sure everything you've told me is the truth, but perhaps you haven't told me everything. Maybe if I were to voice my own suspicions, it might persuade you that we're on the same side.'

The young couple nodded but remained silent. Agatha folded her hands in her lap and gathered her thoughts. 'I regret to say that Dicky's initial response to the matter of the will and to Nippy's life interest does him no credit. He was clearly in a panic because of the dire financial situation he found himself in. It appears that, in the search for a way out, he confided in Mr Smallwood, whose advice seems to have been to locate all copies of the amended will and suppress them. His master stroke, however, was to grant Nippy an estate cottage for a peppercorn rent. This was a move that worked well with local public opinion, but did not give Nippy the security that was implicit in Cuthbert's revised will. By the way, I have not seen the revised will, so these are broad assumptions I am making.'

Agatha took a sip of her coffee. Peter and Terri waited for her to resume her account.

'In this version of events Smallwood is a man of subtle mind and dubious ethics coming to the aid of an old college friend. But something doesn't ring true. Smallwood hadn't been in touch for years and suddenly it's almost impossible to keep him away. The palaver of his becoming the buyer of the Hall through his trust fund and bringing his uncle and then a surveyor to inspect the premises doesn't feel quite right. There is an air of pantomime about it all. One feels that Smallwood had already targeted Dicky for some other purpose and the matter of the will was a convenient cover.

'Clearly I have come on the scene later than both of you, but I have had the opportunity to spend some time with Smallwood and his uncle, Sir James Milne, and my first impression was that the uncle was as bogus as the nephew. But I had no proof. My suspicions were just the product of some sixth sense. They were guests here and we prepared an evening meal, which went off rather well. Towards the end of the evening, Dicky passed around the port and at one point I thought I saw the uncle tampering with the decanter after having poured a glass for himself and Smallwood. I suggested to Dicky that he'd already had enough to drink, but he objected to what he saw as an attempt by me to control his drinking. Soon he said that it had been a long day. He apologised but said that he needed to go to bed. I thought it best to feign tiredness myself, even though I had poured most of my own glass into the cheese plant. Sir James and Smallwood said that they'd turn in too.

'I slept lightly and at three o'clock I heard movement in the house and saw Milne and Smallwood leave the house and take Dicky's car. I heard them return at about five. They sat in the dining room for a while and talked. I slipped downstairs and went into the kitchen. I could hear them through the serving hatch. It became clear that what concerned them was what they referred to as the Helios machine. They said that it needed to be destroyed, but not before someone properly qualified had taken a look at it and interrogated the people involved. This was also the point, as I mentioned last night, when the words Larkspur and Hemlock were mentioned.

'Putting this together with the document you saw briefly and the fact that it was Smallwood who purloined it, one starts to get the feeling that what we're dealing with here is some kind of undercover operation. I wonder if you could provide any further insights from your own enquiries that would confirm or disprove that thesis and how it is that Nippy's preposterous machine could ever be of interest to shadowy figures like Smallwood and Milne.'

Despite her own earlier reservations, Terri threw caution to the winds and said, 'There's another machine in an underground bunker below the perpetual motion machine.'

Agatha laughed dismissively. 'That rather sounds like something from a James Bond movie.'

'But that's exactly what it's like, except the bunker is not as big as Dr No's. It's more like a cellar. But it does contain some large electronic equipment. I think that's more probably what Smallwood and his uncle were referring to.'

This piece of information got more of a reaction from Agatha. 'I see. What kind of machine are we talking about here? A computer?'

'Yes, that's what we think.'

'And how did you find the bunker or cellar? Presumably Nippy didn't tell you about it.'

Peter felt he could make a contribution here. 'We were sunbathing by the lake and we saw Smallwood go into the barn, when we knew that Nippy was in Standon. So we guessed that he didn't have explicit permission to be there.'

'How do you know that Smallwood found the cellar? Presumably it's not obvious that it's there.'

'Because when we got in there, we found one of his cigarettes.'

'Well, well, Mr Smallwood really is rather careless with his smoking. He ought to be more careful about smoking in a barn especially one containing electronic equipment. So what did you make of all this?'

Terri resumed the account. 'Well, it now looked as if Nippy and Cuthbert might be spies and that they were being investigated by the security services. I didn't want to believe that. Smallwood just didn't seem to be a good guy. While we were arguing about it, we heard someone coming down the ladder, so we hid in a curtained off part of the cellar which we found led to a tunnel. We then realised that it was Nippy. I suppose we should have revealed ourselves and faced the music, but we didn't really understand what was going on. It was still just possible that it was Nippy who was the spy. So we decided to follow the tunnel which came out in the cellar under the Hall.'

Agatha crossed her arms. 'I see. So you think that Nippy is a spy, a Soviet spy one imagines. And presumably Cuthbert was too.'

Terri was defiant. 'No, it's Smallwood who is the Soviet spy, and his uncle, whatsisname, Sir James Milne.'

'So how do we explain what Nippy and Cuthbert were up to then?'

Peter explained his theory. 'We think that Mother Goose is, was, Cuthbert. We think that Cuthbert was murdered, but it was made to look like a heart attack. Larkspur and Hemlock are code names used by the Russians for double agents in British Intelligence. We think that someone high up in British Intelligence, perhaps Night-shade, was the person to whom Cuthbert took the preliminary results from Helios.'

Agatha held up her hand. 'One moment. You just said Night-shade. This is the first time Nightshade has been mentioned. Where does this name come from?'

Terri could help here. 'It was one of the other codenames in the folder that Smallwood took. We only saw it for a few minutes, but later we wrote down what we could remember.'

Agatha nodded. 'Thank you. That is very useful.'

Peter continued with his analysis. 'This person, Nightshade say, realised that the entire network of double agents was likely to be uncovered. So Smallwood was sent to locate the dossier. What the double agents didn't know about, at that stage, was Helios. As soon as Smallwood found the Helios, he rushed back to London to tell Milne.

'We'd worked out that much by last week. But we can now add your information. Smallwood brought Milne down to see the Helios. Then Milne organised an expert to come and look at it to try and figure out how it works and whether they need to worry about any further information coming out of it. That presumably was the surveyor yesterday. Next they will arrange to have it destroyed.'

Agatha was impressed. 'My goodness, you two really have thought this through.'

Terri was reluctant to take the credit for their analysis. 'No, Peter worked most of it out. He's brilliant.'

Peter looked bashful. 'It was a joint effort. I would never have dared get into the cellar without Terri.'

Agatha smiled. 'So the question is what are we going to do now? What can we do? Presumably Smallwood is already back in London giving his report to Milne.'

Terri was glum. 'I don't know. Until we saw Smallwood at your party yesterday, we thought that perhaps they'd got all the information they needed and that they'd now leave us alone, well Nippy, alone. But if what you overheard is correct, not only are they going to destroy Helios, but they're also going to interrogate the people involved with it first.'

Agatha nodded. 'That means that Nippy is in danger.'

Terri suddenly sobbed. 'Yes, that's what I'm afraid of.'

Agatha stood up and put her arms around Terri. 'I'm sure we can sort this out. It must have been very stressful for you two. I hope you'll let me help you.'

Terri sniffed. 'Yes, but you're just a woman and we're teenagers.'

Agatha smiled. 'I think it's time we stopped underestimating certain categories of people. Do you really feel inferior to Smallwood? Or even my beloved? I certainly don't. It may also be to our advantage that we are not considered threats.'

Terri dried her eyes. 'But what can we do?'

'Well, first of all, you need to show me this machine. And there is no time like the present.'

'But what if Nippy is there? Or if he arrives while we're there?'

'Leave it to me, should that eventuality arise. If you wouldn't mind waiting for a few minutes while I change into something more suitable for clambering about in cellars.'

Agatha went up to her room and returned ten minutes later in jeans, checked shirt and plimsolls.

Terri's jaw dropped. 'Aggie, you look great.'

'Well, thank you, dear. To tell you the truth, this is closer to my usual get-up. But it is true that we could almost be sisters.'

Peter didn't know what to say. He sensed that there was a lot going on between the two women that he didn't really understand.

Agatha suggested that they go to the Hall in the TR3. It'd be a bit of a squeeze, but she thought Terri would fit on the little back seat, if she sat crossways. Peter had never been in a sports car before and loved the noise it made and the way Agatha swept through the village. He decided instantly that this was the kind of car he wanted when he was older. When they got to the Wyvern Hall barn, to their collective relief there was no sign of Nippy. Agatha had thought to bring Richard's key to the front door of the Hall and so it took only a few minutes to fetch the key to the barn from the utility room, climb down into the cellar and show Agatha the Helios and the tunnel that connected to the cellar under the Hall. Agatha spent some minutes peering at the control panels of the main unit. She then sat down at the desk that was positioned in front of it and said, 'I'm sorry this is going to take a few minutes. I want to have a close look at the contents of this desk.'

She put the bunch of keys on the desktop and then opened the first drawer and brought out a large manilla folder. She put it on the desktop and opened it. As she did so, she caught the bunch of keys with the edge of the folder and they fell down at the back of the desk.

'Oh, how clumsy of me!'

She pushed her chair back and got on her hands and knees and felt around at the back of the desk, but couldn't reach the keys. Peter offered to try, his arms being somewhat longer. Agatha accepted his help. Peter took off his jean jacket and hung it on the back of the door. He then got down on his hands and knees under the desk and felt around for the keys. It did not take him long to find them and return them to the top of the desk. He then noticed that his hands were covered in some kind of oily substance.

Terri said, 'You can wash them in the sink in the little kitchen.'

Peter went through to the kitchen, ran some water into the sink and soaped and scrubbed his hands and wrists until they were clean. He looked around for a hand towel, but had to make do with a tea towel. As he dried his hands he noticed that there was a mug with a small amount of black coffee in the bottom and an ashtray with a half-smoked cigarette resting in it. He put the tea towel down and picked up the cigarette butt. It was a Balkan Sobranie. He went back into the main room.

'Smallwood has definitely been in here again. There's another one of his cigarette butts. I threw the previous one we found in the bin.'

Agatha did not seem surprised. She had now finished going through all the drawers. She closed the small notebook she had been writing in and returned her attention to the main unit, this time looking at the switches. For a moment Peter thought that she was going to try and turn the machine on. But after a moment she turned around, hands on hips and said, 'Well, someone has been having fun.'

Soon they were speeding back to The Priory. Agatha asked Peter and Terri to stay for some lunch. There were all sorts of nice things left over from the previous night including some of the lovely white wine they'd been drinking. She bustled around putting things on the big kitchen table. Peter considered asking for a glass of water, but decided that he might as well act as if drinking wine at lunchtime was an everyday activity with him. Terri caught his eye and indicated with a little smile that she had every intention of making the most of Agatha's hospitality.

When they were all seated at the table, Agatha raised her glass and said, 'You two have done a very good job. Well done.'

She took a mouthful of wine and then said, 'But I want you to promise me that you won't return to the Helios cellar or indeed to the Hall and its meadows until I tell you that it's safe to do so.'

Neither Peter nor Terri responded immediately. Terri put her glass down. 'But how will we get to see Nippy?'

'Well, I think that it'd be better if you didn't see Nippy for a few days either.'

Peter said, 'Is that because you think that Nippy actually is a spy?'

'No, I don't think he's a spy, at least not in the usual sense of the word, but I do think that he's got himself mixed up in something rather worrying and perhaps dangerous. And it could be dangerous for you too.'

Terri was outraged. 'Nippy's not a spy. And the meadows are where Pete and I spend most days.'

Agatha smiled. 'Well, I know you two are at that stage when you can't get enough of each other's company and you could do with a bit of privacy. So I will give you the key to The Priory's summer-house and you can use that and the swimming pool for the rest of the summer. I'm sure Dicky won't mind. You can come and go as you please. But I want you to promise me that you won't go to Wyvern Hall until I tell you that it's safe to do so.'

Terri wasn't yet ready to make that promise. 'But when will that be?'

'Honestly, Terri, I don't quite know what's going on here. I need to have a little chat with Nippy. I promise that I won't mention that you showed me the Helios.'

Terri was still not convinced. Agatha decided to up the stakes. 'If you are not prepared to make that promise and accept my offer of the key to the summerhouse, I'm afraid that I will have to talk to your father and to Flo and make it clear what the new modus operandi is.'

Peter realised that Agatha was not bluffing and said, 'Okay, we promise.'

Terri glared at him, refusing for the moment to endorse the promise. Agatha took another sip of wine. 'Terri?'

Finally, Terri gave in. 'Oh, alright. But I don't know why you're acting so seriously all of a sudden.'

'Because I now think this is a serious matter.'

'So what do you plan to do about it?'

'I don't know right now. I think I will have to get some advice. I have a friend who knows something about these matters.'

After lunch, Agatha took down a key from the row of hooks in the kitchen and handed it to Terri. 'This is the key to the summer-house. The other key is to the side gate to The Priory on the other side of the pool beyond the trees. I know that you know your way around The Priory, so why don't you show Peter the summerhouse? I'm afraid the water in the pool isn't heated, but it's probably no colder than the pool in Standon.'

Terri had started to adjust to the situation. 'Would it be okay, if we had a swim this afternoon?'

'Of course. But before you go, one other thing. What we have talked about is just between the three of us. Please don't mention it to anyone else. Not even to Nippy. Nor to Flo or Fred and Doreen. And most importantly don't mention it to Dicky. I am relying on you to be sensible here.'

Peter and Terri agreed to the additional conditions.

As they walked across the broad expanse of lawn in the direction of the summerhouse, Terri's mood brightened. 'I think Agatha is over-reacting, but this isn't bad compensation for not being able to go to Wyvern's for a couple of days.'

A few minutes later, Peter saw what she meant. The summer-house was screened from the main house by a stand of elegant trees. It was an elaborate gothic chalet with a verandah overlooking a small swimming pool. Terri unlocked the door. Inside there was a sitting area the width of the building furnished with rattan chairs and a sofa. At one end there was a fireplace, the grate of which at that moment was full of large fir cones. At the other end of the room was a bar. It had seen better days and was not fully stocked, but nor was it totally devoid of alcoholic beverages. To the rear of the building on one side was a small kitchen and to the other side a lavatory and shower room.

Terri was delighted. 'It looks like we've found just the place we've been looking for.'

'I'm not sure what you mean.'

'Think about it. What could we do in our own private space, with something comfortable to lie on and a shower room and which would involve Durex?'

Peter saw what she was driving at, but mention of the word Durex reminded him of where his were. They were in one of the top pockets of his jean jacket. And he now realised with a degree of alarm that he had mislaid his jacket.

'Oh, no, I've left my jacket in the Helios cellar. I took it off when I was looking for the keys under the desk. And the Durex are in it.'

Terri looked at him in despair. 'Oh, Pete! We've promised not to go there until Agatha says it's okay.'

'It's okay. I'll get some more.'

'Where from?'

'There's a vending machine in the gents at The Fox.'

'Okay. Let's go there for a drink this evening.'

Peter nodded. 'There's just one other problem.'

'What now?'

'You'll have to lend me the money. My wallet's in the jacket too.'

Terri screamed with laughter. 'You sure know how to make a girl feel wanted!'

Peter put his hand on Terri's arm. 'Hang on a moment. Will your dad be in there this evening?'

'He might, but he's not going to know the real reason you're going into the gents. That's not the way his brain works.'

Peter wasn't so sure.

WHILE TERRI AND PETER had been having their mid-morning coffee with Agatha, Smallwood was on the train back to London. He was reflecting on the events of the previous day. Things had gone surprisingly well. The military attaché from the Russian embassy had been distinctly taciturn, which was just as well because his Russian accent was fairly obvious. Consequently, they had exchanged few words on the journey up. Smallwood had buried himself in his copy of *The Times* and the attaché had stared morosely out of the window. But once they had got to Wyvern Hall, he seemed to know precisely what he was doing.

To begin with they had made a bit of a pretence of inspecting the Hall itself, but soon moved to the cellar under the barn. Smallwood had settled himself in a chair and spent the next hour smoking while his companion looked carefully at the Helios, taking detailed photographs and making notes in a pocketbook. His only concern was that Nippy might appear at any moment and then he would have had to assert that they had been fascinated by the perpetual motion machine, had noticed the trapdoor and found what they imagined was the control room beneath it. But in the event, they were left in peace. He and the attaché had strolled into the village and had lunch at The Fox. Smallwood had called a taxi to take the attaché to the station and then Smallwood had checked into his room and spent the afternoon dozing on his bed.

He had been rather looking forward to the party at The Priory, but to say that he had been surprised at the reason for the celebration would have been an understatement. He knew plenty of men of his disposition who got married in order to advance their careers; sometimes the wife was aware of the underlying situation, more often not. But Warren had no career to speak of and, in his day, had not been at all discreet about his activities. Clearly there was a strong bond of friendship between him and the somewhat obnoxious Miss Ponsonby, but that was scarcely a reason to tie one's hands so securely. Mind you, Warren had said something when they had been sitting on the bench at the top of the big Wyvern meadow about sacrificing his urges in the interests of begetting an heir. Smallwood had thought it guff at the time, but no doubt the landed gentry were more motivated than most to ensure patrilineal continuity.

The other surprise of the evening had been when Warren had taken him to one side and apologetically informed him that Wyvern Hall was no longer on the market. Privately, Smallwood had been delighted. It meant that it would no longer be necessary to claim in a day or two that the survey had thrown up some worrying findings. Nevertheless, he had feigned irritation and had said that he would be out of pocket over the surveyor's fee. Warren had said that he would see him right. Agatha had a bit tucked away and that was why it was no longer so pressing to dispose of Wyvern Hall. Of course, Nippy was still a bit of a problem, but he was sure that Agatha would be able to sort the situation out. She was good at that kind of thing.

Smallwood thought it was somewhat ironic that his own clandestine activities would soon solve that particular problem for Warren. With luck, Nippy's demise in the conflagration at the barn would be seen as a terrible accident consequent on a short circuit in the electrical equipment that powered the bogus perpetual motion machine. Everyone would shake their heads sadly and then get on with their lives. The matter of whether there was a revised will with a life interest clause would be by the by. On top of that, the Mother Goose dossier and the means of decrypting it would be destroyed. The identity of the members of the network would remain safe and the Soviet overlords might also have gained some technological intelligence from the analysis of the Helios conducted by the attaché.

Smallwood had to admit that Rafferty really was a master of the craft. But Smallwood felt that his own contribution was not without merit. He just wondered who Rafferty had in mind to handle the interrogation and termination. He had no doubt that he would have to be involved in the operation, but with luck Rafferty would be able to call on an expert in such matters. That was an aspect of the job for which Smallwood himself really had no appetite.

OVER SUPPER THAT EVENING, Agatha said, 'Dicky, I hope you won't be annoyed with me. I spent the morning with Terri and Peter.'

Richard slurped his soup. 'I did notice at the party that you had become rather thick with them.'

'They're a nice couple of kids. They were telling me how crowded the pool at Standon gets at this time of year. So I gave them permission to use the pool by the summerhouse.'

'Really? Don't you think that they might invite the riffraff of the village to join them?'

'No, I think they're at that stage in their relationship when they just want to be with each other. I also gave them keys to the side gate and to the summerhouse so that we wouldn't have them passing the front of the house and so that they could get changed decently.'

'Oh, I say, Aggie. What's behind all this largesse? Are you sure you're not being swayed by the girl's hemline?'

'Well, she is rather cute, but at the moment I think she only has eyes for young Peter. Anyway, it'll only be for a few days, a couple of weeks at the most. You never use the pool yourself.'

'But *you* like a swim?'

'I do, but that's another thing I wanted to talk to you about. I've got to go back up to my place in Bourton-on-the-Water for a couple of days. Something's come up.'

'Shall I come with you?'

'Not this time, dearest. But I do look forward to showing you off to my friends. And of course my cottage will be a nice little pied-à-terre for both of us, especially when there's racing at Cheltenham.'

'Oh, that is a pleasant prospect, but if you are going to be away for a couple of days, I might pop up to York myself and stay with a racing chum for two or three nights.'

Agatha raised an eyebrow, but made no comment. Having killed two birds with one stone, she steered the conversation towards more inconsequential matters like the guest list for the wedding reception.

LATER THAT EVENING, PETER and Terri were walking the short distance from the Hammonds' accommodation over the butcher's shop to The Fox at the further end of the High Street. Terri was chattering away about this and that, trying to distract Peter from the challenge that lay ahead of him, but Peter was not so easily distracted. Acting nonchalantly was not something that came naturally to him. An impartial passer-by might well have supposed that he was actually on his way to some very unpleasant encounter, a tooth extraction or boil lancing perhaps, rather than an evening in the local pub with his girlfriend.

They pushed the door of the pub open and Peter was pleased to see that it was not as busy as it probably would be later. He would make his trip to the gents as soon as he had bought their drinks. They found a table in a corner and Terri gave him a ten-shilling note from her purse. He got her half a pint of shandy, a pint of bitter for himself and a packet of crisps to share. Carrying them back to the table, he said, 'I'll go and get them now. Get it over and done with.'

Terri nodded with a mock serious expression on her face. Peter was back a minute or two later. Terri was impressed. 'That was quick.'

Peter hissed, 'I haven't got them. I need a two-bob bit.'

'Well, go and ask Tom to give you some change.'

'But he might ask me what it's for.'

'No, he won't. Go on.'

Peter went over to the bar and a moment later, with a twinkle in his eye, Tom exchanged a florin for the handful of change that Peter had proffered. With a look of amusement on his face, Tom then watched Peter cross back to the door leading to the gents and re-emerge a minute or two later. As Peter scurried for the safety of the table where Terri was sitting, Tom sang out, 'Sorry, son, didn't realise that you wanted the two-bob for the johnny machine. I could have told you it was empty. Should be restocked for tomorrow evening though. Hope it wasn't for tonight.'

One or two of the old blokes sitting at the bar, who had followed the exchange, chortled into their beers.

Peter attempted a cocky thumbs up and, turning to Terri, hissed, 'The machine's empty.'

Once again Terri was reduced to uncontrollable laughter. 'Oh dear, the menfolk of Fordham are clearly panic buying rubbers. Who would have thought it?'

'I don't think that was very kind of Tom actually.'

'He just likes a bit of fun.'

'It's humiliating.'

'If you want to be accepted in the village, you just have to accept that kind of joshing. I think they're all pretty impressed that you're my boyfriend now and not Mike.'

'Well, they've got a funny way of showing it.'

'Pete, you've got to be a bit bolder. Anyway, think about my position. That lot at the bar will lose no time letting my dad know, when he comes in, that the boy who's going out with his daughter was on a mission to buy some rubbers and failed. Dad won't know whether to be pleased or outraged.'

Peter was suddenly sure of one thing. 'Terri, I don't want to be in here when your dad comes in. Let's go as soon as we've finished our drinks.'

Whereupon Peter proceeded to try and dispatch his pint in fewer draughts than was probably advisable, while Terri, sensibly sipping her shandy, watched him in wry amusement. He had almost drained his glass when the door of the pub opened and Professor Sage stepped into the room. He took in the young couple, noticed that their glasses were nearly empty and said, 'Good evening, we meet again. Allow me to replenish your glasses.'

Peter tried feebly to say that he'd had enough, but Sage was already heading purposefully towards the bar. He returned a few minutes later with the drinks and said, 'May I join you?'

Peter rose from his chair, offering it to the Professor, and moved around to join Terri on the chintz-covered banquette.

As usual, Terri took a proactive approach to the situation.

'Professor Sage, you mentioned that if Peter or I were thinking of applying to Cambridge, you might be able to advise us.'

'I'd be delighted to, but my expertise is really quite narrow. Are you by any chance interested in philosophy?'

'I am, but I'm worried that philosophy might not be the best qualification for getting a job.'

'That is a point. Of course it is one of the better qualifications if you actually want to be a philosopher. And also a subject that teaches you how to think must be useful in many walks of life. What subjects are you studying for A-levels?'

'I'm doing maths, Latin and French.'

'And what about you, Peter?'

'I'm doing French, German and English.'

'Well, they're all suitable subjects, if you wanted to apply to read philosophy.'

Peter had never even thought of doing philosophy at university. And it was the first time he had ever heard Terri mention the idea. Whatever she was up to, she was wasting no time in steering the conversation in a particular direction.

'But aren't character and personality just as important as intellectual skills in dealing with other people and isn't most work about dealing with other people in one way or another?'

Peter was only slightly less shocked by this sweeping assertion than the Professor.

'My goodness, I wish I'd realised that before I became head of the faculty. Is that an insight of your own devising?'

'Well, I got it from one of Russell's books where he says that work is of two kinds, first, altering the position of matter at or near the earth's surface; second, telling other people to do so.'

'I say that's rather good, isn't it? Good old Bertie.'

'Which did you do?'

'Neither. I certainly altered the position of very little matter myself and no one seems to have taken much notice of me when I requested small re-positionings. That I am afraid is the lot of the philosopher.'

'Is that why Marx said that philosophers have only interpreted the world; the point is to change it?'

The professor laughed. 'I will write a letter in support of your application immediately.'

'But was Marx right?'

'Well, I certainly used to think so.'

'When was that?'

'Oh, between the wars.'

'Does that mean you were a communist?'

Peter could see what Terri was at now, but he wished she'd be more circumspect.

'Well, for a while it was quite fashionable to be a communist. I'm not sure any of us really were. It's rather like today's existentialists.'

'But didn't that make it difficult to get a job later on?'

'Well, as I said, I wasn't really one for repositioning matter at or near the earth's surface. I was in the business of rearranging ideas, most of which were only loosely attached to the earth's surface anyway.'

'So in that sense you *were* trying to change the world.'

'I suppose I must have been.'

'My dad says you told him that you and Cuthbert were friends at university.'

'That's true. We were at the same college and subsequently we both became dons, but in different subjects fortunately.'

'Was Cuthbert a communist too?'

'Oh, no, quite the opposite. On that point we differed, but it didn't affect our friendship. That's partly why I retired to Fordham.'

'So what did you have in common?'

Peter thought Terri was becoming almost impertinent, but Professor Sage seemed happy to answer her questions.

'Well, of course, being at the same college was an important factor. But if I had to choose one particular thing, it was that we both loved playing chess. I'd have to say that I was a rather better chess player than a philosopher. I did win at Hastings in the early thirties. But Cuthbert and I were very evenly matched and were the stalwarts of the varsity chess team. Do either of you play?'

Peter said, 'Yes, I'm a member of my school team and I have played some matches. I also had a number of games against Cuthbert last summer. He thrashed me each time, but it was useful to be able to play against such a good player.'

'Yes, when it came to chess, he was utterly ruthless. Pitting my wits against Cuthbert helped me raise my own game. So, what's your favourite opening as white?'

'Ruy Lopez, I suppose.'

'I see. And if I opened with the Queen's Gambit, what would your response as black be?'

'Probably the Nimzo-Indian defence.'

'Excellent, we must have a game then. How about next Friday afternoon? And Terri, please come too, whether you play or not, and we can talk about useful books to read if you are serious about philosophy.'

As Peter was walking Terri home, she said, 'I knew you could play chess, but I didn't know you were an expert.'

'I didn't know you were a philosopher.'

'You gave away your tactics.'

'It was a bluff.'

'Can you bluff in chess? Sounds more like poker.'

'Well, you can before you have your first game with someone. Anyway, where did you get all that stuff about Marx and Russell?'

'Just things I've read.'

'Sage seemed pretty impressed.'

'I just wanted to find out more about him.'

'You certainly managed to do that. He must have felt he was being interrogated.'

'Well, we now know that he had communist sympathies.'

'A long time ago.'

'And Cuthbert didn't. So Sage might be mixed up in all this?'

Peter was sceptical. 'We have no real reason to think so. He didn't work with Cuthbert, Flo and Nippy in the war and it seems unlikely that he would have got a job in an intelligence agency if he'd had a youthful dalliance with Marxism.'

'Alright, but getting to know the professor better might help one or both of us get into Cambridge, so not an entirely unsuccessful evening.'

'Apart from the Durex.'

Terri laughed. 'Apart from the Durex.'

'And on the plus side, your father hasn't forbidden us to have carnal relations.'

'He wouldn't know what that meant. But I'm pleased to see that you are now at least seriously considering the idea.'

FIRE

THE NEXT DAY THE weather, which had been fine for the most part
since Peter's arrival in Fordham, turned to rain. Peter had arranged
to meet Terri at the side gate to The Priory at eleven-thirty, but by
ten-thirty the rain was even harder and interspersed by flashes of
lightning and crashes of thunder. Flo thought it was not a good
idea to swim in such conditions and offered to drive over to the
Hammonds' to pick Terri up. She and Peter could spend the day at
The Croft listening to records and doing the jigsaw puzzle. Their
progress had slowed down considerably recently. Peter phoned
Terri and relayed Flo's suggestion. Terri had thought that they
could hang out in the summerhouse, but she accepted that there
was no music there and no food either. An hour later they were
settled in Flo's dining room poring over the jigsaw puzzle on its
baize cloth, listening to the Beatles LP playing on the radiogram.

By lunchtime they were starting to make good progress with the
puzzle. After lunch, when Flo had gone up for her nap, Terri said,
'Why don't we go to the Regent in Bishop's Stortford on Wednesday? There's a great new film called *Jason and the Argonauts*. The bus
leaves at eleven-thirty and will get us there in time for the matinée.
We could also go to Steven's, the record shop next door, and listen
to some records in one of the listening booths and maybe even buy
a couple of singles or an LP.'

'Yeah, that's a great idea, but I'll need to get my wallet from the barn.'

'I can lend you the money.'

'Thank you, but I can't go on borrowing money from you. And to be honest I'd like to get the Durex too. I don't fancy another visit to The Fox for a day or two.'

Terri beamed at him and squeezed his hand.

'Okay, then we'll have to pop into the Helios room quickly tomorrow, so we can make an early start the following day.'

'I don't mind doing it on my own. Then only one of us will be breaking our promise to Agatha.'

'No, if you're going to break your promise, I will too. Anyway, I've got a vested interest now.'

So that was agreed and they returned to the puzzle. Over tea and biscuits, Flo invited Terri to stay for supper, but she said that her mother had asked her to help with the supper that evening and took advantage of a gap in the showers to go home.

CONTRARY TO WHAT SHE had said to Richard, Agatha was not in fact driving to her cottage in Bourton-on-the-Water, but to her office in London. The drive would give her time to think over what Terri and Peter had told her and the information she had garnered from a long telephone conversation on a scrambled connection with her director the previous evening.

When she had conceived the idea of putting the proposition of a *mariage blanc* to Richard, she had not expected to find herself in a situation with a bearing on her professional expertise. But she now understood that Rafferty and Smallwood were suspected of being double agents. She was somewhat surprised that they had not identified her as a fellow spook, but then there was a considerable gulf between the different services and she was still in quite a junior position. And in any case they were encountering her in a context that did not suggest that she was an intelligence analyst. Presumably they thought that anyone presenting herself as Richard Warren's future wife must share the woeful intellectual horizons typical of the landed gentry and so they had failed to check her background. More fool them, if so.

She also now knew that Cuthbert had been one of the leading lights at Bletchley and that Nippy had been his assistant. But what was more surprising was that Flo had also been at Bletchley, working as a linguist. After the war, Cuthbert and Flo had continued in the service and had moved from Bletchley to GCHQ's first base at Eastcote. Cuthbert had not, however, made the subsequent move to Cheltenham in 1954, having in the meantime left the service under something of a cloud. He had retired to Wyvern Hall, his country seat, to lick his wounds and devote himself to retirement pursuits. It was little surprise that Nippy had followed his boss to Fordham, and it was only a little more surprising that Flo had also ended up in Fordham when she had had to take early retirement because of her bad leg.

But it now seemed from what the teenagers had discovered that Cuthbert's retirement had been devoted to building an advanced computer. Clearly he must have held onto a batch of signals intelligence and was attempting to decrypt them at the time of his death. Perhaps he had been trying to settle some kind of score, a not unusual occurrence among passed-over operatives. But what was strange was that Rafferty and Smallwood had got wind of what Cuthbert was up to before, it would seem, MI5 had. How had that happened?

The fact that Smallwood had made several visits and had even involved Rafferty, who normally kept a very low profile, suggested that they, or Moscow, thought it was important. It was clear from what she herself had overheard and from the information that the kids had gleaned that Rafferty and Smallwood were Larkspur and Hemlock respectively. But who was Nightshade?

The worrying aspect of all this, from what she herself had heard, was that the ring was not just gathering information. They were clearly worried about the Mother Goose dossier and had plans to destroy the machine and to extract from Nippy, the only other person who had been identified as being involved in the project, how the signals had been decrypted. They would no doubt claim to be interviewing him as bona fide members of the British intelligence services, an approach that was unlikely to intimidate Nippy. In which case they were much more likely to use extreme violence.

The kids had done a good job in figuring out what was going on, but clearly they weren't one hundred per cent sure and were worried that it might be Cuthbert and Nippy who were working for the Soviets. And they were now a problem, because they could get caught up in what was about to ensue. She needed to get them out of the way, which was why she had offered them the use of the summerhouse. With luck they would be so romantically involved in each other that they would forget everything else. In the meantime she needed to get authorisation to bring a team of agents back to Fordham to protect Nippy and to apprehend the agents sent to deal with the Helios. Time was of the essence. She would aim to get back with her team as early on Tuesday as she could and to get them in position.

When she got to London, she asked to see her director urgently. She outlined the situation and asked for a team of six armed Special Branch officers to meet her at The Priory in Fordham as early as possible the next day. Her director felt that she should operate through the usual channels, but Agatha pointed out that not only would that take some time to put in place but when Cuthbert had tried something similar he had ended up dead. On this latter point she got her way and then, after making a few phone calls, headed back to her flat so as to make an early start the following day.

RAFFERTY AND SMALLWOOD ARRIVED in Fordham at ten o'clock on Tuesday morning, parking some way away from the village centre on the Standon Road. They were both dressed as if they were ramblers or bird watchers. Rafferty knocked at the door of Nippy's cottage, while Smallwood stayed in the car. Had Nippy been in, Rafferty would have drawn a gun on him and then called Smallwood over, but there was no answer. Rather than sit in the car for an indeterminate period of time, which might arouse suspicions, the two men stationed themselves in a field opposite Nippy's cottage, from where they kept it under observation, taking it in turns to scan the area with a pair of binoculars. The minutes ticked by and then one hour turned into two, at which point Smallwood spotted a woman walking up the path to the cottage and knocking at the door. There was no reply, which at least confirmed that Nippy had not slipped into the cottage without their noticing it. As she turned to walk away, Smallwood realised that the woman was Warren's paramour. Which was hardly surprising and scarcely worth mentioning. Another two hours passed. Fortunately, they had brought a Thermos flask and sandwiches. Just when they were beginning to wonder whether they might need to modify their plan, they caught sight of Nippy coming up the path from the direction of the barn.

Rafferty waited until Nippy had got inside the cottage and then went across the road and tapped on the door. He took his pistol out of his pocket and waited. A few minutes later Nippy opened the door with a quizzical look on his face. He didn't often get visitors and those that he did get came to the back door. Rafferty raised the pistol. 'Don't say anything, just step back inside. You may notice that this pistol has a silencer on it. If you try anything, I will have no hesitation in shooting you.'

Nippy took a few paces backward and Rafferty crossed the threshold. 'Sit down.'

Nippy did so.

'Long time, no see, eh, Neville?'

'I would have been quite happy never to have seen you again.'

'The feeling's mutual, I can assure you. But there we are. Somebody's been raking over the coals.'

A moment later Smallwood stood in the doorway with a leather bag in one hand and a large rucksack on his back. Nippy said, 'You! I might have known you were up to no good.'

'Now, now Mr Nippy. There's no need to take that kind of tone.'

'What do you two want?'

Smallwood put his bags down. 'My friend here would like to see your machine. Not the one with the big wheels, but the one in the cellar beneath it. You are going to take us down there now and answer one or two questions.'

'You won't get nothin' from me.'

161

'Nevertheless, you will take us down there now. You will walk in front of us and if you try any funny business, we will shoot you. So let's go.'

The three men made their way back down the path that Nippy had just walked up, Nippy walking in front as ordered. They went around to the front of the barn and Nippy opened the wicket door. All three stepped inside and then Smallwood pulled the wicket door shut behind them.

'Open the trapdoor.'

Nippy did so and then Smallwood said, 'I am going to go down the ladder first, then you will come down, Nippy. We will both have weapons trained on you, so once again, no funny business.'

Once inside the Helios chamber, Rafferty took charge. They made Nippy sit on a chair and Smallwood tied his hands behind his back around the back of the chair. Rafferty then sat down on another chair and said, 'Right, now you are going to answer some questions.'

Nippy looked defiant. 'As I said, you won't get nothin' from me.'

Rafferty smiled balefully. 'Oh, I think we will. But it's rather up to you how painful you want to make things.'

To emphasise the point he stepped forward and punched Nippy hard in the solar plexus and then as his head came forward gave him a hard blow to the face with the other hand. Nippy's head snapped back and a trickle of blood came from his nose. Rafferty flexed his knuckles. 'Right, let's begin again.'

Half an hour later, Nippy had still not uttered anything but expletives. He was now on the verge of unconsciousness and Rafferty's hands were sore, despite the stout pair of black leather gloves he was wearing. Irritated by Nippy's resistance to punishment, he turned his anger on Smallwood. 'Come on, man. Don't just stand there watching, get those charges laid. They all need to be linked and we need some up in the barn, so that the whole lot goes up. We'll site the timer up top, so we can set it as we leave. Get on with it.'

Smallwood unpacked the bags he had been carrying and placed the incendiary devices at strategic points around the cellar, running a wire from each device out to the ladder and up to the level above. He then went up into the barn and placed a couple of devices there, bringing all the wires to a single point for connection to the timing mechanism.

When he got back to the cellar, he found that Rafferty had poured some water over Nippy's head in an effort to bring him back to consciousness, but without much success. All he was getting from Nippy were some weak groans. Smallwood was somewhat surprised at how unscientific Rafferty was at inflicting pain, but he was loath to suggest another approach, because he had no desire to be asked to demonstrate what he had in mind. Frustrated, Rafferty cuffed Nippy around the head and then sat down and lit a cigarette.

Smallwood was concerned that even after an hour of being pummelled, Nippy had not provided a single scrap of information. He thought it pointless to continue and that they should set the charges and leave. The longer they stayed the more likely they were to be detected. But Rafferty was now locked in a battle with Nippy and was determined to break him. He was losing sight of the main objective and risking failure because of the slight to his skill as an interrogator. To make matters worse, Nippy had lost consciousness again. Smallwood looked at his watch. It had just gone three.

At that moment, there was the sound of footsteps overhead. Rafferty made a gesture with his hand to indicate that Smallwood should switch off the lights, which he proceeded to do. They then heard the sound of the trapdoor being opened and footsteps coming down the ladder. A moment later the door opened and a hand reached into the room and felt for the switch. As light filled the dark underground space, Terri and Peter stepped into the room to be confronted by Rafferty and Smallwood, both with pistols pointing at them. For a moment nothing was said on either side. Rafferty was the first to regain his composure.

'Don't move. These are not toys.'

Terri suddenly caught sight of Nippy with his head slumped on his chest. 'You monsters, what have you done to Nippy?'

Rafferty strode over to Terri and slapped her hard in the face. 'Shut it. I don't know what you think you're doing here, but it's the worst for you.'

Tears welled from Terri's eyes. Rafferty pulled up two more chairs and motioned to Terri and Peter with his pistol. 'Sit. Smallwood, tie their hands.'

Smallwood took some rope from his bag, cut two lengths and bound the teenagers' hands behind their backs and around the back of the chair in the same way that he had done with Nippy.

Rafferty sat down again and resumed smoking his cigarette. 'Well, this is a fine how-do-you-do. Where do you two fit into things?'

The two glared at Rafferty, but said nothing. Smallwood said, 'They're local kids. I've seen them around the village.'

Rafferty said, 'I'd assumed that much. The question is how did you know about this place and, what's more, know how to get into it?'

The kids remained mute.

Rafferty rose and flicked his cigarette away. 'Right, I'm getting fed up with this.'

He went over to Peter and repeated the punch to the solar plexus and the face that he had used on Nippy. Peter started crying, gasping for breath from having been winded. Blood poured from his nose.

Rafferty loomed over Terri. 'Let's try again. What do you know about this machine and how is it that you seem to be able to just come and go as you please?'

Terri looked terrified and with a quivering voice said, 'Nippy is our friend and he told us that he would show us how his perpetual motion machine worked.'

Rafferty scoffed. 'His what? His perpetual motion machine! Do you expect me to believe that?'

Smallwood coughed quietly. 'Actually, Larkspur, um, Rafferty, that's what everyone around here thinks the machine is.'

Rafferty glared at him, furious that he seemed to be corroborating the girl's story. 'What a load of nonsense.'

He grabbed Terri by the throat. 'Tell me the truth, you little hussy or I'll kill you with my bare hands.'

Terri started to scream hysterically to the extent she could with a constricted windpipe. Rafferty released the grip he had on her throat, but gave her another hard slap across the face. The noise of her screaming brought Nippy back to consciousness. Realising that Terri and Peter were now also captive, Nippy, seeking to buy time, said, 'Alright, Rafferty, I'll tell you what you want to know. Just let the kids go.'

Rafferty turned to the newly conscious Nippy and sneered. 'How touching! The hard man turns out to have a soft spot for a couple of kids.'

'I always had my suspicions about you, Rafferty.'

'Well, it's taken you a long time to act on those suspicions and I fear that you have now left it too late.'

'No, we knew about you and this young fool here, the Larkspur and Hemlock double act.'

'But you still don't know who Nightshade is, do you? And as long as you don't know the real identity of Nightshade, I think my young friend and I here will be left in peace.'

Nippy bridled. 'I wouldn't be so sure of that if I were you, Rafferty.'

'Oh, but I am sure. So much so, that I feel confident in telling you that not only was Nightshade one of Cuthbert's oldest friends and a university colleague, but that person is also a local resident. Something to ponder in your final moments, eh?'

Nippy was about to reply, but Rafferty hit him hard in the face again, knocking him out.

At that moment Smallwood rejoined Rafferty in front of the captives. 'Right, it's all wired. How much delay do you want on it?'

'Fifteen minutes should be enough.'

'Okay, I've arranged the wiring so that each of the circuits connects in the barn.'

'I don't want to know the details, just go and connect it now and then come back down when it's all ready to prime.'

A few minutes later Smallwood reappeared. He looked troubled. 'Do we have to involve the kids? They have no idea what this is all about.'

'We didn't involve them. They involved themselves. I don't suppose you want to be on the first plane to Moscow tomorrow morning.'

'Not exactly.'

'So what do you suggest then?'

'I don't know, but they seem so young.'

Rafferty shrugged. 'Get your equipment together and let's get out of here.'

As Smallwood knelt down to put his things in the backpack, Rafferty hit him hard across the back of the head with the butt of his gun. Smallwood slumped to the ground and didn't move. Terri screamed and Peter looked white with fear.

Rafferty unscrewed the silencer from his pistol, dropped the silencer into his pocket and slipped the pistol back into his shoulder holster. He then rolled Smallwood over with his foot and picked up Smallwood's pistol. He unscrewed the silencer, ejected the magazine and put both in the backpack that Smallwood had been loading. Terri was still screaming. He looked witheringly at Terri. 'No one can hear you. Save your screaming for later. Time to say goodbye.'

He hoisted the backpack over one shoulder and moved to the door. He looked back once more and then disappeared into the outer room. Terri and Peter heard his steps on the ladder and the sound of the trapdoor being opened and slammed shut. Then they heard something heavy being moved over the trapdoor and after that silence.

Peter said, 'Terri, are you okay?'

'Yes, what about you?'

'Yes, I think so. We need to try and get out. They've laid explosives or something and set a timer. He said fifteen minutes.'

'Why did he kill Smallwood?'

'I don't know, but if we don't do something quick, we'll be dead in fifteen minutes too. We need to try and undo these ropes. Let's turn the chairs back to back and see if one of us can undo the other's knot.'

They shuffled the chairs around until they were back to back. Peter said he'd try first. He felt for the knot, but it was difficult with his hands behind his back and one over the other. After trying for thirty seconds or so, he started to lose the strength in his fingers and gave up. 'You try and undo mine.'

Terri worked at his knot. 'I think I might be moving it.'

'I could try and stretch my hands apart.'

'No, that will just make it tighter.'

After a minute she too gave up. Peter had an idea. 'He didn't secure these knots to the chair. I might be able to slide my arms up over the back of the chair.'

A few moments later he had freed himself from the chair, but his hands were still bound.

'You try.'

It was more difficult for Terri because she was not quite as tall, but eventually she too was freed from her chair. They tried once again to undo each other's knots, but even though they could get closer to each other, they were still unable to undo the knots.

Peter said, 'If only we had a knife.'

Terri said, 'I have. You know I always have a knife. But I can't get to it. It's in the front right pocket of my jeans. You might be able to reach it.'

'I'll have a go.'

Peter positioned himself so that he could get his right hand into Terri's pocket. He wriggled his hand to the bottom of the pocket and felt for the knife.

Terri kept as still as she could as he tried to withdraw it. He managed to pull it out without dropping it, but he was unable to pull the blade from the hasp.

'I'll hold the knife and you pull one of the blades out.'

After a few moments Terri said, 'I've managed to pull the saw-tooth blade out. I think that'll be the best one to get through these ropes.'

'Okay, but this is not going to be easy. I'll try and angle the blade away from your wrists.'

Peter started sawing. On a number of occasions Terri yelped as he nicked her skin, but soon he had cut through the rope and the binding fell away. Terri then took the knife and did the same to Peter's binding, somewhat more easily because she was able to see what she was doing.

'We've got to free Nippy too. You make sure he doesn't fall and I'll cut his rope.'

Nippy was starting to come around, but he was still not fully conscious. Peter said, 'We haven't got enough time to get out through the barn even if we could open the trapdoor. We're going to have to get out through the tunnel. You go and open the door on the other side of the kitchen and I'll drag him.'

Terri was shocked. 'Drag him?'

'He can't walk. I'll be careful. I'll put my arms under his armpits.'

A few minutes later they had Nippy in the tunnel. Terri said, 'What about Smallwood?'

'He must be dead. Rafferty hit him very hard.'

'But if there's a chance he's alive, we need to try and save him.'

Reluctantly, Peter went back into the cellar. Smallwood looked a mess. Blood had congealed on the back of his head, but he did seem to be breathing, if only shallowly. Peter hoisted him up under the arms and dragged him into the tunnel. He'd hardly got through the door when the charges went up. Fortunately, they were incendiary charges, rather than explosive ones.

Terri shouted, 'Shut the door.'

WHEN AGATHA GOT BACK to The Priory just after midday on Tuesday, she was annoyed to find that her team of Special Branch officers had not yet arrived. She went into the house and made some phone calls. They were on their way, but had got lost in the country lanes. Agatha made herself a cup of tea and sat staring out of the window. At two-thirty she saw three squad cars turning in at the gates and she went out to meet her team. She invited them inside and showed them a map of Wyvern Hall and explained what the operation entailed. Their target was one or more persons who were British agents working for the Soviet Union. Most probably it would be a team of two. It was possible that there might be a third person, whose activities they'd been aware of for some time, but whose identity remained unknown. It wasn't possible to say how long the operation would take, but she thought the targets would make a move in the next day or two, although it might be as early as that same day. Their objective was to destroy the barn on the Wyvern Hall estate and the machine it contained. Secondarily, they might harm or threaten to harm Neville Smith, known locally as Nippy, who had built the machine. The machine itself was a

Heath Robinson-esque computer, which was being used for freelance and, strictly speaking, illegal decryption of signals intelligence. Ideally, they would intercept Nippy and bring him to The Priory, mainly for his own safety. He was an elusive man, however. Agatha had called at his cottage earlier, but he had not been there.

She wanted the officers to form themselves into two watches, who would take over from each other around the clock. Each watch would comprise three men, who would monitor the front and back of the barn, and the front of the Hall itself. They would need to stay in radio contact with each other and with her. She would remain at The Priory, but at the first sign of action, they should radio her and she would be there within five minutes. The team off duty were welcome to use the facilities at The Priory. She would show them where the guest bedrooms and bathrooms were. Clearly, they should keep as low a profile as possible and everyone should be armed. She suggested that the whole team should take the first two hours together to familiarise themselves with the terrain. She would accompany them. They should all assemble in the Wyvern Hall car park as soon as possible.

Fifteen minutes later Agatha was standing with the pair who were observing the front of the barn, when one of them said, 'There's someone leaving the barn, ma'am.'

Agatha peered through her binoculars. 'It's Rafferty. We need to apprehend him. I'll call the others in.'

Rafferty circled the barn and set off towards where he'd left the car on the Standon Road. He was not aware that he had been spotted. The two officers with Agatha crossed the meadow keeping the body of the barn between them and Rafferty. Meanwhile Agatha radioed through to the two watching the rear of the barn and ordered them to detain the middle-aged man walking towards them. They should take care because he was likely to be armed.

Ten minutes later, the group of officers and Agatha were surrounding Rafferty, who was prone on the ground with his arms handcuffed behind his back. He had been disarmed and the officers were going through his backpack. One of them said, 'It looks like equipment for laying charges or explosives.'

Agatha said, 'Get him to his feet.'

Two of the officers lifted Rafferty up and turned him to face Agatha. 'Sir James, we meet again. Or is it Mr Rafferty? Or indeed Larkspur?'

Rafferty sneered. 'I didn't think there was something quite right about you. I thought it unlikely that that nancy-boy friend of Smallwood's would be getting married.'

'Ah, Mr Smallwood. I presume you mean Hemlock.'

'Oh, you really have done your homework.'

'I'm rather surprised that Mr Smallwood isn't accompanying you.'

'Smallwood had a bit of a headache and decided to stay put.'

'Yet, somehow we find you exiting the barn of Wyvern Hall.'

'Yes, odd, isn't it?'

'May I ask how you got in?'

'Mr Smith let me in.'

'Presumably not of his own free will.'

'My, you are quick. You have a great future in the service.'

'In which case, can you tell me the purpose of the equipment in this rucksack?'

'Ah, well in another minute or two, it should become quite obvious.'

'And where is Nippy now?'

'That's a good question. Presumably still in the cellar under the barn with Mr Smallwood and a couple of teenagers. Quite a party, really.'

The implication of what Rafferty was saying sent a chill down Agatha's spine. She had a terrible feeling that the two teenagers were Terri and Peter. Why Smallwood was also with them though was a mystery. Agatha's ruminations were interrupted by one of her men shouting that the barn was on fire and as she turned to look, she could see smoke pouring from the eaves of the barn and flames starting to lick around the edge of the big double door.

Rafferty said, 'Ah, that must be the incendiary devices going off. Oh dear, it looks like the little gang aren't going to get out in time. I'd suggest that you don't ask your men to attempt any heroics.'

Agatha didn't hold back. 'You bastard!' Addressing one of her men, she said, 'Take him to one of the cars.'

Another officer radioed for the fire brigade to be called, but given the distance to the nearest fire station, it was clearly going to be some time before a tender arrived. Agatha was cursing herself. She had moved too slowly. She should have been more open with Nippy and the kids and impressed upon them the danger they were in. It hadn't helped, of course, that the kids must have broken their promise to her.

At that moment, her radio crackled and one of her men who was watching the front of the Hall said, 'Ma'am, we've got a girl here in hysterics, saying that there are injured people in the basement of the house.'

Agatha snapped into action. 'Keep her with you. Don't let her go back in. I'll be right over.'

A few minutes later Agatha found the two officers who had been covering the front of the house holding Terri who was kicking and screaming and shouting that she needed to rescue Nippy and the others.

Agatha wrapped Terri in her arms, noticing how bruised her face was and that her tee shirt was covered in blood. 'Terri, Terri. We'll get them, but you've got to tell me the precise situation.'

Terri calmed down, feeling safe in Agatha's embrace for the first time since she and Peter had walked into the Helios cellar. 'Peter left his jacket in the cellar last week. It had his wallet in it. We went in to get it. I know we shouldn't have, but he needed some money.'

Agatha stroked Terri's hair. 'You can give me all the details later. Right now, you need to tell me where the others are.'

'They're in the cellar under the house. Nippy and Smallwood are badly hurt, unconscious.'

'We'll get them out, but you're going to have to show my men where they are. Do you think you can do that?'

Terri nodded. 'Yes, I don't want any of them to die, not even Smallwood.'

Agatha hugged her again. The barn was now burning fiercely. It wasn't directly attached to the house, a range of outbuildings stood between barn and house. But the breeze was already fanning the flames in the direction of the outbuildings.

Agatha took Terri by the shoulders and looked at her poor, bruised face. 'Do you think you're ready to go back in?'

Terri nodded again. Agatha waved her team over. 'This is Terri. She's had a bad time and been hurt, but she will show you where the three men are. Two are in a bad way, perhaps unconscious, and one is a teenager. One of the men is an accomplice of Rafferty. He will have to be detained. Be quick.'

Having called an ambulance, Agatha went over to talk to the officers who were holding Rafferty in one of the police cars. She told them that she had decided that it would be better if Rafferty was taken to London without further ado.

As the two officers climbed into the front of the car, she opened the back door of the Wolseley and said to Rafferty, 'These officers will take you to London where you will be interviewed. I am afraid you will not be allowed access to a solicitor for forty-eight hours. We wouldn't want you tipping Nightshade the wink, so that he can get on the next flight to Moscow.'

'I really don't know what you're talking about.'

'Oh, I think you do. And if you think your activities have gone unnoticed, you are sadly mistaken. We have had our eye on you for some time, but really it was Nightshade we were after.'

Rafferty held her gaze. 'I would say you are holding a busted flush.'

'Ah, so you do know what I'm talking about.'

'Miss Ponsonby, I sincerely hope we never meet again. Please ask your men to get me to the comfort of my cell as quickly as possible.'

Agatha slammed the door of the Wolseley and stood and watched it exit the gates of Wyvern Hall.

In the meantime Terri led the officers back into the house and down into the cellar. Peter looked terrified when he saw her coming down the steps of the cellar escorted by four large men. She saw the look on his face and held her hands up, almost in a gesture of surrender. 'It's alright. They're police officers. They're here to help us.'

At the sound of voices, Nippy groaned softly, but Smallwood was still out cold. Two of the officers helped Nippy to his feet and guided him carefully up the stairs, with Terri following. Meanwhile the other two officers asked Peter if he'd hold Smallwood's head as steady as possible while they carried him, since he was in no state to walk. They took him gently by the arms and legs and carried him up the stairs with Peter making sure his head didn't move too much, then out onto the front lawn of the house where they laid him down on the grass and covered him with a coat. Without regaining consciousness, Smallwood seemed to be trying to move and was groaning feebly. One of the officers took over holding Smallwood's head from Peter and said, 'Keep still, mate, you're safe now, but you've had a nasty blow to the head.'

Nippy too was lying on the grass, with the jacket of one of the officers covering him. Peter stood in the middle of the lawn, not quite sure what was going on. Terri rushed over and hugged him. He did his best not to flinch, but his ribs were very painful, as was his jaw, and his face was caked with blood.

'How did the police get here so soon?'

'Agatha. It seems she's some kind of spy herself.'

The flames had now reached the first outbuildings and the smoke was billowing into the sky. A number of local residents, having noticed the smoke, had arrived to see what was going on. The two officers not tending to Nippy and Smallwood did their best to keep people back, but they were outnumbered. Fortunately at that moment two fire tenders arrived and swept up the drive. The leading firefighter of the first tender jumped out to try and assess the situation. Agatha went over to him and pointed out that they could take the tenders down the track to the side of the house and that there was a lake not far from the barn if the tenders' tanks ran dry.

As they were talking, an ambulance arrived and Agatha left the firefighters to talk to the ambulance crew. It did not take them long to examine Nippy and get him into the ambulance, but Smallwood's condition was more serious. With the help of two of the police officers they managed to get him onto a stretcher without jolting his head and neck too much and then into the back of the ambulance. It was clear that Smallwood needed emergency attention and probably an operation. One of the medics radioed ahead to warn the hospital. While he was doing this, Agatha ordered the two officers who had been attending Smallwood to follow the ambulance to the hospital and to mount guard on him until she was able to organise a detachment to relieve them. If Rafferty had wanted Smallwood dead, there was at least one other person who might share that wish.

But Agatha was also concerned about Terri and Peter. Peter's jaw looked swollen and he was holding his side. At the very least he had a broken rib and perhaps worse. She went over to Peter and Terri and said, 'I want you to go with the two officers who are going to keep an eye on Smallwood so that the medics can check you out. It looks like you've both been hit quite hard.'

Terri started to protest. 'My parents will be expecting me back…'

Agatha stopped her. 'You must do as I say. I will let your parents know that you are in safe hands.' And turning to Peter, she said, 'And I'll let Flo know too. If the medics discharge you, two of my men will bring you back to The Priory. I'm afraid I will need you both to make a statement.'

Several hours later, having both been examined, had their cuts cleaned up and in Peter's case been x-rayed, they were released to a new pair of police officers who were waiting to drive them back to Fordham. One of Peter's ribs was cracked, but his jaw was merely badly bruised. There was no explicit treatment for either injury other than to take it easy for the next week or two. Terri had asked to see Nippy before she went, but the sister in charge had said that that was impossible and that they would have to come back the next day and even then it would be a matter for the police as to whether Nippy would be allowed to have visitors.

In the back of the unmarked police car, Peter and Terri held hands wondering what was involved in making a statement. The Priory was a hive of activity when they got back. There were two uniformed officers at the main gates and several vehicles parked outside the house. Inside there were several officers, one on a radio, another on the phone, and a clerk was typing up notes. Agatha was striding around bellowing at people. Peter and Terri stood in the main lobby until Agatha spotted them and came over.

'I understand that you've both been pretty badly roughed up, but you'll be okay. I need you to sit down with one of my officers and tell him exactly what happened, as you saw it, today. You will be interviewed separately, I'm afraid. When you've done that, you can have some food. I've got someone in the kitchen rustling up some sandwiches. I've spoken to both your families and told them you're safe and that you're staying here tonight. I will show you where you're sleeping. You both probably need a good night's sleep.'

Terri wanted to know how Nippy was, but Agatha said that she had no more information than Terri had herself, but that as she understood it, he was out of danger. Agatha called over one of her officers and said, 'This is Terri Hammond and Peter Marshall. They were in the cellar. They are ready now to make their statements. Please don't make the interviews too long. They have had a very difficult day.'

The officer took them to the library and asked Peter to wait outside. A female officer joined the first officer and they took Terri into the library. Twenty minutes later, they asked Peter to come in and Terri was taken to the dining room to have some food, where Peter joined her when his own interview was finished. As Peter was finishing his sandwiches and a cup of tea, Agatha came into the room and sat down with them. She was starting to look tired now. Someone brought her a cup of tea. She took a sip and then put the cup back on the saucer. She fixed Peter and Terri with a steely gaze and said, 'I'm very annoyed with you. You broke your promise to me and you very nearly got yourselves killed.'

Peter squirmed in his seat, but Terri looked defiant. Agatha took another sip of her tea.

'But you have also both been very brave and resourceful and not only have you saved Nippy's life, you have also saved Smallwood's and if he survives the fractured skull he has received, he is likely to be a very useful source of information for us. And as a consequence you have saved my professional bacon. You probably now realise that I work for one of the intelligence agencies and Rafferty, or Larkspur as we can also call him, nearly got the better of me. But thanks to your disobedience and bravery, I will probably now get a commendation. So I am in your debt and I am not sure how to repay that debt at the moment. However, because we are not quite certain if there are associates of Rafferty and Smallwood in the vicinity, I am going to have to insist that you stay here tonight. Rooms have been made ready for you upstairs and an officer will be on guard on your landing. Have you any questions? I am afraid that I will probably not be able to answer everything you might want to know.'

Peter was too tired to think of anything to ask. He just wanted to get to bed. But Terri said, 'Where's Richard? Has he been arrested too?'

Agatha laughed. 'Oh goodness me, no. I know he is a friend of Smallwood's, but I'm pretty sure that he didn't have the foggiest idea of what was going on.'

'So where is he then?'

'Oh, he's in York, at the races. It's been rather convenient to have him out of the way. But it's going to be a job to calm him down when he sees the place crawling with Special Branch officers though.'

Terri was still not convinced. 'Does that mean that you and he are not really getting married? It was just a front to disguise the fact that you are a spy yourself.'

'Ooh, Terri. You are a sharp one, aren't you? I think we might have to ask you to apply for a job with my department when you've finished university. But, even though your question is an absolutely reasonable one to ask, I can assure you that Richard and I are still intending to get married as long as he doesn't call it off when he realises what I do for a living.'

Agatha finished her tea. 'Right, I'll show you to your rooms.'

They went up to the top floor. Police sentries were posted on each floor. Agatha led them to a pair of rooms.

'These rooms have been made ready for you. There is no one else staying on this floor, but a police officer will be stationed by the stairs all night. If you have any worries, you can call him. I will be sleeping on the floor below. I can be with you in two minutes. You are covered in blood and smoke. Each room has its own bathroom. I suggest you get out of those clothes and have a nice long bath. It will help you to get a good night's sleep. I will try and get you a change of clothes for tomorrow morning, but I can't guarantee it.'

Then somewhat unexpectedly, Agatha gave Terri a hug and a kiss and then did the same to Peter, but slightly more carefully, conscious of his bruised jaw and broken rib. As she was walking back down the corridor, she said over her shoulder, 'Terri, I don't suppose you'd consider being my bridesmaid?'

Without waiting for an answer, she nodded at the sentry and then disappeared down the stairs.

Peter said, 'Which room do you want?'

'Don't mind.'

Terri opened the door closest to her and went inside. Peter opened the door to the other room and lay down on the bed, suddenly overcome with tiredness. A moment or two later an internal door connecting the two rooms opened and Terri came in.

'Do you think she realised that there was a connecting door?'

Peter shrugged.

Terri said, 'I was going to ask her if we could share a room, but I didn't want her to think that I was scared.'

'I think she already knows you better than that.'

'Exactly, so she's done it on purpose, so we didn't have to ask.'

Peter wasn't sure that was what had been uppermost in Agatha's mind, but didn't have the energy to challenge the interpretation. Terri moved towards the door of his bathroom. 'I'll have the first bath.'

He was about to point out that she had her own bathroom, but she was already running the bath. A few moments later he heard her get into the bath and soon he thought he could hear her singing quietly to herself. He then slipped into a shallow sleep, from which he was awoken a little later by Terri swathed in towels and another wrapped around her hair.

'Your turn.'

Peter wanted to sleep. 'Terri, I'll have a bath tomorrow morning.'

'You need a bath now. You need to wash all that bad stuff off.'

Peter sat up with some difficulty, gingerly swung his legs over the side of the bed, wincing with the pain in his side, and stood up. He started to unbutton his shirt, but stopped at another sharp stab of pain. Terri looked concerned. 'Here, I'll help you. Sit down and I'll slide your shirt off. I'll start with the side that doesn't hurt.'

She slipped the sleeve of the shirt off his right arm and then very slowly pulled the other sleeve off his left arm.

'Right, now stand up.'

She started to unbutton his jeans.

'Terri, I can do it myself.'

'It doesn't look as if you can.'

Without waiting for permission, she unbuttoned his jeans and lowered them gently.

'Okay, sit down now.'

He did as he was told and she pulled the jeans off, then took his socks off.

'Now the pants…'

'Terri, I can do those myself.'

Terri laughed. 'Spoilsport.'

Peter didn't feel able to respond positively to her humour or her coquettishness. 'Terri, there's a policeman at the end of the landing.'

'I don't think he's there to stop me helping you get your pants off.'

Peter made his way into the bathroom. He slipped off his underpants, stepped into the bath, and, using his good arm, let himself down into the warm water. It was delightful and he was grateful to Terri for persuading him to have the bath. Terri had followed him into the bathroom and now lowered the lid of the toilet and sat on it, watching him carefully as he soaked away the fear and the hurt. After a while she said, 'Don't fall asleep.'

He stood up very carefully, the water streaming down his body, too tired to bother to shield his genitals. He stepped down onto the bathmat. Terri held the towel out. He wrapped it around his waist. She noticed the bruise on his side and also the one that was forming on the right side of his face.

'Let me dry your back.'

She took another towel and patted his back dry and then his chest, doing her best not to put any pressure on his ribs. She took a pace backwards and, holding his gaze, undid the towel that was knotted over her breasts and let it fall.

'Pete, I know that your side is hurting you, but I need you to hold me. I haven't allowed myself to be scared all day, but now I'm terrified just thinking about what nearly happened to us.'

Peter didn't know what to say. He wanted to hold her too, but was apprehensive about his side. And not just that.

She stood in front of him, her pale breasts and belly contrasting with her brown arms, legs and midriff. She smiled as she noticed his eyes scan her body then leant forward and unwrapped the towel from around his waist.

'We can't sleep in damp towels.'

She pressed her naked body against his. He put his arms around her, but winced as he did so with the pain in his side. Afraid that she might hurt him, if she reciprocated the embrace, she dropped her hands lower.

'Well, thank goodness, other parts of your body are still operational.'

Peter groaned, this time with pleasure, and said, 'I need to lie down.'

'We both do.'

She took his hand and led him to the bed, gently helping him stretch out on the bed, and then slipped in beside him on his uninjured side. They lay there, both trembling, until she pulled the bedclothes back over them.

After a few moments, she said, 'We nearly died earlier today and if we had, it would have been without making love. I don't want to risk that again. I want to make love to you now.'

'Terri, I want to make love to you too, but my jacket and its contents have gone up in flames. So not only have I lost all my money, but the Durex too.'

'Forget the stupid Durex. If something happens, we'll sort it out. And what's money anyway!'

Even with their cuts and bruises the next half hour or so was considerably more ecstatic than either of them had expected. Peter's cracked rib meant that not only did they have to go about things gently, but that a certain amount of ingenuity was called for too. While Peter had thought about sex a lot, and particularly sex with Terri, when it came to the mechanics of the act, his ideas were decidedly conventional. So he was surprised and delighted that Terri, as a way of minimising any hurt to his side, suggested that she got on top. The upward perspective afforded by his supine position and the element of restraint consequent upon Terri straddling him heightened his pleasure and, he hoped, hers in ways that he had not previously imagined.

Soon they were asleep and if they weren't exactly cradled in each other's arms, they were as close to each other as two young, loving bodies could be.

AFTER THE FIRE

WHEN PETER WOKE THE next morning, he was thrilled but also alarmed to realise that the warm naked body curled against his own equally naked body was not the oneiric vestige of an erotic dream, but the very tangible and lovely body of Terri. He was about to roll over and remind himself of her corporeality, when he let out a yelp as a sharp pain seared through the right side of his torso. Terri opened her eyes at the sound and, having established that Peter was not in serious pain, greeted him with a dazzling smile. She snuggled in closer to him and was in the process of moving her hand down his body, when there was a sharp knock on the bedroom door and even before they could respond, Agatha walked into the bedroom.

She smiled at the alarmed couple. 'Excuse me for barging in like this. But I am glad to see that you made use of the interconnecting door. It would have been wrong of me to suggest you share a room, but it was obvious that it was what you both needed.'

Peter, as usual, didn't know what to say, but on this occasion even Terri was lost for words. Agatha sat on a chair. She looked drawn and tired. Clearly she had had very little sleep.

'I came in earlier when you were asleep and removed the clothes you were wearing yesterday. You would not have wanted to put them on again, covered in blood and smoke as they were, but in fact they are also needed for forensic analysis. I was going to go

181

around to your families and pick up some clean clothes, but I realised that first of all we were going to have to come up with a story that would make sense of the injuries you've sustained and at the same time provide a rational explanation for how you came to be in the cellar. So I'm afraid we're going to have to get this right between us before you are allowed to rejoin your families.'

It dawned on Terri that the proposed conversation might take some time and it was now becoming apparent that she needed to empty her bladder. Interrupting Agatha's explanation, she said, 'Agatha, I need to go to the loo. Do you mind…?'

'Oh, of course not, my dear. I'll get you a towel.'

Terri said, 'It doesn't matter.'

She threw the bedclothes back, hopped out of the bed, and glided nimbly across to the ensuite bathroom before returning a couple of minutes later and slipping back under the bedclothes. Agatha watched her with what she hoped was an impassive gaze, registering Terri's neat breasts, her taut belly and the little smudge of down shadowing the cleft at the top of her thighs. It was not often these days that Agatha got the chance to contemplate a young, unclothed, female body and for a moment she experienced a feeling of infinite regret. Terri noticed the way that Agatha's eyes followed her and suppressed the thought that to some extent she was being provocative in flaunting her naked body for an older woman. Peter, on the other hand, oblivious to the electricity crackling between the women, took it for granted that the display was for him and felt himself responding in the time-honoured manner.

Agatha looked at him. 'Peter?'

Peter blushed. Had she noticed through the bedclothes the effect that Terri's naked body had had on him? He stammered, failing to say anything sensible.

Agatha, conscious that Peter lacked the boldness that came so naturally to Terri, said, 'Would you like to use the lavatory too?'

In fact, now that the question had been raised, Peter realised that he would feel much more comfortable if he could empty his bladder. But he would have to wait a moment or two until he was in a position to do so. He had no intention of emulating Terri, if that was what was being suggested. Agatha, sensing the reason for his discomfort, said, 'I tell you what. I'll nip downstairs and get us all a cup of tea. That'll give you two time to sort yourselves out. And the sooner we can agree what we're going to say to the good folks of Fordham, the sooner I can get you some fresh clothes to put on.'

As soon as she was out of the room and had closed the door, Terri burst out laughing. 'You should have given her a flash, Pete.'

Peter didn't see the funny side to it. 'It's all very well for you, but it's not under my conscious control.'

'So I've noticed. And I'm not complaining.'

She reached down again. Peter pushed her hand away. 'Stop it, Terri. I need to have a pee before she gets back.'

Terri giggled mischievously. 'You'd better get in there quick then.'

Peter knew she was right. He sat up with a grimace as another stab of pain went through his side, swung his legs over the side of the bed and made his way self-consciously to the bathroom, trying to will himself into a state of flaccidity. He went to the sink and splashed his face with cold water. The sight of his bruised face in the mirror brought back the events of the previous day and a chill ran through him at the thought of how close he and Terri had both come to death.

Having relieved himself, he opened the door to the bedroom to find that Agatha had returned with the teas. He was about to step back inside the bathroom and find a towel to wrap himself in, but reluctant to have his timidity confirmed and satisfied that he was no longer in the earlier state of arousal, he walked across the room and got back into bed, not without a modicum of aplomb, but certainly not as elegantly as Terri had managed it.

Agatha set a mug of tea beside each of them. Peter took a grateful sip, at the same time reflecting that even though the previous twenty-four hours had been the strangest period of his life, sitting in bed with his girlfriend, both of them naked, while a female member of the security services served them tea was beyond anything that he might ever have imagined happening.

Agatha sat down again. 'Right, let's get this straight and then we can get you two back to your respective families.'

Twenty minutes later Agatha had coached both of them in what they could and couldn't say. She was adamant that neither of them should mention anything about Rafferty or Smallwood's presence, nor their treatment of Nippy, nor Rafferty's attempt to murder Smallwood. Agatha was pretty certain that Smallwood had been whisked into an ambulance before any of the townsfolk had turned up. Nor should there be any mention of the Helios. The fire and the injuries sustained by Nippy, Peter and Terri were to be put down to a malfunction in the perpetual motion machine. Nippy's survival was a consequence of Peter and Terri's quick-wittedness in dragging him into the tunnel. Agatha's own involvement should be played down too. It was just lucky that she'd been passing. She hoped that none of the locals who had turned up realised that she had assumed authority over police officers and emergency services alike. But if it was mentioned, Peter and Terri should say that they had not noticed. Privately, Peter thought that anyone who had even a passing acquaintance with Agatha would not be in the slightest bit surprised that she had assumed command at a critical moment.

Terri asked why it was necessary to go to such lengths to cover up what had really happened.

Agatha laughed. 'Terri, you disappoint me. I thought you had it all worked out. The reason is so that Moscow doesn't realise for at least a couple of days that we have arrested Rafferty and have Smallwood under armed guard in a hospital. For this reason it is vital that none of these details find their way into the newspapers. The story has to be about the tragic end of an English eccentric's engineering project, a man whose life was saved by a couple of plucky teenagers. If we manage to make this version of events stick, and if Smallwood survives, then we have a good chance of turning him, and maybe even Rafferty. If they agree to our demands, there will be no trial and no criminal sanctions. We will keep them in place, but only after they have revealed the details of their network and in particular the identity of Nightshade.'

Peter was aghast. 'But that's like letting them get away with…', his voice faltered, '…murder.'

'Yes, it is. And I understand that it might make you angry. After all you were very nearly their victims. But I can assure you, it will not be a comfortable position they will find themselves in. They will always be having to look over their shoulders. Moscow would have no hesitation in arranging for their demise if it ever had reason to believe that they had been turned. Also if we ever get the impression that they are still in the business of betraying their own country, their liberty will be short-lived.'

Terri was thoughtful. 'So this is all about uncovering who Nightshade is.'

Agatha shrugged. 'Yes, I'm afraid it is.'

There seemed nothing more to say. Agatha finished her tea and said, 'Right, you two get yourselves cleaned up. No more canoodling. I'll go and see Flo, and Fred and Doreen and be back with your clothes as soon as I can. And one more point. I will make it quite clear that, of course, you had separate rooms when you were staying here and I was constantly on the *qui vive*.'

While Terri and Peter reluctantly abandoned the comfort of their bed, Agatha drove around to the Hammonds and then to The Croft.

Flo opened the door with a concerned look on her face. 'Oh, Agatha, is Peter alright?'

'Yes, he's fine. I've come to reassure you on that point and give you more information about what happened.'

Flo said, 'Come in.'

They went into the kitchen and Flo bustled around, making a pot of tea. 'I am rather annoyed with Peter. He had been given strict instructions not to trespass on the Wyvern Hall estate.'

Agatha seated herself at the kitchen table and said, 'Yes, but it's just as well, on this occasion, that he broke the rules, because he and Terri were able to rescue the hapless Nippy from the inferno. Unfortunately, they picked up some minor injuries themselves. But they have had a thorough check-up at the hospital, although it was so late by the time that they were discharged that I thought it better to put them up at The Priory. I hope you got my message in that regard.'

'Yes, from a police officer. Is Peter still at The Priory?'

'Yes, that is my other reason for coming around so early. Their clothes are covered in blood and soot. I've been around to the Hammonds to pick up a set of clean clothes for Terri. Would you mind giving me a set for Peter, then he'll be able to return to The Croft, looking less like a wounded soldier?'

Flo went upstairs and returned with a small pile of clothes and a pair of plimsolls. She handed them over.

Agatha said, 'Don't be too severe with him when he gets back. He's still in a state of shock.'

Flo nodded. 'How's Nippy?'

'He's alright, but the medics decided to keep him in for a couple of days.'

'I must go and see him.'

'I'm sure he'd appreciate that. I've arranged for him to have a private room.'

'That's very generous of you, Agatha.'

'It's nothing.'

Flo took a sip of her tea and, tilting her head at a quizzical angle, said, 'It's fortunate you were on hand.'

'Yes, I don't think I would have been aware of the fire if I'd been at The Priory, even though the smoke was rising high into the air, but fortunately I happened to be passing in the Triumph.'

'And I too only became aware of the blaze when you came around, by which time most of the excitement seemed to be over. I imagine that that's the end of Nippy's machine.'

'I think that's most certainly the case.'

The two women fell silent. Agatha drained her cup. 'Right, I'd better get back to The Priory with these clothes.'

RICHARD ARRIVED BACK AT The Priory on the Wednesday evening after several delightful days in York with an old pal. He was surprised to see a policeman on duty at the gate, who saluted him as he swept into the drive in the Lagonda. He was even more surprised to see two large official-looking cars parked next to Agatha's Triumph in front of the house. What on earth was going on?

Agatha was waiting for him at the top of the steps.

'Dicky, how was your trip?'

'Splendid. But would you mind telling me what's going on?'

'Let's go into the kitchen and have a nice cup of tea and I will explain everything.'

Once they had their teas in front of them and Richard had found the packet of Rich Tea biscuits, Agatha started cautiously on her account.

'The first thing you need to know is that the barn and some of the outbuildings of Wyvern Hall have burned down. Nippy was injured, and Peter and Terri rescued him from almost certain death, picking up some minor injuries themselves.'

'My goodness. How did it happen?'

'It's not quite clear, but the investigators think it was caused by a wiring fault.'

'So that's the end of Nippy's machine.'

'Yes, I'm rather afraid it is.'

'Is he cut up about it?'

'Not really.'

'That's a relief.'

'Another good thing is that I've checked your insurance policy and had preliminary discussions with a firm of loss adjusters. It doesn't look like there should be too much trouble there either.'

'You mean we might get some money too?'

'Yes, it looks like it.'

'Would we have to rebuild the barn?'

'I don't think that will be necessary. Since it would be ludicrous to build a replica of a mediaeval barn, I think we may be able to remodel the back of the house to our own taste.'

'Well, that all seems rather satisfactory, injury to Nippy apart. So why are we being guarded by the boys in blue?'

'Inevitably there had to be some investigation to make sure there was no skullduggery involved. I invited the Inspector to make this his base for the duration. They've almost finished and I imagine they'll be off shortly.'

The proximity of police officers always made Richard slightly nervous. So the fact that they were soon to depart was some relief.

'Was the Inspector appropriately grateful?'

'Yes. Actually, I knew him.'

'Really, I didn't think those were the circles you moved in.'

'Yes, I'm afraid they are and it's time for me to own up to what I do.'

'You're not a police officer yourself, are you?'

'Not exactly.'

'Not exactly?'

'I work for the Government.'

Richard was shocked. 'You surprise me. You and Smallwood.'

'Yes, something similar, I'm afraid. So I can't go into too much detail. Are you upset?'

'Not really. In the short time that we have been affianced, it does not seem to have impinged much on your time.'

'No, but there will be times when I will have to be away for several nights.'

'I have no problem with that. I don't expect you to be permanently chained to the kitchen, although I do hope there will be the odd evening when we have Boeuf Stroganoff for supper again, if only to remind us of our courtship.'

'Of course, my darling. There will always be the Stroganoff to remind us of our liaison.'

At that moment, there was a tap on the door and a middle-aged man in a belted gabardine raincoat and fedora hat took a step into the room. 'Sorry to disturb you, ma'am. We're finished here now. Thank you for allowing us to use The Priory as our base.'

'It's a pleasure, Inspector. May I introduce you to my fiancé, Richard Warren? Darling, this is Inspector Pitlochry.'

'Pleased to meet you, Inspector.'

'And you, sir. Shall I dismiss the constable at the gates, ma'am?'

'Yes, please, Inspector. I hope you have a straightforward drive back to London.'

When the officer had gone, Richard said, 'It makes a nice change to get a bit of respect from one of those chaps.'

'I'd rather not know about any of your earlier encounters with the law, Dicky. From now on things will be different.'

'Aggie, going back to what you were saying about Nippy, should I go around and make it clear that I in no way blame him for what has transpired?'

'I think that would be a lovely thing to do, but they are keeping him in hospital for a day or two. And in any case there are other matters to attend to this evening.'

'Oh, Aggie, you're not expecting me to do a bit of inseminating tonight, are you?'

'No, you have another week to restore the motility of your semen. That means no furtive letting off tension for the next week.'

'Oh, I got rid of all the tension in York.'

'Dicky, I do not wish to know any more in that regard. No, I have decided that we need to tidy the grounds up and also apply a lick of paint here and there before our nuptials. I'd like you to cast your eye over the arrangements I've made, if you wouldn't mind.'

Richard had absolutely no objection to casting an eye over Agatha's plans, so long as he was not being required to find the funds to pay for them or to wield a spade or paintbrush himself.

GRADUALLY, THINGS GOT BACK to normal in Fordham Market. If in the previous weeks Terri and Peter had applied a somewhat liberal interpretation to the ban on entering The Wyvern Hall estate, there was no way now of not observing it. The place was crawling with fire investigators, local authority officers and the occasional police officer. Once these people had completed their work, the demolition team moved in and started to clear the site of the barn and those outbuildings that were beyond repair.

Fortunately, Richard had agreed to an extension of Agatha's original offer to Terri and Peter to use The Priory summerhouse and pool. Consequently, for the next few days, they spent many hours there. Initially, they had imagined that it would give them enough privacy to resume their *amours*. But it soon became clear that The Priory was also now a lot busier. Not only did Agatha seem to have a constant stream of visitors, some of whom accompanied her on strolls through the grounds, but it also seemed that an extensive team of groundsmen and gardeners had been employed to restore the grounds to some semblance of their former glory. While this activity certainly deterred them from total abandon, it didn't stop them indulging in the usual intimacies that teenagers resort to. But after the ecstasies of that night in The Priory bedroom, the furtive fumbling involved seemed tame stuff.

One day as they were sunbathing on the apron of the pool, chatting inconsequentially, comfortable in each other's company, they became aware that Agatha was standing on the other side of the pool observing them quietly. She was glad to see that their cuts and bruises were healing well. What it was to be young! They jumped up and greeted her. She walked around to their side of the pool. 'I've got some good news. Nippy is coming home tomorrow. He's still in pretty bad shape, but he's on the mend. He will be housebound for some time and I'm sure he could do with some company and people to help him with his shopping.'

Terri said, 'You can rely on us.'

'Thank you, dear. The other matter is that I'm afraid the arrangement relating to the summerhouse and pool will have to be terminated. The workmen are going to start restoring the whole area tomorrow. I'm sorry. If the work doesn't take too long, we may be able to resume the arrangement before the end of the summer, although there is now not much left of the school holidays.'

Terri was initially downcast, but the thought of being able to spend time with Nippy soon cheered her up.

As Agatha prepared to go and attend to some other matter, Terri said, 'How is Smallwood? Is he recovering too?'

'I'm afraid that the ban on talking about Rafferty or Smallwood remains. We have done a good job of blaming the whole thing on Nippy. With his agreement, I might add. But from now on, I am not prepared to answer any questions about those two gentlemen. Please don't put me in a difficult position. I – we are very grateful for everything you did, but it is better if you consider the whole thing some kind of collective bad dream and things will now return to normal.'

As Agatha walked away across the lawns, Peter said, 'Phew, well, that's telling us. And if it was a bad dream, it had at least one very real consolation.'

Terri flashed Peter a bright smile, but then frowned. She had considered Agatha a friend, but now she wasn't so sure.

When Agatha was out of earshot, Terri said, 'I know that Agatha said that we shouldn't talk about Rafferty and Smallwood, but surely that's just with other people. Or it means not to ask her any questions. But I don't see how she can stop us talking between ourselves.'

Peter shrugged. 'What's there to say?'

'Well, I've been thinking about something Rafferty said to Nippy just before he knocked him out. He said that not only was Nightshade one of Cuthbert's oldest friends and a university colleague, but he was also a local resident.'

'I just thought he was being beastly, saying whatever would hurt Nippy most.'

'But what if it was true? The only academic I can think of around here is the professor and we know from what he told us in the pub that he and Cuthbert were friends when they were undergraduates. We also know that he used to be a communist and maybe he still is.'

'Well, in that case, he'd certainly fit Rafferty's description. But it's hard to imagine that he had any secrets to give away or if he did, that anyone would understand what he was saying.'

'That's true, but who else is there?'

'I wonder if what Rafferty said made sense to Nippy.'

'If he remembers. That was immediately before Rafferty punched him.'

'Well, when we see him, we can ask.'

Peter tried to imagine Professor Sage as a double agent mastermind, but he just seemed too genteel and otherworldly. On the other hand, that was probably the perfect cover for a double agent. In any case, he had other worries on his mind.

'Terri, I hope you don't mind me asking you, but when do you expect your period?'

Terri laughed. 'Are you worrying that I might be pregnant?'

'Well, yes. Aren't you?'

'Not yet.'

'I was just wondering what we would do if you were pregnant.'

'I'd have to come down to London and we'd get a flat together. Or you could come down here, but I don't think it'd be much fun for us to be cooped up with Fred and Doreen, with me expecting a baby.'

'Terri, neither of those options seems practical.'

'So, what? You're going to leave me to have the baby on my own.'

'No, I love you, but I'm worried and I just wanted to talk about it.'

191

'I'm sorry, Pete. I'm teasing you. I'm pretty regular, so two weeks at tops, perhaps sooner.'

'Okay, I might be able to stretch my stay in Fordham until then, if Flo doesn't mind.'

Terri leaned forward and put her arm around Peter. 'Pete, let's not talk about parting. I can't bear the thought at the moment.'

'Nor can I. I don't ever want to leave you.'

They embraced tenderly, with tears in their eyes.

WHEN TERRI AND PETER walked through the back door of Nippy's cottage, they found him sitting in an armchair staring listlessly into space. At the sight of the two young people his face brightened and he said, 'What took you so long? I'm dying for a cuppa.'

Terri laughed. 'You're obviously feeling better.'

While Peter filled the kettle, Terri sat down beside Nippy and held his hand. 'Welcome home, Nippy. We've missed you.'

'And I've missed you too. And Master Peter. I haven't had a chance yet to thank you both for getting me out of the cellar under the barn.'

'We weren't going to leave you there.'

'But for all you knew, they'd laid explosives.'

'There wasn't time to think it through. We treated Smallwood exactly the same way. We thought we ought to if there was a chance that he was still alive. Has he pulled through? They seemed to think he might have a fractured skull.'

'Daughter of the dragon, I am sure that you have had the same lecture that I have from Miss Agatha. We're not to talk about Rafferty and Smallwood or the Helios machine.'

'But surely between ourselves? I mean we can't scrub out the memory, even though I would quite like to.'

Peter brought a mug of tea over for Nippy and put it on the little table beside him and then put his and Terri's on the kitchen table. Nippy took a big slurp of his tea. 'As I said. I've been dying for a nice cup of tea.'

Terri took a sip of hers and said, 'If you make us a list, we'll go and get some shopping for you.'

'Thank you, but Miss Agatha has stocked the larder with so much that I won't need anything for several days.'

'Anyway, are you going to tell us whether Smallwood is going to be okay or not?'

'Well, I can tell you that he was still alive when I left the hospital. But I'm not sure that they'll keep me informed of his progress.'

'Why do you think that Rafferty tried to kill him?'

'I don't know. Perhaps because he knew too much.'

'But surely he knew what Rafferty knew.'

'Maybe not. That's why Rafferty wanted us all dead. He'd said more than he intended and must have regretted it almost immediately.'

Terri shook her head. 'I can't remember what he said. You've confused me now.'

Nippy called her bluff. 'Well, if you can't remember, I'm not going to tell you.'

Peter, who had been listening carefully to the conversation, decided to bring the sword fencing between Nippy and Terri to a conclusion. 'Rafferty said that Nightshade was one of Cuthbert's oldest friends, a university colleague, and a local resident.'

Terri laughed, 'Well, at least that excludes Nippy. I don't imagine he is loaded with academic honours.'

Nippy bridled. 'I'm going off you rather rapidly, daughter of the dragon. You have no idea what my qualifications are.'

Terri was crestfallen. 'Oh, Nippy. I was just joking. There are all sorts of reasons why you're not Nightshade.'

Nippy sniffed. 'Yes, well, you know how to hurt a person.'

'Nippy, Nippy, I'm sorry.'

Peter thought he'd better intervene again, to stop the exchange ending in recriminations. 'I know my knowledge of the local population is not as extensive as either of yours, but the only eminent academic I'm aware of is the professor.'

Nippy scoffed. 'Don't be ridiculous.'

'Well, the professor told us that he and Cuthbert were friends when they were undergraduates. And he also told us that he used to be a communist.'

'That's true. But the professor helped me build the Helios. Why would he do that, just to arrange to have it destroyed?'

Neither Peter nor Terri could quite comprehend what Nippy was saying.

Finally Terri said, 'The professor helped you build it?'

'Well, he advised me on the structure of the central processing unit. He's an expert logician. If he'd wanted to put a spanner in the works, he could have done it much more subtly.'

Terri was confused. 'But he didn't work with you and Cuthbert during the war.'

'All the more reason why he wasn't Nightshade. Look you kids almost got yourselves killed poking your noses into stuff that doesn't concern you. You need to do what Miss Agatha says and drop the subject.'

Terri was pleading now. 'But it's not that easy. If Rafferty had said that Nightshade was a doctor living in Manchester, we would have thought no more about it. But for it to be someone who lives in Fordham.'

Nippy's attitude softened. 'Yes, I see that. But I think you might find the implication very difficult to take, indeed, very painful.'

Peter suddenly didn't want the conversation to continue. He had a terrible feeling that he knew who Nightshade was and didn't want confirmation. But it was too late, Nippy had decided to confide in them.

'Right, I'm only going to tell you this because I owe you a debt of gratitude. And because I trust you to treat the information with sensitivity. But I also think you're going to find it upsetting.'

Nippy paused wondering if he'd regret what he was just about to tell Peter and Terri. But it was too late. At some point they were going to have to have this conversation.

'Everything points to Nightshade being Flo.'

Terri gasped. Peter felt sick.

Nippy looked at Peter with pity in his eyes. 'I'm sorry master Peter, but it's probably better you know.'

Terri was in denial. 'But it can't be Flo, she wasn't an academic.'

Nippy nodded. 'That's true, strictly speaking she didn't have a PhD or an academic post. But it's not quite as simple as that.'

'I don't get you, Nippy.'

Nippy finished his tea and wiped his mouth with the back of his hand. 'Well, in the early 1930s, the Master was a lecturer at Cambridge in Russian and Slavonic literature and Flo was his star pupil. But one of the absurdities of Cambridge University at that time was that women students were not awarded a degree at the end of their studies.'

Terri was aghast. 'Why not?'

'I don't know. Misguided ideas of tradition? Fear, probably. Many, perhaps the majority of the chinless wonders moving smoothly from public school to Cambridge might not have found their progress quite so assured if the allocation of places had been strictly on merit. Anyway, that meant that when Flo finished her undergraduate studies her chances of academic employment were limited. The other problem was that Flo was in love with the Master and so was reluctant to do postgraduate work at another university. However, the Master, though extremely fond of Flo, was not of that persuasion, if you know what I mean. So in the end she went off and studied in Germany for a few years.'

'So, in a sense Flo *was* an academic.'

'Yes, exactly. And she was a recognised linguist which meant that when the war started both she and the Master were recruited to work at Bletchley, a top-secret government department which monitored German and, for a time, Russian military transmissions. That's where I got to know them. I'd worked for the Post Office Telephones before the war and I was seconded to give a hand with electronic communications.'

'That's the three of you in that photograph.'

'Yes, we were a good team and had some great successes in cracking Soviet codes. But we were also involved in an internal enquiry, because there had been some leaks to the Soviets and it was thought that it might have had something to do with our department. In the end no proof was found and the matter blew over.

But we weren't together long because once Russia entered the war on Britain's side, we had instructions to cease monitoring Soviet transmissions. It seems a very short-sighted move now, but I think at the time there was some concern that British Intelligence had been comprehensively penetrated by Soviet agents.'

Peter had been listening closely. 'What happened then?'

'We were deployed onto other projects. Then, when the war finished, I went back to Post Office Telephones. But the Master and Flo remained in the security services. With the start of the Cold War, Russian language experts were suddenly as much in demand as German language experts had been just a short time before.'

Peter realised that Nippy's voice had become rather croaky. 'Nippy, would you like another cup of tea?'

'Thank you, master Peter, I would.'

Peter busied himself with the tea things. When they all had fresh mugs of tea in front of them, Nippy continued with his account.

'Flo rose rapidly up the management ladder. She seemed to have a natural talent for the job. The Master's prospects on the other hand were not so bright. It seems he was responsible for a number of conspicuous disasters and eventually he was required to resign. He returned to Wyvern Hall to lick his wounds and offered me the job of keeping things running.

'It was then that he confided in me that he attributed some blame to Flo for what had happened to him. And the more he brooded the more he began to suspect that the leaks from Bletchley might also have had something to do with her. He started to make enquiries about the contacts that Flo had made when she was in Germany and to trawl through some old transcripts he had kept. But he was unable to find anything to incriminate her, although in the process he did uncover a ring of double agents operating at the heart of British security. Tying identities to the codenames contained in the Soviet transmissions, however, proved to be more difficult.'

Terri wrinkled her brow, 'Isn't it hard to stay friends with someone if you think they've betrayed you? It must have been difficult with Flo living in the same village.'

'Well, this was before she had moved to Fordham. In the meantime the Master had turned his attention to other things, painting, making jigsaw puzzles, playing chess and so on. But then five or six years ago Flo bought The Croft. As you can imagine this stirred up the old suspicions and the Master went back to the transcripts that he had retained.

The thing is that the Soviets used a system known as the one-time pad that effectively made decrypting their messages impossible. But the Master was aware that some of the pads had been duplicated in a printing error, which could be exploited to enable decryption of some of the material.'

Terri jumped up and said, 'And you built a computer and cracked the code. You're geniuses!'

'Not so fast, daughter of the dragon. We did build a computer, but not one that was capable of cracking the Soviet signals.'

'But how was that going to help you determine who Nightshade was?'

'Well, you can't just look at a machine and work out what it does. If you think you can, it's probably just because it has a visual similarity to other machines or tools with which you are already familiar. So we built a machine that had all the essential parts of a computer, a central processing unit, memory storage and input and output devices.'

'So you built one fake machine inside another.'

'Well, that's one way of putting it. But the Helios did actually work. Not as well as we wanted, but it was still pretty good.'

'Good at what?'

'Playing chess. The professor and I were trying to build a machine that could play chess. If others thought that it was a device for decrypting old Soviet radio messages, that was just a happy coincidence.'

Peter said, 'In that case how were you able to produce the material that Smallwood took from Cuthbert's filing cabinet?'

Nippy chuckled. 'So you know about that, do you?'

Peter blushed. 'Yes, we were looking for Cuthbert's will, so that you'd be able to stay at Wyvern Hall, but Smallwood came back and we had to hide. When we got out of the cupboard, he'd taken the folder with the Helios decrypts.'

'Those decrypts were made by the Master using paper and pencil and exploiting the duplicate one-time pad weakness. Very time-consuming work. But it was important for what we were trying to do, to make it look as if they were produced by the computer.'

Terri was getting frustrated. 'And what were you trying to do?'

'Trying to get the double agents to reveal themselves. We thought that if the output was convincing enough they might feel compelled to find out how the dossier had been compiled.'

Peter was thoughtful. 'That meant you had to get the decrypts into their hands. Which is why you were so relaxed about Smallwood breaking into Wyvern Hall.'

'I didn't think there was any point giving up after the Master died, so I thought I'd give them a hand, which is why, once Smallwood appeared on the scene, I put the Helios decrypts in the Master's will folder.'

'So you saw his amended will?'

'Of course I did.'

Peter laughed, but Terri was troubled. 'But how did Smallwood know that there were these decrypts in the first place?'

'Because the Master talked to Rafferty. He and Rafferty used to be colleagues, until the Master was forced to leave the service and Rafferty replaced him. He told Rafferty that he had uncovered a Soviet spy ring in British intelligence, suspecting very strongly that Rafferty was one of that number. He provided the codenames, but not the evidence. The fact that he knew the codenames and some dates made Rafferty take his claims seriously. The Master was expecting one of the group to try and find the dossier. He just didn't expect to be murdered. Well, maybe he did, but he'd decided to take the risk.'

They all fell silent. Nippy looked at Terri and Peter. 'I know this is all very upsetting, but you've got to deal with it sensibly. Despite what happened to all three of us, I doubt very much that those events will form the basis of a court case. So there will be no formal proof of what I've just been telling you. And I know it's difficult, but you mustn't let it colour how you feel about a certain person. Rafferty may have been leading us all astray on purpose and the Master's suspicions would be very hard to substantiate and might have become distorted by the bitterness he felt at being pushed out of the service that he'd given so much of his life to. I know that these James Bond films make everyone think that the world of spying is sexy and glamorous. But it's not. It's horrible and heartbreaking.'

Terri and Peter nodded disconsolately.

As they took their leave of Nippy, he said, 'Master Peter, please thank Flo for the bottle of whisky she sent around and send her my best wishes.'

On the way back along the top of the railway cutting, Peter said to Terri, 'I don't think I can bear the thought that Flo is Nightshade. She just doesn't seem like a bad person.'

'I know. And it's going to be difficult to keep it out of the relationship. I think that's why Nippy didn't really want to discuss it.'

'And maybe that was why Agatha has been trying to stop us trying to find out any more.'

'Well, we don't know for certain.'

'But once they arrest her, we will.'

'But it sounds like there's no proof, just conjecture.'

'Unless Rafferty and Smallwood confess.'

'Ah, yes.'

They walked the rest of the way in silence. Peter dropped Terri off at her house. For a moment he thought she was going to invite him in for supper, but she seemed even more downcast than he was and disappeared inside almost without a backward look. He was not looking forward to an evening at The Croft. He was afraid that Flo might notice that his attitude to her had changed. He needed to think through how he was going to handle things. Absurdly, he thought a bit of Dutch courage might help. He still had the change from the ten-shilling note that Terri had given him and decided to go and have a pint of BBA in The Fox.

Three-quarters of an hour later back at The Croft, he found Flo preparing the evening meal. 'Ah, there you are, dear. How was Nippy?'

'He was fine. He asked me to thank you for the whisky.'

'Does he need any provisions?'

'No, it seems Agatha has filled his larder.'

'She really is a bundle of energy, that young woman. And how's your side feeling?'

'Much better, thank you, Flo. I've almost forgotten it.'

'And how has your day been?'

'We spent most of it with Nippy. I think he was glad to have the company, but he seems very tired.'

'The loss of his machine would have been a terrible blow.'

'Yes, he seems very sad.'

'Getting old is not much fun. It's hard not to think back on all those missed opportunities. It's not the things we did that we regret; it's the things we didn't do.'

Peter wasn't quite sure how to take that admission in the light of what they now thought they knew about Flo. But it did chime with his own mood.

'I don't really want to go back to London, Flo. I love it down here.'

'Well, I wouldn't mind you staying here for as long as you wanted, but I'm not sure what your mother would think about the idea. Or your school. I understand that you are a promising student and expected to do well in your A-levels.'

'I'd love to stay with you, Flo. You treat me like an adult. People here in Fordham are nicer, more interesting.'

'Peter, you're in love and that colours everything else. Fordham is no better nor worse than anywhere else, but for you it's suffused by the glow emanating from Terri Hammond. When you're in love, the world that you know gets knocked off its axis. Everything is magical. You want to be with your love all the time. You want to be close to her, to watch her, touch her and all the things that follow from that. I'm not going to tell you what you should and shouldn't do. But I can tell you you're not the first person to feel like that. And I do know that as lovely as it is, it is also very painful.'

Suddenly, Peter found himself sobbing. Flo came over and hugged him. 'My dear chap, I think we both need a pre-prandial drink.'

She fixed them a large Cutty Sark on the rocks each. They clinked glasses and Flo said, 'To love.'

Peter sobbed again and took a mouthful of the firewater.

Flo looked at him across the top of her glass. 'I know that what I have been told about the other night is not the full story. And I know that you and Terri were in terrible danger and that you both behaved bravely. I am afraid that for the best of intentions you have become caught up in something dark and connected to very dangerous currents of power. I don't want you to make any admissions, but I do think that you should stop trying to get to the bottom of the mystery. We are certain of little in this life. At best we have working theories. But we also expose ourselves to danger if we don't maintain a level of doubt or scepticism. No answer is the final answer. The desire for utter certainty can only drive us mad. As John Keats said, we need to be capable of being in uncertainties.'

Flo finished her drink and said, 'Now, let's eat and promise to be friends whatever happens.'

Peter finished his own drink, kissed Flo on the cheek and sat down at the table.

PETER WAS LYING ON the grass outside the railway cutting den, listening to Terri playing his guitar and singing. She really had a nice touch and a fine voice. She was wearing a skirt again and a white blouse. He thought she looked so beautiful, with her long brown arms and legs. As he listened to her sing, the thought of returning to London filled him with gloom. The summer was coming to an end, even the weather was changing. It was still warm, but large threatening clouds had been building up during the course of the morning.

Terri finished playing and laid the guitar down carefully. She jumped up. 'Right, let's have the last two beers.'

'But we haven't got anything to open the bottles with.'

'Of course we have. I always have my pocket knife.'

'That skirt doesn't look as if it has any pockets.'

'Don't you like it?'

'I like it a lot. I was just wondering where you kept the knife.'

'Ah, that would be telling. I'll leave it to your imagination.'

She disappeared into the hedge and returned with two opened bottles. They clinked the bottles together and took a couple of mouthfuls of beer.

As they were drinking, the first drops of rain started to fall. Terri said, 'I'd rather not go back to The Croft just yet. I'm fed up with jigsaw puzzles. I suppose we could go up to Nippy's.'

Looking up at the sky, Peter said, 'The rain might pass over. Why don't we stay here? We could shelter in the hedge, get the ground-sheet and the towels out.'

Terri needed no second bidding. Soon they had organised the space inside the hollowed out hedge and were lying next to each other listening to the rain pattering on the top of the thick hedge. Terri was lying on her back with her hands behind her head, Peter lying on his side. He reached over and, kissing her on the cheek, started to unbutton her blouse. Terri looked up at him. 'Pete, what are you doing?'

'I'm undressing you. You said you wanted me to undress you.'

Terri smiled at him. 'Are you sure you're not just looking for my pocket knife?'

'Well, that too.'

Kneeling beside her, he had soon removed her blouse. Through-out the process, they held each other's gaze. Then he unhooked her bra and slipped it off. As he did so, the pocket knife slipped out of her bra. She covered her breasts with her hands and said, 'Now you know my secret.'

He laughed. 'There weren't many other places to look, but perhaps I'd better make a thorough inspection.'

He found the zip on the side of her skirt, slowly unzipped it and gently pulled the skirt off. She raised her bottom slightly to help him. Finally, he leaned forward, kissing her lower torso and re-moved her knickers. As soon as she was completely unclothed, she removed her hands from her breasts and opened her arms as if to invite him to embrace her, but said, 'Are you going to remain fully clothed?'

'I wasn't planning to.'

'I'm glad to hear it.'

In next to no time, Peter had removed his own clothes and lay down beside Terri. The rain was pouring down and the occasional drop was coming through the canopy of the hedge, but it was not enough to dampen their ardour. After a while, as their embraces were moving towards a point of inevitability, Terri said, 'So you're no longer worried about getting me pregnant?'

Peter smiled. 'I've stopped worrying about the consequences of the night of the fire. Whatever happens, happens. But I have not come unprepared this time. I have some Durex in the pocket of my shorts.'

Terri laughed. 'Where did those come from?'

'The vending machine in the gents at The Fox. After I dropped you off yesterday evening, I didn't want to go back to The Croft immediately. So I went to The Fox and had a pint. Tom told me the machine had been refilled and I went in and bought a packet.'

'That was very bold of you.'

'I'm fed up with being timid. I want to be more like you and some of the other women I've met in Fordham. I've learnt a lot over this summer.'

Initially, these fine words were undercut by the difficulty Peter seemed to have in donning the condom, much to Terri's amusement. 'Shall I help?' she offered.

'No, I'm in charge for a change.'

Terri squealed with delight. 'I am in your hands, Mr Marshall. Do with me as you will.'

Some time later, all three condoms had been deployed and Peter and Terri had missed lunch, but they didn't care. They lay in each other's arms, profoundly in love.

THERE WAS A KNOCK at Nippy's back door. A moment later, Agatha poked her head into the kitchen. 'May I come in?'

Nippy snapped out of the drowsy state he'd been in and said, 'Oh, Miss Agatha, it's you. Yes, please come in.'

'I've brought you some fresh bread and milk, and a few other things.'

She put the supplies on the kitchen table.

'Shall I make us a nice cup of tea?'

'That would be very welcome.'

A few minutes later, steaming mug of tea in hand, Agatha said, 'I'm afraid I've got some bad news. Rafferty committed suicide in his cell. And Smallwood never recovered from his injuries.'

Nippy cleared his throat. 'Well, I can't say I'm really sorry. Still, no one wants to end like that.'

'Quite. It will be kept quiet, of course. But I thought I ought to let you know, seeing that they were planning to kill you. And very nearly did.'

'If it hadn't been for Peter and Terri.'

'Yes, if it hadn't been for Peter and Terri. However, I think it would be better if they didn't know this detail. In fact, the less discussion there is about these matters and the likely identity of Nightshade with those two, the better. They are only young people.'

'That is true, but they are also good people. I am certainly happy to keep the news of the deaths of Rafferty and Smallwood to myself, but I am afraid the three of us have already had a conversation about the Master's history and who Nightshade might be.'

'Oh dear, Nippy, that really is most unfortunate.'

'Miss Agatha, just before Rafferty and Smallwood set the timer on the incendiary devices, Rafferty, annoyed that he'd got no information out of me, felt sufficiently confident that the three of us would be dead before he got back to his car that he as good as told us who Nightshade was.'

'And Peter and Terri heard this?'

'They could hardly not.'

'And when you say as good as told you, what do you mean by that?'

'He said that Nightshade was one of the Master's oldest friends, a university colleague, and also lived locally.'

'And he said this before he slugged Smallwood?'

'Yes, but I didn't witness the attack on Smallwood, because after identifying Nightshade he hit me again and knocked me out. But the kids saw and heard it all and also believed they were going to die. After all that, you could hardly expect them not to need to talk about it. We no longer live in times when people are expected to keep schtum about the bad stuff they've been through.'

'They didn't mention this in their interviews. Nor did you, for that matter.'

'They were probably in a state of shock and what Rafferty was saying wasn't news to me anyway.'

'You knew already?'

'Knowing something is not the same as having proof.'

'Yes, indeed. In that case I am afraid that I am at a disadvantage and that all three of you possess more information than I do. I presume that the obvious inference is the false one.'

'I'm not sure that Rafferty was aware of Professor Sage as a resident of Fordham, so I think he was being explicit. The kids, of course, did think that he was referring to the professor, because the alternative was unthinkable. And in any case, they had no reason to know that Flo had an academic background.'

'So, now they do have reason to believe that Flo is Nightshade.'

'Yes, I'm afraid so, even though I attempted to put it in the context of what happened during and then immediately after the war. I also made it clear to them that there would probably not be any public confirmation of these matters or at least not for a very long time.'

'Do you trust them to keep this to themselves?'

'Yes, Miss Agatha, they're good kids. I trust them completely.'

'Yes, so do I. And enough of this *Miss Agatha* nonsense. We're old friends. You don't have to continue with all the forelock tugging. I'm going to drag Dicky and the rest of Fordham into the twentieth century.'

Nippy laughed. This was the first moment of levity in a conversation he had not been looking forward to.

Flo sat opposite Nippy and stirred her tea. 'So, how are you feeling now, Nippy?'

'Not too bad. I can get around, but it's slow going.'

'Do you need any help?'

'I'm getting plenty of help from Terri Hammond and your great-nephew, thank you, Flo. They have been marvellous.'

'I'm glad to hear it. And I'm sure you're more fun to be with than I am.'

'I wouldn't say that. I spend most of my time sleeping.'

'Ah, well, that probably gives them more scope for kissing and cuddling.'

'I couldn't possibly say, Flo, but they seem to me to be decent young people with all the usual appetites.'

'I have absolutely no objections in that respect and you, of course, have every reason to see them in a positive light.'

'I'm not sure what you're trying to say, Flo.'

'I am not convinced by the explanation I have been given about how the accident happened.'

'Well, I am not sure what exactly has been said to you. The truth of the matter is that I was unconscious for a considerable time and my recollection of events is a little hazy.'

'I see.'

'I can assure you that Peter and Terri have behaved impeccably.'

'But perhaps they have not told me all that transpired.'

'They're young people. They're happy to help others and they are not marked by the past. Not yet, anyway.'

'Well, they're lucky to have you as their champion. What do you think of Agatha Ponsonby?'

'I can only say that Richard could do a lot worse than throw in his lot with her.'

'Yes, it is a curious match, but it will be much to Richard's advantage, other than in matters of the heart.'

'I wouldn't know, Flo.'

'No. You never thought of marrying?'

'Not really. Who would have had me?'

'Oh, come on, Neville. Everyone knows Nippy is a disguise, one that you forgot to take off at some point.'

'We all wear masks, Flo.'

'True. You know Cuthbert hurt me, a number of times.'

'I know. What had been a bee in his bonnet grew and grew until it became some terrible monster.'

'Why did you stay with him?'

'Surely, it's obvious. Because I loved him.'

'But he didn't reciprocate?'

'No, the times were different, not in terms of love, but in terms of class.'

'Ah, yes. That rings a bell. So we were rivals.'

'Not really. Flo, I can't change what happened. Or really, what didn't happen.'

'He did his best to destroy my career.'

'That sounds just like the things he too used to say. I don't understand why you chose to retire to Fordham.'

'I thought that there might be enough time for us to put all that behind us.'

'I'm not sure I quite believe that.'

'Well, no doubt there were other motivations, even so, we didn't do too badly in those final years. But all the time he was looking for proof that I had destroyed him, wasn't he?'

'There's no point in my confirming or denying your surmise. You are certain about what you believe.'

'You could have tried to prevent him.'

'I could hardly do that, but I did try to divert him. It all went wrong when he went to see Rafferty.'

'Ah, Michael, not a nice man. What induced Cuthbert to do that? Rafferty was the last person he should have trusted. He should have consulted me.'

'Even you must see that it was impossible under the circumstances.'

'But why did you keep the pantomime going after he died, the so-called dossier and the toy computer under your perpetual motion machine?'

'Because it would have been what he wanted.'

'Well, I can only admire your loyalty. What are you going to do now?'

'I don't know. What are *you* going to do?'

'Oh, I will move away once I've dealt with Miss Ponsonby. There's no reason for me to stay here now.'

'Flo, let it go. It's a new world.'

'I'm afraid I don't see it that way. The war is not over yet. Anyway, thank you for being so frank with me. Whatever you may think, I wish you well.'

With that, she rose from her chair and walked slowly to the door, putting her cup and saucer in the sink as she went.

After she had gone, Nippy sat quietly in his chair, tears running down his cheeks.

'FLO, THANK YOU FOR agreeing to talk to me. You know, of course, who I work for. And you may also have realised that the fire that destroyed Nippy's perpetual motion machine was started deliberately, but not by Nippy or indeed anyone local. Nippy agreed for the fire to be thought a fault in the wiring of the machine, so that we would have time to interrogate Michael Rafferty and Tony Smallwood, who were arrested at the scene.

'We have had some interesting admissions from Rafferty and Smallwood as to why they were so determined to destroy the Wyvern Hall barn and its contents. I wonder if you could tell me about your relationship with Rafferty and Smallwood.'

Flo composed herself. Agatha noticed a thin smile play over her lips.

'I certainly did know a Michael Rafferty when I worked for the firm, but that was a long time ago. I only know Mr Smallwood through his connection with Richard. I can tell you that Mr Smallwood would never have found preferment in the firm in my day.'

'What if I were to tell you that both Rafferty and Smallwood have made confessions and quite independently identified you as Nightshade?'

'I would say that they are deceiving you.'

'Why would they do that?'

'To protect someone else, I suppose. Or to buy time. Of course, if you think you have corroborating evidence, then you will no doubt make it available to my solicitor.'

'Flo, we do not see any reason for this enquiry to be conducted in public or to come before the courts. In fact, there may be advantages to both sides that we come to some understanding.'

'I am all for an understanding, namely that I have never been an agent of the Soviet Union and that I had nothing to do with leaks at Bletchley or the failure of Cuthbert's career. I have had to put up with this sort of innuendo for a long time and, quite frankly, I am fed up with it. I am not Nightshade. The identity of Nightshade has been a mystery for years. I think suspicion fell on me because of Cuthbert's bitterness and paranoia. It became an obsession with him and coloured everything he did.

'But if you really believe what Rafferty and Smallwood are telling you, then you should act on that belief. Otherwise please leave me alone.

'I am sure you will do very well in the service, but I would warn you against a feeling of certainty. Has it not occurred to you that there may be no Nightshade? Or that a particular individual may have more than one codename? This job does strange things to the mind.'

Agatha stood up. 'Very well. I will reflect on what you have said. Unfortunately, it was my responsibility to come and talk to you. I will have to leave it to others to decide what happens next.'

'Of course, my dear, I understand your situation all too well. There is really no need for this to cause any rift between us. I am very happy to have you as a neighbour in Fordham and I look forward to your wedding to Richard. It is just the thing to cheer us all up.'

Agatha took her leave. Once in the TR3, she banged her fists on the steering wheel and screamed quietly. She had had no doubt that Flo was Nightshade. She had felt confident that if she could persuade Flo that Rafferty and Smallwood had been turned and had incriminated her, she would confess. She had sought permission from her director to give her plan a go. He had done his best to warn her that tangling with Flo was a dangerous business. She had a reputation for being a tough adversary. With Rafferty and Smallwood dead and the Helios a smouldering pile of junk, he felt there was little to gain. He would have preferred to consider the case closed. In the end, reluctantly, he agreed. Agatha would have to learn the hard way. And he had been right. Top-notch professional that she was, Flo had simply batted away Agatha's gauche attempt to intimidate her. She had comprehensively called her bluff.

The thing that now bothered Agatha was that it was almost as if Flo already knew that Rafferty and Smallwood were dead, even though the news had been embargoed. Who might have told her? Surely it wasn't her director who had alerted Flo? That thought was too terrible to entertain. But very few other people knew about the deaths. In fact, one of those few was Nippy. The possibility that it was Nippy who had passed on the information to Flo about the deaths of the two double agents made what were already very turbid waters even muddier. Why on earth had she told him about the deaths? It was now clear that she had made an elementary mistake. What had she been thinking? Not that she believed that Flo and Nippy were in cahoots. Really, what evidence did she have for assuming that?

Or had she got this all wrong? What if Flo wasn't Nightshade? Who else could it be? She had originally dismissed Rafferty's reported remarks about Nightshade being a local person and a friend of Cuthbert's from his university days as purposeful misdirection and not just an act of gratuitous cruelty. But if it was true, then the idea that it was actually Sage who was Nightshade was not so improbable. Especially since Agatha had discovered from recent debriefing sessions that whilst Sage had not actually worked *with* Cuthbert at Bletchley, he had in fact worked there in another department.

The whole thing was a hall of mirrors, one created by the poisonous atmosphere of the security war that had been waged almost since the turn of the century, a war that had now entered a more lethal phase with the build-up of immense stockpiles of nuclear weapons by the great powers. To survive in this new world, you needed to resist all feelings of certainty, as Flo had suggested. Otherwise you would end up chasing a will o' the wisp.

Once you let paranoia take hold, almost anyone could be Nightshade. Or no one. Indeed, it was not impossible that Rafferty and Smallwood's handler had actually invented an entirely fictional double agent to confuse British counterintelligence. Such things were not unknown. It could even have been an earlier codename for Rafferty, which would account for the absence of references to Nightshade in Soviet signals in recent years and Rafferty's confidence in telling her that she was holding a busted flush.

And why stop there? If it was a matter of disappointed love, it could indeed have been Nippy. Or even, in an act of ultimate cunning, Cuthbert himself, whose well-advertised suspicions about Flo might have been designed to deflect suspicion from himself. Perhaps there was no answer. Perhaps there never would be an answer. She started the car, put it in gear and drove thoughtfully back towards The Priory and her next assignment.